Pr

D1457064

"*Montana Cherries* is a heartwarming yet heart-wrenching story of the heroine's struggle to accept the truth about her mother's death—and life."

—*RT Book Reviews*, 4 stars

"An entertaining romance with a well-developed plot and believable characters. The chemistry between Vega and JP is explosive and will have you rooting for the couple's success. Readers will definitely look forward to more works by this author."

—*RT Book Reviews*, 4 stars (HOT) on
Caught on Camera

"Kim Law pens a sexy, fast-paced romance."

—*New York Times* bestselling author Lori Wilde on
Caught on Camera

"A solid combination of sexy fun."

—*New York Times* bestselling author Carly Phillips on
Ex on the Beach

"*Sugar Springs* is a deeply emotional story about family ties and second chances. If you love heartwarming small towns, this is one place you'll definitely want to visit."

—*USA Today* bestselling author Hope Ramsay

"Filled with engaging characters, *Sugar Springs* is the typical everyone-knows-everyone's-business small town. Law skillfully portrays heroine Lee Ann's doubts and fears, as well as hero Cody's struggle to be a better person than he believes he can be. And Lee Ann's young nieces are a delight."

—*RT Book Reviews*, 4 stars

Montana PROMISES

Also by Kim Law

Montana
PROMISES

Kim Law

J-KO

Published by J-Ko Publishing

ISBN: 978-1950908028

Cover Design Copyright © 2019 The Killion Group, Inc

My tushie was saved with this one due to a middle-of-the-night phone call. Thank you so much, Terri Osburn. This one's for you!

Chapter One

Nate Wilde watched the activity on Main Street from where he stood on the second floor of the new storefront, amazed that this late in the day, the grand reopening still had people lined up, anxious for a sampling from his family's cherry-themed gift store. He was equally amazed at the number of items, both packaged and prepared foods as well as utensils, cookbooks, and the like, that he'd witnessed being purchased before he'd retreated to the quieter space above the sales floor.

But what *didn't* surprise him—and how he understood enough about her to know this, he wasn't sure—was the way Megan Manning continually coaxed customers *back* into The Cherry Basket. Even after they'd left.

From his perch at the one-hundred-year-old window, Nate had watched more than a handful of people step outside the front door, bags weighted with their purchases and their bank accounts clearly having been relieved of a chunk of change, only to be stopped on the street by Megan. She'd smiled, enveloped them with her obvious charm, and a short time later, a good number of those very people had turned around and headed right back into the store. And they'd exited the second time with another bag!

He shook his head in disbelief. She was like some sort of mystical sales goddess who'd been sent to them at the best—or more likely . . . the *worst*—possible time.

Actually, what she was, was the recent ex-girlfriend of his youngest brother. The brother whose proposal to *another* woman had kicked off the day's festivities. And that blew his mind, as well. Because Megan—who was also friends with the new girl-friend, *now fiancée*—didn't seem to be in the least fazed by the recent turn of events. In fact, she'd helped plan it.

Nate shook his head again, silently swearing that he'd never understand women, then glanced over his shoulder at the sound of footsteps coming up the narrow back stairs.

Five seconds later, one of his older brothers appeared in the office doorway.

"How's Dad?" Nate asked. Cord was a doctor, in town from Billings for only a couple of days, and had headed to the rehab facility to check on their dad shortly after the ribbon cutting.

"Wishing he were here," Cord answered. He stepped into the room. "But he's also making progress. The pain is less today."

Their dad had lost his leg—and damned near his life—ten days prior in a tractor accident on their family orchard. "Gloria still planning to keep staying with him?" Gloria was their dad's wife of two years.

"Says she intends to stay until they release him. They brought in a bed for her."

"He's in good hands then." That was one less thing for Nate to worry about.

He turned back to the window, and Cord crossed to stand beside him. Neither said anything else for a few minutes, as they both got drawn into the activity below. Jaden—he of the new fiancée—was making his way back from the other end of Main Street, Arsula and her parents in tow, all four of them looking as bright and shiny as new pennies. And Nate couldn't help but be annoyed at the sight. Not that he begrudged Jaden love. *Nor* a fiancée. Hell, if that's what the man wanted, then more power to him.

But damn. Jaden had met Arsula only two months before. The same night he and Megan had broken up. *And*, he and *Arsula* had broken up two weeks before today. This was a make-up, take-me-back type of engagement, and one that Nate worried about.

"You think that'll last?" Cord voiced Nate's thoughts, and Nate glanced at his brother.

"You don't?"

Cord didn't look at him. "I didn't say that."

"Then what are you saying?" Nate turned back to the window, his gaze flicking between Megan—who remained just outside the store's front door, looking as bright and shiny as a penny herself—and Jaden. Neither of them seemed in the least concerned about the other, yet Nate couldn't help but believe it couldn't be that easy to get over someone. Not after dating for four years.

"I'm not saying anything, I guess," Cord said under his breath, and Nate followed along with his train of thought. Jaden was in love. He was happy. Life was good.

But he was also their little brother, who thought he had life all figured out.

Who'd also thought he had life figured out just two months before.

Someone in their family had to maintain some common sense.

"You next in line, then?" Nate asked, unable to contain the ghost of a smile.

"For marriage?" The sentiment finally pulled Cord's gaze from outside. His eyes narrowed along with the thinning of his lips. "Tell you what. I'll board that train just as soon as you do."

Nate snorted. Their other four siblings, as well as their dad and Gloria, had all gotten married over the last few years. All blissfully in love. All seeing stars and rainbows and freaking glittery unicorns. It was like a damned epidemic around there.

Except, their dad was now down a leg, and the orchard stood on the brink of disaster.

So much for happily-ever-afters.

Nate jammed his hands into his jeans' pockets. "I suspect that's one train destined to spend eternity in the boneyard."

"I couldn't agree more."

They turned back to the street again, this time with Nate catching sight of a group of senior citizens, most with balloons bobbing above their heads. They'd formed a line behind the stage that had been set up for the day and were waiting for the bus that would return them to their retirement community. Along with the group of retirees, two of Birch Bay's fire trucks had also shown up, as well as the entire police force, the mayor, most local business owners, and all of the town councilmen. And, of course, darn near every person who lived within the confines of their small town—and quite a few who didn't.

Megan voluntarily giving up her high-paying computer programming job last month and asking to stay in Birch Bay as the permanent store manager might have surprised them all, but that had been nothing compared to her plans for making sure the citizens of Birch Bay, Montana, had only positives to associate with The Cherry Basket.

And dang . . . what a way to kick things off.

Too bad all the hard work might be for nothing.

The back door on the first floor slammed, the sound barely audible above the clamor of customers' voices and the continuous shuffling of product being pulled from shelves, and in the next instant, several sets of footsteps headed up the stairs. Nate watched out the window as Jaden glanced down at his phone then up to where Nate and Cord remained at the window, and with a quick kiss to his fiancée's cheek, he turned and headed for the store.

"Guess we can't put it off any longer," Nate muttered. He turned to face the door.

"Family meeting at its finest." With a less than excited tone, Cord also turned. Both of them waited, leaning back against opposite sides of the window frame and tucking their hands into their jeans' pockets, and both wore long faces of concern.

All six of them had spent the last ten days focused on any and everything *not* related to the subject utmost on their minds. The last four weeks, really. Ever since the arctic blast that had blown through town on the tail end of a warm spell, dropping the temperature from a mild sixty degrees to negative forty in a record-breaking matter of hours, no one had talked about the what-ifs.

What if it wasn't *just* a manageable portion of the orchard's trees they lost due to the weather . . . but the majority of them?

What if it wasn't financially feasible to replant?

What if their dad had died when he'd gone out before dawn to check on the trees instead of merely turning his tractor over and losing his leg?

Nate swallowed, still not wanting to think about the last one. And even while understanding all they needed to talk about today—and the potential impact of every single what-if hanging out there—he still planned to add his news to the mix. Because he'd already caused too much damage by sticking around too long.

His sister, Dani, was the first to make it down the hallway, her shoulders pulled back as she entered the room as if going into battle. She was followed by Gabe, the next oldest sibling. Nate's twin Nick came in after them, and then the runt of the litter could be heard thumping loudly up the stairs in his recently acquired walking boot.

Jaden, slightly out of breath once he reached the small room but still looking as damned happy as he had since Arsula had accepted his ring, pushed his way in and closed the door behind him. Nate opened his mouth, ready to begin the conversation and get the whole topic over with, but then he closed it again when he realized that Cord had shifted to stand with the rest of them. Five sets of blue eyes, all matching Nate's own, now stared back at him.

"What?" How had *he* become the focus of this meeting? This was supposed to be a discussion on the future of their farm. On the fact that their dad had been diagnosed with Parkinson's—as well as having hallucinations with the disease—and not a one of them had known about it until they'd shown up at the hospital ten days before. "Did you all change this to some kind of intervention and not tell me?" he joked. It had been years since he'd needed one.

"Of course we didn't—" Dani began, and then she frowned. "Is there a *need* for an intervention?"

Nate didn't bother to answer. "Then what's going on?"

As soon as the question passed his lips, he had another thought.

He jerked his gaze to Cord's. "Is it Dad? Did something happen that you didn't tell me?"

"No," Gabe answered before Cord could. He held both hands up and took a single step forward. This positioned him slightly in front of everyone else. "Dad is fine." He looked briefly lost before adding, "As fine as he can be, anyway."

Gabe and Nick had also gone out to the rehab center after the ribbon cutting, while Dani had stuck around to help at the store.

"This isn't about Dad," Gabe continued.

Dani shifted so she stood with Gabe. "Not completely."

Nate looked from one to the other, unsure what to say next. What to *do* next. Clearly, they all had something on their minds other than the future of the farm. And clearly, they'd all been talking about it without him . . .

Talking *about* him . . .

He blanked any expression. "Then what *is* it about?"

Jaden's gaze slid off to the side, his jaw going tight, and the entire thing suddenly made Nate snap.

"Just spit it out," he barked.

Dani reached out for him, but Nate shrugged out of her reach. "Nate—"

"Don't," Gabe interrupted their sister, and Nate, tired of whatever game this was, ignored both Gabe and Dani and turned to his twin.

He scowled at his brother, and without preamble, Nick said, "We need you to stay." The words landed flat.

"You need me to stay?" Nate repeated. He looked at each of his siblings in confusion. They never "needed" him for anything. And it was too damned bad if they did, anyway. He'd been there for two months. He'd stayed too long as it was. "For what, exactly?"

And why were they bringing this up now? He hadn't even told them yet that he was leaving.

"To help with Dad," Gabe answered.

Nate frowned at his oldest brother, then he eyed their sister. "You said this wasn't about Dad."

"I said not completely."

"So, you lied."

She made a face. "Quit being prickly before you even hear us out."

"Quit being prickly?" If he hadn't already been standing with his back to a wall, he'd have put several additional feet between them. "We're all here today," he reminded them, "because we're *supposed* to be having a meeting about the farm. About the fact that our dad very nearly lost his life because we tossed that very responsibility back into his lap three years ago due to none of us being willing to deal with it any longer." Their dad had originally passed the farm on to the six of them when he'd retired almost a decade before. However, none of them had ever truly appreciated the "gift." "Yet you five show up," he went on, "all staring me down, as if *I've* done something wrong? And you accuse *me* of being prickly?"

He shook his head, knowing instinctively that he didn't need to hear anything else.

"I'm not being prickly, dear sister. I'm being *me*. I don't like whatever the hell this is, and I'm not going to smile and pretend it's okay." He shoved his way between Dani and Gabe, finished with the conversation, and elbowed Nick to the side. But as his hand closed around the time-aged brass doorknob, Jaden finally spoke.

"We know you're planning to leave. I saw you put your bag in the truck this morning."

Nate stopped. That's where this had come from? He and Jaden had both been staying at the farm together the last couple of weeks, so it would be hard to go unnoticed even if he wanted to.

He turned back. "So? I always leave. What's the big deal this time?"

"Dad lost a leg, Nate." Dani's soft words punched him in the gut.

And their dad hadn't *just* lost a leg. Due to a hallucination while he'd been out on his tractor, he'd steered directly into a decades-old tree. And then he'd lain there bleeding out . . . none of them the wiser. All because . . .

Nate forced a neutral expression, not wanting to go back to that morning. To that fear. "I'm *aware* of what happened to our father, Dani." He was also aware that it was entirely his fault.

"He also has Parkinson's." This came from Gabe. "And *that* isn't going anywhere. You can't just disappear again. Not when we don't yet know how Dad's going to be able to get around. How much help he'll need."

Nate glanced around the group of them again, noting that Cord had yet to say anything and also taking in the fact that Nick had slid to his right, putting himself between Nate and the door. "So, what are you saying?" Nate once again faced Gabe.

"That you need me to stick around and play babysitter?" He knew the words were harsh, but he couldn't let himself be soft. Not right now.

"We're saying that we need you"—Dani began, then she let out a shaky sigh, and the pain suddenly darkening her eyes had Nate glancing away—"we just *need* you, okay?" she finished in a hoarse whisper. "To be here. To be one of us."

"Of course I'm one of you." He'd been born to the same parents as the rest of them, after all. And if being siblings and growing up together wasn't enough, the six of them also had plenty of shared miserable experiences.

Yet biology and a shit childhood didn't take away from the fact that he had also always felt like an outsider. And even more so since the day he'd turned eighteen.

"Dad has Gloria," Nate reminded them. "Who isn't about to let him want for anything." He forced his tone to be calm and soothing, in the way one might address a child. "As well as four out of the five of you, each who lives within five miles of him. You don't *need* me. He'll be back home in a matter of weeks, and you all know as well as I do that at least one of you will be stopping by every day. He's going to have plenty of help."

"Then stay for me," Jaden added, and Nate literally laughed out loud.

"Stay for you?" He looked down his nose at his baby brother, peering into the lenses that only Jaden had been burdened to wear. "I stayed for you two months ago when you snapped your ankle in two, remember?" Jaden had been in for Gabe's wedding, and due to the accident, he had been unable to return to Seattle. "Even though the last thing you wanted was *my* help."

"It wasn't that—"

"I *stayed*," Nate interrupted. "I've been here to play chauffeur —which is the only thing you've ever allowed me to do, by the way—and now I'm leaving. End of story. Your fiancée can drive you wherever you need to go at this point."

"Then stay for the farm." Nick's words held no emotion, and once again Nate laughed.

"The *farm?*" He turned in a full circle, taking in the agreeing nods, before stating what no one had yet been willing to verbalize. "Only fifteen percent of our trees currently have any buds on them. That's no longer a *farm*. That's a *hobby*."

"No," Gabe argued. "It's early yet. There might still be more that make it. We won't know for a couple more weeks."

Nate twisted his mouth. "You don't believe that any more than I do."

"Well, even if it is only fifteen percent"—Dani jumped back into the conversation—"that's still enough to supply the store. The farm is still viable."

Nate shifted his gaze to his sister then, the movement slow, and found himself feeling bad for what he was about to say. He knew how much she wanted both the orchard and the store to last. How much she always had. He also knew that she had a history of not exactly seeing reality at first glance.

"That *was* enough to supply the store," Nate explained. "*Before* we moved it here. *Before* we became the new 'darlings of downtown.'"

"Hey." Jaden's chest puffed up at the mimicked catchphrase Megan had coined. "Don't blame Meg for this. All she's done is try to help. She didn't know we were going to lose the trees."

Nate turned back to his youngest brother. "And how about *you* don't take up for her? You broke up with her, remember?"

The words fell into silence, with more than one of his siblings now wearing a perplexed expression.

"Fine." Nate rolled his eyes at the absurdity of the moment. "I know. *She's* the one who broke up with him. And the two of them are still great friends." *Whatever.* It still annoyed him how they both acted as if their feelings had just turned off.

No one said anything else for several seconds, and Nate simply waited, still standing in the middle of them, being surrounded as if they'd closed in bully-style instead of their earlier firing squad attack.

And then someone did speak.

And the words could have knocked him over.

"Is something . . . going *on* . . . with you and Megan?" Nick asked the question slowly. Carefully. And Nate just as purposefully turned his head and stared at his twin.

"Something . . . like *what?*"

He narrowed his eyes at the person who knew him best, and Nick wisely didn't voice any more of his thoughts. But Nate could feel the question now not only pulsing through Nick but also circling around each of his siblings. Disgust rolled through him.

Really? This was what they thought of him?

"Fuck you all," he gritted out. He did *not* have the hots for his baby brother's ex.

And he owed Nick an ass-kicking for even going there.

He forced his way back between Dani and Gabe and crossed back over to the window, then he pulled in a deep breath and once again turned to his family. His patience had vanished. "We're supposed to be talking about the farm," he repeated his earlier reminder. "Have all of you forgotten that? We're supposed to be addressing the fact that our dad almost *died* because of the farm. Not ambushing me. Not bringing up"—he shot Nick a scathing look—"*ridiculous* accusations."

"No one is accusing you," Cord finally joined the conversation. "Nor ambushing you."

"Well, it sure as hell feels like it." He glared. "And I *am* leaving, by the way. Tonight. If someone needs to stick around to care for Dad, then how about you do it? You're the doctor."

"It's not that easy."

"Right. Like you would, anyway." A muscle jerked in Nate's jaw. Cord had been the first of them to move away.

"You're right." Nick pushed his way forward until he stood directly in front of Nate. "We *can* take care of Dad. And yes, one of us will likely be over there every day once he gets home. But we do need help with the orchard."

Again, Nate laughed. "What orchard?" He stretched his arms wide, and his voice took on heat. *"We. Have. No. Orchard."*

The rest of them went quiet again, everyone contemplating the reality in their own way, before Cord finally cleared his throat. They all dragged their gazes to his, and hesitantly, he brought up the question they each knew had to be addressed. "Is it time we discuss selling?"

Everyone else remained silent, but slowly, one-by-one, they all glanced at Dani.

Eventually, she spoke. "Not yet." She shook her head. "We never wanted to—"

"You never wanted to," Gabe corrected softly.

"And you do?" Dani shot him a look, and the two of them locked into a full-fledged stare off.

"First things first. Dad will need a place to come home to." Nick's tone was genial, but it did little to ease the tension. "It's been his home again since Dani and Gabe turned over running the farm, so whatever happens in the future, we can't just kick him out right now. And whether we do decide to sell down the road, or whether we replant, at the moment there's still fifteen percent of the trees that need tending to."

Nate scowled at his twin. "I am *not* sticking around to run a non-existent orchard."

"Well, it's not like you've been doing anything else lately." Nick fired back, and as Jaden had done when the conversation first started, his gaze immediately shifted off to the side.

Nate swore as realization dawned.

"Jaden told us that you haven't been out on a crab boat in over a year," Dani offered.

"And crabbing isn't the *only* thing that I do," Nate rebutted. "It's seasonal. Did you all forget that?" He didn't take his eyes off Jaden. He knew he never should have admitted anything to his "all-too-helpful" brother.

"Do you have something lined up that you actually need to get to?" Nick asked. "Or are you just running?"

Exhaustion suddenly swamped Nate at the no-nonsense tone, and he dragged a hand down over his face. "What would I possibly be running from, Nick?"

Two beats later, Dani said, "Us?"

Though the question came as a surprise, Nate didn't even have to consider the answer. Not like he once would have.

He shook his head, the lump in his throat keeping him from speaking at first. The truth was, he didn't *have* to go. And he didn't even know where he might end up. But he also couldn't stay.

"I'm not running," he denied. Not *from* them, anyway.

He was running to save them.

"Then stay." Nick nodded in encouragement. "Even if only fifteen percent survive, that means eighty-five percent won't. We've all been so focused on getting the store moved and reopened that we haven't looked past today. Dad's going to need a ramp put in. Other modifications. The orchard will need a wood chipper working overtime. I can help around my classes and work. We all will help. But we need someone there full time."

Nate replayed the words before reacting. Thought about what really may need to be done for a seventy-year-old who was down a leg and had rapidly progressing Parkinson's.

His siblings may be asking him to stay simply because it was the easiest option for everyone, but they weren't wrong. This wasn't the time to have anything less than all hands on deck. If he did this one last thing before he went . . .

He stared at his brother and promised himself that he wouldn't stick around for longer than a couple more weeks. He wouldn't get to the point where he'd rather stay.

"The fifteen percent," he finally spoke. "If the trees actually make it and don't need to be cut down themselves, I'm not sticking around to take care of them. I'm not running a dilapidated orchard."

"Fine." Cord spoke up before anyone else could. "Then stay long enough to hire someone to do it. Or to hire someone to replant. Whatever is decided. But stay to help get Dad settled."

"And *then* leave if you have to," Nick added. He shared a knowing look with Nate. "Whatever you need to do. We're here for you. But *we* need you to be here for us right now."

Chapter Two

❧❧❧

"That's right, Mrs. Kerry. We should have more of the cherry-and-orange scone mix in by Wednesday at the latest." Megan opened the door for the last two customers of the day. "And I promise to call you the *second* some hit the sales floor." She wished the fifty-something couple a good evening and closed and locked the door behind them.

Then she turned, put her back to the door . . . and she smiled. What an exhilarating day!

Success had whispered in her ears all day. As customers had come in—and left grinning ear to ear—as moans and groans sounded when bites of cupcakes or muffins were sampled, as the register had continuously been worked. But the biggest success had been screamed from the size of the crowd that had shown up that afternoon. Birch Bay *loved* The Cherry Basket, that was for sure.

The store had been cherished before, no doubt. In all the years it had been open, sales had never been "bad." But according to the books, they *had* flatlined over the last couple of years. With the new downtown location, though, as well as the revamp of the website and the work both she and Dani had put into the new marketing plan, it was now—so it seemed—a place which would be sought out on a much more frequent basis. And she couldn't be happier that she'd been a part of that.

That she'd been the *reason* for it.

She turned back to the door, the smile still on her face, and peered through the glass. There was still a crowd lingering. Not huge, but enough to continue giving off a party atmosphere outside. She supposed with it being Friday afternoon, less people were in a hurry to get home and start any end-of-day routines.

Some of those who remained had also rolled up their sleeves and were helping with cleanup. There were tables, tents, a stage, even strings of old-fashioned Edison lights draped from tree limbs that branched out over the street. It all had to come down, and no one stood around waiting to be paid in order to pitch in. This was simply their town, and there was something that needed to be done. So they were doing it.

That was one of the reasons she'd wanted to set down roots in Birch Bay.

One of the reasons she wanted it to be *her* town, too.

Her gaze flickered over the crowd, her managerial instincts kicking in to ensure her employees—whom she'd sent outside with the Wilde family when they'd returned from their meeting thirty minutes earlier—were doing their part. She should probably head outside herself, if for no other reason than to be a part of things. But she wanted a few minutes to be alone first. A few minutes more to revel in the fabulousness that was the day—as well as to wonder what *tomorrow* would bring.

The smile slipped from her face. "Tomorrow" being more metaphorical in her mind than the actual day, but the future nonetheless. Because no matter what today's success implied, if there weren't cherry trees to be harvested come late summer, she wasn't sure what would become of The Cherry Basket.

Moving to the front counter, she logged in to the point of sale system and began closing out for the day. All the while, she kept an ear tuned for any sounds from above. Because though the majority of the Wilde family was outside helping with breakdown, Nate was *not*. He hadn't returned with the rest of them earlier, nor had she heard a peep out of him since the meeting had broken up.

She glanced at the ceiling, wondering what he could possibly be doing up there, then she shifted her gaze to the hallway that led to the stairs and the back door. Maybe he'd come down and left when she hadn't noticed?

She shook her head slightly. She didn't think so. First of all, previous instances of being around Nate told her that he wasn't the type to "tiptoe" anywhere. He had a presence when he entered a room. And second, she'd been actively listening for him. Because she wanted to know the outcome of today's meeting.

She'd hoped that Dani, who she reported to as manager of the store, would give her a heads-up when they'd come down. Or even Jaden. She'd known the family had planned to meet today to discuss both the future of the farm as well as the state of the cherry trees, and both of those things pertained to her since they pertained to the store. Yet not one word had been spoken by any of them. They'd simply filed through the crowded store, all of them either focused on getting outside to start cleanup, or—as in Dani's case—heading for a baby anxious to be fed.

Megan tapped a final key and sent a report to the office printer, then closed out the software system. They'd had a wildly successful day in terms of sales, which meant that her next step should be taking inventory. An order would need to be placed tonight so product could be restocked the first of next week. Otherwise, all this success would quickly backfire. However, going to the stockroom was the last thing she wanted to do at the moment. There was a man loitering on the floor above her. And she intended to stop him on his way out.

Grabbing a notepad, she decided to work on a personal task while she waited. Now that the store had been moved and reopened, it was time to concentrate on her apartment. She'd rented the place two months before, and honestly, since it had come furnished, there wasn't a lot that she *needed*. But she *wanted* to make it her own. Until now, she'd never lived fully on her own, and as each day passed, she found more and more that she liked about it.

Drawing a line down the middle of the sheet, she started two lists. Things that remained in storage from the apartment she and Jaden had once shared in Seattle, and items she wanted to buy new.

Tangerine-colored dish towels.

Honeysuckle-scented soaps for the bathroom.

A girly comforter set.

Laughter from out on the street reached her ears, and her earlier smile returned. This was her life now, and she couldn't be happier.

She continued jotting, jumping from list to list as ideas came, and even making a couple of smaller sub-lists. She became so engrossed in what she was doing, in fact, that she physically jerked when someone cleared their throat.

The pencil went flying, and her hand slapped to her chest.

"Nate!" The man stood directly in front of her.

The corners of his mouth quirked up. "Scare much?"

She smirked. "Creep much?" She stooped to search for her pencil.

"I didn't creep." He leaned over the counter and watched her. "I even said hello as I came into the room."

From her position squatted on the floor, she looked up. "You spoke . . . as in, out *loud?*"

Her question had him chuckling. "Is there any other way to speak?"

She shot him another smirk. Then she snagged the pencil out from under the edge of the storage cabinet and stood. Though she'd met Nate three years before when she'd first visited Birch Bay with Jaden, she hadn't really gotten to know him until the last two months. And what she knew, she still could probably fit on the tip of her pencil. But since she'd been staying with Max and Gloria when Nate had first come home for Gabe's wedding, their paths had again crossed. They'd both been under the same roof for those few days, and since then, he'd been a help in finding the store's new location, as well as in getting it up and running. In that time, her opinion of him had morphed from strictly troublemaking, do-what-he-wanted loner brother to *possibly past* troublemaker, *definitely* do-what-he-wanted loner, but a brother with a potentially good heart.

She'd also come to the conclusion that though he was a smartass—which she could fully appreciate—he was also surprisingly funny. And he seemed to embody the type of protectiveness that would have him kicking anyone's rear who dared threaten his family. Not exactly the man she'd originally thought him to be.

"So, what has you so focused down here?" he asked now, and Megan's eyes dropped to the counter.

She slid the notepad closer. "Just working on a to-do list." Flipping the pad over, she pointed to the ceiling with her other hand. "What kept you so focused up there?"

His gaze followed her finger. "Just working on my own list."

He pulled a rolled-up clump of papers from his back jeans pocket and peeled off a single sheet.

"My list," he announced. He waved the piece of printer paper in front of her before cramming it back into his pocket, then he handed over the rest of the papers. "And your *amazingly impressive* sales report."

"Ah," she murmured, pride once again fluttering in her chest. She took the report. "Thank you very much."

"I think we're the ones who should be thanking you." Nate's voice was deeper than the rest of his brothers'. And that was saying a lot. He curled both hands around the front edge of the counter and leaned in, looking over the report as she did. "I have to say, you seem to be a genius at this whole retail thing."

The flattery warmed her. "I am pretty good, aren't I?" She couldn't contain her smile, and she found herself laughing freely. "Imagine that . . . a bachelor's *and* a master's degree, both in computer science, and I turn out to be exceptional at selling things."

"Well"—Nate straightened—"a degree doesn't always mean what a person might expect it to. I've known others to get one and not use it."

"Yeah? Who else do you know?"

His gaze suddenly clung to hers. His eyes could be so expressive at times. The only problem was, she'd yet to figure out the meaning behind any of the expressions.

"Why are you still in here, Manning?" Nate nodded toward the windows spanning the front of the store, rather than answer her question. "Instead of out there being loud and rambunctious with everyone else?"

She wanted to ask him the same thing. She also wanted to ask why he'd changed the subject. She suspected he wouldn't answer either question, though. That was another thing she'd picked up about him. He only answered the questions he felt like answering.

Which wasn't a lot.

"I was waiting for you," she admitted, and that had him stepping back.

His stance went from friendly to back off. "Why would you be waiting for me?"

The trigger-fast tension, now sitting high and tight in his shoulders, had her wondering at the change. What was his issue?

She narrowed her eyes as she stared back at him, and he mimicked the action.

So, she crossed her arms over her chest.

He did the same.

His movements had her sighing with a long, drawn-out sound. The man could be ridiculously difficult.

"I was waiting for *you*," she explained, her patience now gone. "Because the rest of your family went out the door the instant they came back downstairs, and I didn't get a chance to speak to any of them."

He glanced toward the windows again at the dissipating crowd.

"And because I want to know how the meeting went."

Her words brought his gaze back, but his shoulders didn't soften. "What meeting?"

Her jaw twitched. "*Seriously?*" Why was that even a question? She jabbed a finger toward the ceiling. "The meeting that you and your family had up there just a short while ago. I know you guys were discussing the farm, and you have to know that's important to me. It impacts the store. My job."

He picked up a cherry-filled chocolate bar from one of the impulse bins. "Are you worried about your job?"

"Oh, for goodness' sake." She shook her head. "No, Nate. I'm not worried about my job. As we've already discussed, I'm more than qualified. I can find another job if I need one. Heck, I can be the hermit living in a basement writing apps all day. But I am worried about your family. About the farm. Are you guys going to sell or not?" Her voice had risen as she'd spoken, and though she doubted anyone could have heard her outside, it seemed as if those remaining within eyesight all suddenly looked her way.

She didn't want to think about the Wildes selling the orchard. She loved the place. She loved the whole Wilde family.

And that meant she also absolutely *hated* what Max was going through.

She expected Nate to avoid her question again, just because he liked to be difficult, but instead, he shook his head. It wasn't a large movement but enough to tell the answer was a definite 'no.'

"You're *not* selling?" Relief flooded her.

"We're not . . . *yet.*"

"*Oh.*" Her chest deflated.

"And maybe not at all," he quickly clarified. "We don't know yet."

Her prior relief idled at the side, hopeful for a chance at a return. "Well, that's something, I suppose." She did her best to sound hopeful. "And the trees?" she asked. "Are they—"

"Mostly a loss."

"*Oh,*" she said again, and this time followed it with a tired sigh.

"Yeah. *Oh.*" He appeared to be as devastated as she felt. "But there are some still alive. We don't know for certain how many yet, but at least fifteen percent." Now it was he who seemed to put in the effort to be hopeful. "In the coming weeks, I'll be working on cleaning up the place," he explained. "Running dead trees through the wood chipper, figuring out what we do and don't have."

"Wait..." She held up a hand to stop his words, then she finally came out from behind the counter. "You mean, you aren't leaving?"

He dropped the candy bar back into the bin. "Why would you think I'm leaving?" He looked down at her—she stood beside him now, and there was at least a foot of height difference between them.

"I just—"

"You tired of seeing my ugly mug around here, Manning? Ready for me to go?"

The question threw her, and something new simmering in the air now had *her* taking a step back. Also, he had the complete opposite of an ugly mug. The man was cover-model perfect.

As were all the Wilde boys.

"Why would what you do matter to me?" she asked, mostly because she couldn't think of anything else to say.

"It wouldn't. I was just joking." He didn't look away. "But why would you think I'm leaving?"

"Because Jaden told me you were."

Nate closed his eyes at that, and the temporary "weirdness" that seemed to hover in the air evaporated. When his blue eyes once again looked her way, they did so along with a tight smile. "That boy sure likes to share what he knows, doesn't he?"

"Who? Jaden?" She didn't understand why Jaden telling her would upset him. "I'm sorry . . . was he not supposed to say anything about it?" Megan lifted her shoulders in a shrug. "To be honest, I don't think he even knew that he'd told me. He was just nervous earlier as he waited to ask Arsula to marry him. He was rattling off at the mouth a bit."

"Right. That's my brother. Rattling off at the mouth."

When he didn't say anything else, just continued to look ticked, she ignored the direction his thoughts had taken and asked her question again. "So . . . you're *not* leaving?"

"No, I'm not leaving. Not yet. But I *definitely* will be." With his announcement, he turned and headed for the door. "I'll be sure to have Jaden tell you when the time comes, though."

He put his hand on the keys still hanging from the lock.

"Try not to scare any bears out there, Wilde."

He stopped with the door halfway open and looked back with a startled expression. Shouts from outside filtered into the building, and she heard someone call out for Nate.

"You know?" She apparently had to explain herself. "Because of your grumpiness? Don't scare the bears . . . because *they're* supposed to be the ones who are scary?"

The man didn't even crack a smile. "You're cute, Manning." His sarcasm couldn't be missed. "Jaden really missed out when he lost you."

"I know," she deadpanned in return. "But he wasn't man enough for my charms."

She maintained her lack of emotion until Nate rolled his eyes and shook his head, and when he once again turned for the door, she tossed out another tidbit.

"What you do may not matter to me, but I'm still glad you're staying."

He glanced back at her again, and this time she flashed him a legit smile. Difficult or not, she liked the man. He made her laugh, and he pulled no punches. She also felt a kinship with the loner side of him. "I also know it'll make your dad happy," she told him. "He loves it when all of you are around."

That seemed to pain, as well as to please, him. "You think so?"

She nodded without hesitation. "Absolutely. He mentioned you often while I was staying with them." She hadn't returned to Seattle after she and Jaden had visited for Christmas due to the previous store manager having to leave unexpectedly because of a family emergency. "I'm just sorry that I didn't—" Her words faltered as she tried to continue, feeling tears pushing at the back of her eyes. A chill ran down both sides of her neck. "I'm sorry I didn't notice that anything was wrong with him. I mean" —she lowered her chin and ended up staring at Nate's chest—"I *did* notice a couple of things. *Maybe.*" She shook her head in uncertainty. "But I brushed them off. I assumed it was nothing."

Nate didn't say anything else for a moment, but he did let the door swing closed behind him. They stood there, facing each other, but not looking at one another, until Megan had her emotions back under control. When she did, she once again lifted her gaze.

And the fact that she could read what was in Nate's eyes floored her.

He was riddled with pain.

"It's not your fault he's sick," he informed her.

"I know that." And she did know. But she *had* lived with the man for eight weeks.

And she *had* seen a few things that should have raised a red flag.

"*Nor* that he lost a leg," Nate stressed.

"I know that, too." She'd picked up on a shift in his voice. Tightness now squeezed around each of his words. "But it's not *your* fault either," she told him.

Is that what he thought?

But why would he? His father had been out before daylight on a tractor!

"Right." Nate gave a short nod with the single, tautly spoken word, and the look in his eyes told her more than words ever could. He one hundred percent believed it was his fault.

He looked over her head then, taking in the mostly empty shelves behind her—and likely seeing only whatever ran rampant through his head. When their gazes reconnected, his expression had returned to blank. "But Dad losing a leg or not, you know we've likely also lost more trees than can support this place, right?"

That was the other thing she'd been afraid of. "So, we replant. Don't you guys always have to replant a few trees each year anyway? And I'll help. I'll pitch in however I can. I've got plenty of free time. Plus, I like to stay busy. Just say the word and I'm there."

She knew she was now the one rattling, but she meant the words. She'd do whatever it took to make sure the Wildes' cherry orchard didn't go under.

Nate opened the door again, that time by taking a step backward and pushing with his backside. "You want to stay busy, Manning?" He glanced to his right, as if scoping out what remaining work there was to do out on the street. "Then buy yourself a pair of work gloves." He looked at her again. "And show up at the farm. I'll be glad to teach you how to use a wood chipper."

He slipped out the door without saying another word, and she stood there watching him walk away. But instead of heading toward his family, he went in the opposite direction. Without speaking to anyone.

Chapter Three

Two beads of sweat raced each other down Nate's back as he hoisted the pile of recently cut deck boards and headed to where the ramp frame connected on the far side of the deck. It was just after noon on Monday and warmer than a normal mid-April afternoon, and with several hours of sunlight remaining, he should at least be able to finish the floor of the ramp. Possibly even get started on the railing.

He dropped the lumber to the ground, finding a sense of satisfaction with the clatter of wood pieces tumbling together, then refit one of his earbuds more securely into his ear. Grabbing the nail gun he'd purchased from the local hardware store, he pressed his phone's volume up a couple of times and got to work.

As quickly as he began attaching the boards, however, he stopped when he caught a flash of a reflection in the black paint of his F250. Someone was coming up the driveway. He leaned to his right, nail gun hoisted at his side, as he waited to see who it was. With any luck, it would only be a delivery person. Once he'd decided to stay, he'd ordered supplies he doubted he could quickly get in town. No need to delay the work to be done.

Luck wasn't on his side today, however, because it was neither a brown nor a white boxy vehicle that pulled up. Nope. It was a shiny red Toyota Prius with a set of sweet custom graphite rims.

He pulled the earbuds from his ears but didn't turn off the compressor. Then he waited for Megan to get out of her car.

It took a minute, as she seemed to need to gather something from her passenger seat, the passenger *floor*board, and from directly behind where she still sat. And the longer he waited, the more effort it took to care that he'd been interrupted. He'd noticed that trait about her before. She was brilliant. *Seriously.* Even smarter than his baby brother. But the inside of her car, the few times he'd caught glimpses of it, always looked like someone's catch-all drawer had exploded.

Fighting the urge to go over and take a peek inside, he waited, wondering what she was doing out there. And when she finally stood from the car, his earlier humor shifted to bafflement.

He put the nail gun down and flipped off the compressor.

"What are you doing, Manning?"

Her head whipped around at his question, making it clear she hadn't yet seen him standing behind the house. In her hands were a set of clear, plastic work goggles, an enormous jug of water, rawhide gloves, a baseball cap, and a bottle of sunscreen.

She juggled the items, switching most of them off in the crook of one arm, until only the gloves remained in the other hand, then she held them up. "I've come to help."

He glanced down her body, taking in the faded jeans and worn T-shirt. "Help?"

"Correct." She juggled her armload back into two hands and headed for the deck. "I've got to say, though"—her boot-clad feet carefully picked their way through the tools scattered across the driveway—"that I kind of had my heart set on running the wood chipper."

At her words, he frowned. She deposited her "supplies" on the third step and surveyed the mess he'd made, hands going to her slim hips, before finally tracking her gaze over to where he remained.

And then she grinned at him. "I'm good with doing this, though. Put me to work, Wilde."

He didn't so much as move. "I am not putting you to work."

"Sure you are." She downed a long guzzle of water, smacking her lips afterward as if she'd just applied lipstick, then she smeared sunscreen over her nose and cheeks. "That's what you do after suggesting someone come over to help."

"But I *didn't* suggest you come over to help." He hadn't even spoken to her since Friday.

"Of course you did." She tugged on her gloves and grabbed her goggles, then paused, goggles positioned just above her eyebrows, while she eyed him from under the protective lenses. "You said that if I wanted to stay busy, I should get myself a pair of work gloves and come help."

She rolled her eyes up as if to point out said work gloves, and he pursed his lips.

He *had* said that.

But he certainly hadn't expected her to take him up on it.

Having no time for delay, he made sure his frown remained intact, narrowed his eyes for good measure, and stomped over to where she stood. "I have a *lot* to get done today, Megan, and none of it involves teaching someone how to run power tools. So please . . . *go home.*"

He reached out, intending to take her by the shoulders and steer her back to her car, but the brown eyes now glowering at him through the protective wear—daring him to put his hands anywhere near her body—had him immediately dropping his arms.

He let out a sigh.

She did the same.

Then as they'd briefly done at the store Friday afternoon, they had a stare off. In the short time he'd gotten to know her, he'd learned that her stubbornness could give his a run for its money. And something told him that today *his* money would be the one lost.

"Seriously, Meg." He continued to scowl.

"*Seriously*, Nate."

He gave it another ten seconds, but in the end, she won.

"*Fine.*" He threw his hands up. "Stay and help. See if I care." He nodded toward the pile of deck boards he'd dropped earlier. "You can hand me the boards."

He headed back to where he'd left off on the ramp, leaving her to follow, but when he picked up the nail gun and turned to hold out a hand for a board, she hadn't moved from her spot. And she looked quite ticked. She now stood with her own arms crossed and one set of toes rapidly tapping out in front of her.

"What now?" He truly didn't want any help. Mostly because as a rule, he preferred to work alone. But also because he didn't want *her* help. He didn't need the distraction.

And hello . . . *distraction*!

He glowered at her. She wasn't a distraction in the way his brother had meant when the asswipe had asked if there was anything going on between him and Megan, though. Because of course there wasn't anything going on. Nor would there ever be. She was Jaden's ex!

But still . . . she *did* bother him. And mostly because he *had* noticed her.

And he didn't care for that one bit.

It hadn't been while she and Jaden had been together, of course. At that point, she'd been nothing more than an assumed future sister-in-law. But given he'd since spent more time around her . . . like it or not . . . he'd noticed.

Like the fact that she always smelled like the pears he'd once harvested in Oregon.

That her smile, when so spontaneous that it even caught her off guard, could wipe all other thoughts from a man's mind.

And he'd also noticed that she didn't put up with crap. From anyone.

That particular trait just *might* have played into his current suggestion that she do nothing more than stand off to the side and hand him boards like a good little girl while he did the heavy lifting.

He bit back a grin as she continued to glare at him. Her cheeks had heated to a splotchy pink, and when she finally did move, stomping over to him as he'd previously done to her, he merely doubled down. "What?" he growled out.

"*What?*" Her eyes snapped, and he darn near whipped his head back to keep from being singed. "I'll tell you *what*." She jabbed him in the chest. "I didn't come out here, Nate Wilde, to play assistant to anybody. And I *won't* stand around and be insulted as if that's all I'm capable of."

"Fine." He didn't look away. "Then go to the store. I'm sure *they* could use your help."

She jabbed again. "The store is closed on Mondays, you jackass."

He knew that. It had always been that way. "Then go *home*, Megan. Or hell, go shopping. Enjoy your day off. I don't care where you go, but just—"

When she jabbed him in the chest a third time, he caught her finger—because darn it, it *hurt*—and they once again had a stare off. Only, this time, he refused to back down. He also found himself having a hard time keeping his smile under wraps. He'd never seen her so riled up, and he knew it was sexist to think it cute . . . but sweet Jesus . . . it was cute.

Or maybe it's just that *she* was cute.

The thought had him letting go of her finger as quickly as he'd snagged it. He had to quit thinking such thoughts. And he had to send her packing.

"Megan." His calmer tone had her switching gears, and her anger seemed to sweep away as quickly as it had appeared. "When I suggested you come out here before, I promise you, I said it as a joke. So, while I *do* appreciate your offer"—he dipped his head as he looked down at her and tried to come off as contrite—"there's honestly no need for you to stay. I can handle this myself." He'd done construction for years. Building a ramp was no biggie.

"But I *want* to help." Her proclamation was as soft as it was determined, and he could see in her eyes that she truly did. They'd lightened with her tone, took on a more amber hue. "I want to do whatever I can," she explained, "because I don't want you all to lose this place. I don't want *Max* not to have a place to come home to."

At the mention of his father, the muscles in his chest contracted. "Dad will definitely have a place to come home to. I promise you that."

He'd witnessed Megan's concern for his dad before. After the accident, when she'd shown up at the hospital. When she'd asked about him practically every time Nate had seen her since. And during each of those times, she'd asked about his dad *before* bringing up any other topic of conversation.

"He won't be home for a few more weeks," he reminded her, "so I have plenty of time to get this finished."

She nodded and looked down at the work he'd already completed. He'd spent the weekend working through the list he'd started at the store Friday afternoon, and after talking to a couple of buddies he'd originally met in Alaska—guys who'd built handicapped ramps more recently than he—he'd double-checked ADA compliance. If he was going to do the work at the house, then he'd make sure to do it to code.

"But I want to help," Megan said again, and this time it was more of a plea than a statement. "It's the least I can do. Because I should have . . ."

When she shook her head instead of finishing her sentence, he reached out. "Don't."

He grazed the backs of his fingers over the upper part of her arm. He knew what she'd intended to say. Because he'd been thinking the same thing for the last two weeks. Only, he'd been thinking it about himself.

"You *shouldn't* have, Megan." He dropped his hand back to his side. "You *shouldn't* have done anything. You didn't know he was sick. He didn't tell anyone."

Her eyes looked hollow. "But I did see him acting 'off' a couple of times."

He hated the hurt shining back at him.

"I did, too," he admitted, and at his words, her gaze reached deeper into his soul than anyone else's ever had. That made his guilt claw at him even more. Because he *had* seen his dad acting off. More than once. He'd been unsteady. Confused. Especially that last morning.

But Nate had been more worried about his own feelings than to think anything of his dad's actions other than that the man was getting old. People did odd things when they aged. Or so he'd told himself.

He'd selfishly avoided the reality staring him in the face for nearly two months.

He'd ignored every blatant sign flashing in front of him.

And he'd done all of that even before that last morning.

"Here." He handed the nail gun to Megan. His dad's loss wasn't on Megan. That was for sure. "I'll cut. You attach."

MEGAN TOOK THE NAIL GUN, surprised at Nate's sudden change in mood, then twisted her wrist so she could see the side of the bracket where the nails came out.

"Megan!"

She jerked her attention back to Nate. *"What?"*

"Don't turn the nail gun toward your face." The man looked ready to pull his own hair out. She scowled at him.

"I didn't." It had been angled across the front of her. Pointed *away* from both of them. She lowered the gun to her side, making sure her finger wasn't anywhere near the trigger. "And anyway, the compressor isn't even on." She nodded toward the connected tank. "I made sure before I looked at the gun."

Again, he sported a pull-his-own-hair-out look, with both hands clenched tight where they rested on the table saw and his jaw just as tense. "But I *just* had the compressor on. Right before you pulled up. It's still pressurized, and the hose is still attached. With only a light touch, the gun could easily fire."

Oh. She gulped. Well, he had her there. She hadn't even thought about that. "Still," she dragged the word out, not quite ready to lose without a fight, "I didn't—"

"Just don't do it again. Okay?" His tone portrayed the strain evident in his entire body, and she pressed her lips together, cutting off her argument. Because he was right. Her actions could easily have been unsafe.

She nodded. "I promise not to do it again." And then the gratefulness that passed over his features pleased her a little too much.

"Thank you." He nodded toward the ramp behind her, and the tension visibly drained from his shoulders. He then went into teacher mode. "After you turn the compressor on, just line the boards up with the outside of the frame, hold the bracket head of the gun tight against the wood, and shoot."

"Easy enough." Turning, she set about her task—and she ignored the silently whispering question as to why making him happy had made *her* happy.

They worked in silence for the next forty-five minutes, her attaching boards and him measuring and cutting, and before she realized it, they'd reached the platform area where the ramp changed directions. She grabbed the measuring tape before Nate could move for it himself, wiped at the line of sweat that had formed along her hairline, and checked the length needed for the platform boards.

"Five feet," Nate said from behind her. "Exactly."

And he wasn't wrong.

When she straightened, expecting to find him lining up

another board to be cut, she instead discovered him within arm's reach, holding out a bottle of Gatorade. But rather than immediately take it, she eyed the bottle with skepticism. Did he have visions of it being filled with poison? If for no other reason than so he could have the afternoon all to his lonely self again?

She managed not to roll her eyes at the likely possibility and, instead, lifted her gaze.

"Thanks," she offered, noting that the stony expression which had appeared when she'd first shown up was once again firmly in place. Then she had the thought that the Gatorade might, instead, be meant as a peace offering. Because the man *had* tried awfully hard to get rid of her earlier.

And she *had* been an excellent source of help.

And stubborn or not, even *he* had to acknowledge that fact. If only to himself.

Taking up the drink, she decided she'd accept the offering as a symbol of peace—no matter how it had been meant—and guzzled a third of the bottle. Once her initial thirst had been quenched, she looked back over at Nate. "I saw your dad this morning."

His brows shot up. "You went by the rehab center?"

"I did." She took another swallow, keeping an eye on Nate. Today was the first time Max had been up for visitors outside of family. "I only spent a few minutes with him," she shared. "Didn't want to wear him out. But he looked"—she shrugged, not knowing how else to describe Max without sounding maudlin—"good . . . considering."

"Yeah . . ." Nate's gaze drifted from her to some spot over her shoulder, not offering any other thoughts on the matter, and Megan turned away to balance her drink on the framed edge of the platform. With both hands now free, she headed for the back of his truck.

"He did mention that you hadn't visited over the weekend." She spoke as she hoisted a twelve-foot length of lumber onto her shoulder. "He asked if you'd left town."

As she dropped the plank beside the saw, she glanced over and caught the same guilty expression on Nate's face that she'd seen earlier—which also matched the one he'd worn Friday afternoon.

"I've been busy." He motioned to the ramp before following her back to the truck.

"That's what I told him."

"Is that right?" He looked down his nose at her when they reached his lowered tailgate, a humored smirk now flirting with his eyes. "Except that you haven't seen me all weekend, Manning. So, in reality, you had no clue *what* I'd been doing."

"Wrong." She swatted his hands away as he tried to stop her from pulling out a board. "I knew exactly what you were doing. I saw Jaden in town this morning, and he told me."

The muscles in Nate's body tensed for a split second, almost as if in the beginnings of some sort of seizure, before he pushed her hands away yet again and slid out a stack of boards. He moved to the table saw, dropped the boards from chest height to clatter loudly at his feet, and when he turned back, the humor that had previously crept into his features was gone.

"Of *course* Jaden told you." His lips barely moved as he spoke, and the words—combined with the obvious sentiment—had her hackles going up.

"What do you mean by that?"

He once again looked down his nose at her. "What I mean is that of course *Jaden* told *you*. Because that's what you two do, isn't it? Keep up with each other. Stay in each other's lives."

"We don't . . . "

Nate's eyes narrowed, and she jutted out her chin.

She and Jaden were still friends, yes. But that was all. And that was important to her.

They'd known each other for years before they'd dated, and granted, their friendship had gone through a definite rough patch after the breakup, but they'd gotten beyond that in the last few weeks. Which was essential, being that she wanted to remain in Birch Bay indefinitely. And even more so, due to her now working for his family.

At least, she *hoped* to continue working for his family. If they ended up selling the farm . . .

She didn't want to think about that. She liked living in Birch Bay. She liked being invested in the Wilde family's businesses.

She *liked* the life she'd laid out for herself here.

No. Nate had this wrong. Nothing but friendship remained between her and Jaden.

"I'm not *staying* in his life, Nate." She allowed her own irritation to show. "Not like that. And you've been around me enough the past couple of months that you good-and-well know it, too."

"What I *know* is that he's now engaged. But maybe *you've* forgotten that."

"Of course I haven't forgotten that." Her anger spiked. Seriously, what was his issue? "I even helped him plan out his proposal."

"Which is *exactly* my point."

She took a step back at his eruption and bumped hard into the tailgate.

"Snarl at me all you want"—reaching behind her, she rubbed at the spot where the tailgate had jabbed—"but your *point* makes no sense. I fully support the two of them as a couple. I was the one who first suggested they go out. And I'm *not*—"

A white Honda appeared in the driveway behind them, and Megan bit off any further argument. It was Arsula and Jaden.

Nate eyed the vehicle until the car came to a complete stop, and then he slowly turned back to her. Both of them glared at each other, both breathing harder than a simple conversation should entail, and Megan wondered how they'd veered so far off path that what had started as pleasant had turned to attacking.

"Hey, guys," Arsula called out as she hurried around the front of her car.

"Hey," Megan and Nate said at the same time. Neither of them sounded very welcoming, and Megan caught Arsula sliding a sideways look their way. Before Arsula could say anything else, though, Jaden spoke from the passenger seat, and his fiancée made a beeline for him. Given the slash of pain across his face, he'd likely just come from a rough physical therapy session.

After Jaden and Arsula made their way into the house, Megan decided to get back to work. She'd come out there to help, after all, not to be accused of something that wasn't true. So, she saw no reason in continuing the conversation.

Nate, however, had other ideas.

"I'm just saying," he started, and from the quieter tone and the fact that the hairs on the back of her neck stood up, she knew he'd moved in closer, "that it's weird. That's all."

"What's weird?" She grabbed the nail gun and shot a pointed look at the table saw.

"Your being involved with Jaden's engagement."

"But *why?*" She didn't see the problem. She'd helped out a friend.

In fact, given how much she and Arsula had gotten to know each other over the past months, and the fact that she'd also created and deployed Arsula's new intuitive coaching website for her, she'd actually helped out *two* friends.

Nate narrowed the gap even more when he put his face directly in front of hers. "Because it's *odd*, Manning. Because you were with the guy for four years. And to hear him tell it, *you* intended to marry him."

True. She wet her lips. The two of them *had* planned to get married. They'd had their plans firmly blocked out for quite a while. He'd finish his master's in Seattle, then they'd both move here where she'd work long-distance in her originally chosen field while Jaden would get certified and eventually open his own office as a family and children's counselor. It had been a solid plan, and that's one hundred percent what she'd wanted. As well as the house and kids they'd not only planned for but had already started saving for.

Only, things had changed after she'd stayed in Birch Bay to

help out his family. Time and distance had been eye-opening. And what she'd discovered was that somewhere along the four years, not only had her and Jaden's passion waned . . . but her desire to spend years coding computer applications had, as well.

Both of those realizations had terrified her. Heck, they *still* terrified her to some extent. Because she'd had a plan, and she was a woman who liked plans. Plans were the perfect counterpart to lists. However, when it came to her decision regarding Jaden . . . she had zero doubts. And the reason for that was simple. She refused to settle.

She refused to marry a man whose chemistry was better as friend than lover. She didn't want someone just because they "fit" or because it was comfortable. She wanted her *person*. And she wanted her person to be as madly, passionately unable to live without her as she wanted to feel toward them. Also, given she'd basically turned her back on her multiple years of education and was actively trying to make her new life in Birch Bay, she really hoped she could find her person *here*.

She put the nail gun back down, pushing away any lingering worries about past decisions. Onward and upward, she thought. Because she had a new plan.

"I'm not with Jaden anymore, Nate." She let him see the confidence she felt with that decision. "And I haven't been for a while now."

"For two months," he lobbed back.

"Exactly. And *I'm* the one who broke up with *him*. Don't forget that."

"I haven't forgotten."

He hadn't moved away either, and they stood there, neither of them angry any longer nor looking ready to spew venom. But he still clearly had a point to make. "So then," she said, "*what* is your issue?"

But this time he didn't have an answer. He just stood there. Staring.

Breathing.

Smelling like testosterone-laden male and the pine-scented Montana outdoors.

The thought whipped through her, causing her to rear back, and the idea of putting distance between them suddenly became priority number one. Her feet began to move. What had they even been arguing about? And why was she now thinking about how the man smelled?

"I need to go." She racked her brain for a reason, already heading for her car. "I . . . have a date tonight." Because yes, she did. "I need time to primp."

She groaned inwardly, but she kept walking. She never needed five hours to get ready.

"A date?"

The dubious tone of Nate's question brought her feet to a halt, and she slowly looked back. Her irritation once again rose. "*Yes*," she drew the word out. "Is that so hard to believe?"

"No. Of course not. I just . . ." His brow creased. "You mean with a man, right?"

Shock had her staring. What? Did he think that being with Jaden had ruined her for all other men or something? That she'd switched to women?

"I mean," Nate stammered. He shifted on his feet. "A date where *he's* paying? Where he's picking you up? That kind of thing?"

The hole he dug only got bigger. "Well, my-my, Mr. Wilde. Aren't you just the traditionalist? Should he also hold every door for me? See me safely back into my apartment? Oh"—she touched a finger to her lips—"I know. Maybe he should also check all my closets and under my bed when he takes me home, too."

She shuddered in mock damsel-in-distress, and Nate flushed in response. And dang if she didn't find that cute.

She turned back for her car. She didn't need to be finding anything about Nate cute.

And anyway, he was too masculine to be "cute." He was more—

"I didn't mean to imply that a woman can't pay for her own meal." He spoke from behind her, and when she once again peeked back, for the first time that afternoon, she got a glimpse of an actual smile.

It was miniscule, but still . . .

Sensual.

The word whispered through her, and she almost nodded before catching herself. That was it, though. The man was sensual.

His smell.

The way his hair was just a little too long. Perfect for a woman to run her fingers through.

The brooding way he watched a person—which, alone, could evoke a full-body shiver.

She opened her car door and stood behind it while also mentally erasing every thought she'd just had. "Then how about the idea of a woman paying for a *man's* meal?" she asked. She eyed his jeans-clad legs as they started her way. "If the woman were the one who'd done the inviting," she went on. "Could you get behind something that forward thinking?"

"I could." He kept moving, and she kept an eye on the shrinking distance. "I could even support a woman paying for whatever form of . . . *entertainment* the date might involve."

His feet stilled with the last word, and neither of them said anything else for a long beat. But from the shocked expression on his face—as well as her own thoughts—she knew that both their minds had sunk into the gutter as far as what "entertainment" could be part of a date.

Finally, Nate hung his head, and his shoulders shook with laughter. "I did *not* mean that the way it sounded."

"No?" She couldn't help it; she chuckled along with him. And the tension that had so quickly wound through her drifted into the wind. "Then tell me, Nate, what other forms of entertainment *were* you thinking of? How do you entertain *your* dates?"

His laughter abruptly ceased, and his blue eyes were once again on hers.

Megan gulped.

"Never mind." She climbed into her car. What was wrong with her today? "It doesn't matter anyway. This is strictly a dinner-as-entertainment kind of date." She slammed her door, but because the window had been down when she'd pulled up, she didn't fully block herself off from the testosterone-laden, pine-air-smelling, cute-cheek-flushing man.

He came to her door.

"I need to go," she said, repeating her earlier assertion, and then she sat there, looking straight ahead instead of at him. And she wondered why her ex-boyfriend's brother suddenly made her itchy between the shoulder blades.

"Megan." The way he said her name, a little soft, a little husky, had her throat going dry.

And she wanted to kick herself. This was *Nate.*

Jaden's *brother.*

"What?" she scratched out.

He wrapped his fingers around the bottom of the open window and squatted down to her level, and she got another noseful of man. "I'm sorry that I upset you."

"About what?"

He nodded toward the house. "About Jaden."

"Oh." *Yeah.* That's what they'd been talking about.

What they'd been *arguing* about.

She glanced over at the house before bringing her gaze back to Nate's. She didn't want any of the Wildes thinking she wasn't over her ex. "I'm not still hung on up him, Nate." Her words swirled into the space between them. "I promise you that. And I truly am happy for their engagement."

"I know." His expression went repentant. "And I also know that *he's* happy with Arsula."

"Then really . . . *what* is your issue?" She stared at him now, this time breathing him in on purpose, if only to prove that there was nothing special about the man. He was just Nate.

"I just don't understand it," he said at last, and as one shoulder lifted, she could read vulnerability in his eyes. "How two people could be . . ." His words trailed off briefly before he added, ". . . and then for you to be okay with him getting engaged so quickly."

His non-question ended with another shrug, and Megan found herself turning in her seat to face him. Then she allowed a moment of pure honesty with herself. One she hadn't let happen before. The quick engagement *had* shocked her. Not because she wanted to be with Jaden. She hadn't been lying about that. But because it *had* hurt a little to know that he'd found that kind of love so quickly.

That she'd been so right in her assessment that *he* wasn't that for her.

"Honestly," she said now, her voice cracking before she cleared it, "I was over him weeks before I ended things. I hadn't fully even admitted it to myself until the night we broke up, but I suppose, that being the case, that plays into me being okay with everything now."

Because she *was* okay with everything.

However, as she'd done far too many times since the moment she'd first considered breaking up with her once long-time boyfriend, she wondered if there was actually someone out there who *could* share that kind of lasting love with her. Or was she doomed to be more like her family?

Doomed to either leave . . . or to be left?

Chapter Four

✦

He stood me up.

Megan tapped Send on her phone four days later and stared at it as she willed three dots to appear in the bottom left corner. When they popped up almost immediately, she let out a breath. Thank goodness for Brooke.

Mark? her friend replied.

Exactly.

The guy you went out with Monday night?

Before Megan could answer, Brooke started typing another message, so she waited. When her phone buzzed in her hand once again, the returned words put a smile on her face.

The "I own 35 pairs of loafers, all in different styles" spray-tanned "out- doorsman" who'd insisted on another date just so *he* could buy dinner this time?

That pretty much summed Mark up. Megan snickered.

`The one and only.`

The dots went to work again as soon as Megan sent her reply, but at the same time, a pair of trouser-covered legs appeared in her peripheral vision. They stopped directly beside her table, and she quickly slid her gaze to the floor. The shoes at the ends of the pant legs were a crisp black loafer—instead of the navy basket-weave pattern of Monday night—and she let a smile inch up. Though he absolutely wasn't forever kind of potential, she'd had a decent enough time on her first date with Mark. At least, good enough to accept a free meal in return.

Only, when she looked up, ready to *consider* forgiving him for keeping her waiting, it wasn't her date who stood before her.

"Ma'am?" The manager of the restaurant offered a tight pull of his lips. "Will you be ordering now?"

It was Friday night, and the Lakefront Grill was a happening place. Her waiter had already stopped to check on her multiple times, as well the hostess and a woman she thought was one of the bartenders. But now she got the big guns. Apparently, her sitting there, ordering nothing more than a Diet Coke for half an hour was the limit of their patience.

"Can I wait a few more minutes?" Not that she expected Mark to show up at this point. She just wasn't ready to skulk through the diners being made to feel like even more of a loser than getting stood up already did.

The manager stared at her, his jaw set and his eyes two squinty little black orbs, and Megan guessed he also fought back a sigh. She simply stared in return.

In the end, he caved. "Ten minutes." But his tone made it clear that in exactly six hundred seconds, he *would* be back. And if she didn't order dinner at that time? He'd personally be escorting her out.

As the man walked away, she pulled a face, then picked her

phone back up. Brooke had sent several more messages—a solil-oquy about the inadequacies of the men in the Birch Bay dating pool—but Megan didn't respond to that line of thinking. Instead, she thumbed out a quick offer.

> Be at the Lakefront in less than ten and I'll buy you the best steak on the menu.

She could almost see her friend's disdainful eyes staring back at her. Brooke's parents owned a meat shop, and there wasn't any better cut of steak out there.

> Please, Megan added, before Brooke could reply. I don't want to eat alone.

But alone or not, she *would* stay and eat, she decided. Because leaving hungry, simply due to some man not showing up when he'd said he would, would be ridiculous.

> I'm actually on a date myself.

Megan blinked at the response. What? Why didn't you tell me?!?

> Last-minute offer. Department head of mathematics.

Brooke was an instructor at the Salish Kootenai College.

> Then why are you texting with *me* if you're on a date with someone else?

The three dots appeared instantly, and Megan dipped her head as she waited, making it so she couldn't see the manager.

The man had crossed to the edge of the bar area and was now staring at her as if it were his life's mission to make her uncomfortable.

Her phone buzzed with Brooke's reply.

Because he's been in the bathroom for twenty-five minutes. He's either escaped out the window or the afterburners appetizers made him sick. Either way, it's a no for me. Dude needs a heartier stomach to hang out with me . . . or he at least needs to HANG OUT WITH ME!

Laughter bubbled up at both visuals of Brooke's date, and she quickly tapped out a question. Have your entrees been served yet?

Ten minutes ago.

Anything good?

Everything cold by this point.

Megan snickered again. Her friend was a bit of a foodie. And she *hated* having to eat her meals cold. Box it up and meet me at my place. We can reheat it and eat out on the patio. I'll provide plenty of wine and turn the outside heaters on high.

As she waited for Brooke to respond, she peeked out from under her eyelashes again, checking to see if the manager was still practicing his scary glare. But her gaze landed on a familiar set of blue eyes, instead.

Nate.

She sat up straighter.

Her follow-up reaction, after scanning all the way down to his cowboy boots and back, was to look away. Because the memory of Monday afternoon, when she'd run from the Wilde place after suddenly finding the brother of her ex intoxicating, was suddenly all too real.

Nate.

Who could be harsh, but was also refreshingly honest.

As well as hot and brooding and sexy and . . .

Sensual.

She closed her eyes and breathed in slowly through her nose. *Nate.*

Whom she'd never *once* thought twice about before Monday afternoon.

She opened her eyes again. What was wrong with her? She wasn't going to think twice about him now, either. He was just Nate. Part owner of the business she worked for and growing friend due to their acquaintance within his family and that business. He was not . . . *Nate.*

Returning her attention to the bar, when she found him still looking her way, she lifted her chin in acknowledgement, not allowing so much as a smile to flicker across her lips. When his greeting was returned in the same fashion, she breathed out a sigh of relief. It was just Nate.

But then the manager appeared directly in front of her, blocking her view, and she had the urge to shove the man out of the way.

"Ma'am?" He scowled at her in a way that reminded her of her mother.

"I'm only twenty-five," she mumbled as she snatched up her phone. She rose from the table, suddenly too tired of his attitude to stick around. "I'm too young to be called ma'am."

The manager gave the impression of neither hearing her

words nor caring whether she'd spoken or not. Instead, he merely held one arm out in the direction of the door and waited for her to precede him. But before she could do more than gather her coat and bag, Nate was there, his eyes latching onto hers.

"Megan." He stepped between her and the manager and took her hand. "My apologies. We must have gotten our signals crossed."

Their signals?

Her confusion quickly fizzled when a glint appeared in Nate's eyes, and he tilted his head ever so slightly toward the waiting manager. "Did we not agree to meet in the bar?" He held up a beer that was two-thirds empty, and she didn't need any additional prodding.

"Oh my *gosh*." Pulling her hand free, she pressed her fingertips to her mouth. "Is that what we said?" She let her eyes go wide. "I'm so sorry. Can you ever forgive me?"

Without looking at the manager again, she retook her seat, somehow managing to keep her giggles inside, and when Nate settled onto the chair across from her, she flashed him a wide, fake-adoring smile.

"Ma'am?" The manager tried once more, but Nate took over.

"It's my fault," he told the man. "I should have checked the dining room before now."

Nate didn't take his eyes off the manager until the other man, huffing under his breath, finally walked away, and when he did turn to Megan, the smile that she'd only caught a tiny glimpse of Monday afternoon suddenly went from miniscule to full-on. White teeth flashed inside generous lips, and she noticed that one of his front teeth had a tiny nick missing from the inside corner.

How had she never noticed that before? She'd seen him smile plenty of times.

Her phone suddenly vibrated in her hand, and she jumped as

if it had zapped her. Looking down, Brooke's picture smiled back at her.

"Do you need to get that?"

"No." She shook her head at the same time she pushed the button to end the call, and that's when she noticed all the texts she'd missed. "But I do need to send a quick message."

"Sure."

She quickly scanned the waiting texts and saw that due to a questionable medical issue, Brooke had not only paid for, but packaged up the meals, and she was now ready to meet up at Megan's. Megan peeked back up, unsure what to do. Was Nate's "rescuing" her also an offer to stick around and have a meal? To truly let her save face?

Or had he merely been wanting to annoy the manager because the man was a douche?

"Problem?" Nate asked. He nodded toward the phone. "Is it the loser who stood you up?"

A quick chuckle slipped out. "Not the loser. And not that I'd bother replying if it was."

"Good to know." He unrolled his silverware and tucked the napkin onto his lap. "Then if it's all the same with you, *I'm* your date now. I didn't really want to eat by myself tonight anyway." He then leaned in and whispered conspiratorially, "Unless, of course, you'd rather pretend I showed up too late, so you can storm out of here, showing 'me' you won't put up with it."

She found it admirable that he'd be willing to be embarrassed like that. "How about I 'put up with it' by sending *him* the bill after we order the best things on the menu?"

When Nate's lips once again curved at her words, she once again noticed the chipped tooth. She also noticed that his lips were almost a sunburned color. But not in a bad sunburn kind of way. More in a completely kissable, totally mind-melting sort of way.

Her thoughts froze. What in the world was wrong with her?

"Megan?" Nate's lips moved to form her name, and mortification engulfed her. Sheesh. All she'd done since sitting down was stare at the man's mouth.

She licked her lips, suddenly wishing she hadn't finished her last Diet Coke. "Yes?"

He nodded once more toward her hand. "Your phone is ringing again."

"Oh." She jerked her eyes downward. She was acting as if she'd never been on a date before.

Not that this was a real date.

Her sense of survival finally kicked in, and, as if the buzzing device was a lifeline in some sort of weird dating-but-not-really-dating game show, she slid her finger across the screen.

"Brooke." She spoke as she brought the phone to her ear.

"Are you okay?" her friend's voice rang out.

"I—"

"This is the third time I've called! Why have you been ignoring me? Did loafer guy show up and kidnap you? Do I need to call the police?"

Megan watched as the corners of Nate's lips quirked up yet again, and this time she found herself smiling back. "No police," she assured Brooke, and as the waiter showed up with menus and fresh glasses of water, she added, "but I do have to back out on our *plans.*"

She stressed the last word, hoping Brooke would understand she didn't want to say out loud that she'd been about to leave the restaurant to have dinner with someone else.

"Plans?" Brooke said hesitantly. And then she groaned. "Oh, for the love of Pete. Please tell me that loafer guy did *not* show up there."

Megan offered the waiter a close-lipped smile as he set down a refill of her drink. "Not him, no." She locked eyes with Nate. "A friend did, though. And I owe him. I'll talk to you tomorrow?"

"Wait . . . *tomorrow?*" Brooke repeated the word in a way that meant far more than Megan had intended, and Megan felt her cheeks heat.

"Not *that* kind of 'tomorrow,'" she gritted out. She offered Nate an apologetic look, as clearly, he could hear every word and read between every line. *"Just* a friend."

Silently, she added that it was a friend who would *definitely* be going home by himself. If only because he wasn't the one currently lusting after the other.

"Well, that's a little disappointing," Brooke bemoaned.

"Not as disappointing as your date having to rush off to urgent care because he couldn't handle a jalapeño."

There was a pause before Brooke added, "Well played."

Her friend signed off, and once Megan had hung up, Nate picked up his beer bottle and held it up in a toast.

"To friends," he said with a wink. "And not to loafer guy."

She laughed with him. "To friends."

And to "Just Nate" sitting across from her.

Dinner became normal at that point, as well as quite enjoyable. Nate was more talkative than usual, so after they ordered, they chatted. They talked about the weather, about how the store's first week after reopening went, about how delicious the food was and how loafer guy was totally missing out, and she also got an update on his dad. Nate hadn't made it back out to the rehab center yet, but his siblings had.

"They're still thinking he'll get to come home in a few weeks?" she asked.

"That's what they say."

She twirled a piece of pasta around her fork. "And how do you think that's going to go?" She watched him as she spoke. "Will he be able to get around in the house okay?"

Will you *be okay?*

She didn't ask the last question, but it resonated inside of her. Because the moment the conversation had shifted to Max, she'd once again sensed the guilt Nate carried.

"The improvements to the house will be done by then." Nate stabbed at a remaining bite of salad. "I've finished the ramp and have ripped out the bath in one of the downstairs bedrooms."

He looked up and explained. "I've worked in construction in past off-seasons, so we're doing a full remodel. Nick is going to help. We'll swap out the shower for a roll-in one, add a lowered sink, rails. The works."

"Sounds like a good plan."

"Yeah. And we're following ADA guidelines to the letter. No need putting out the effort if we don't intend to do it right."

That was a theory she could get behind.

She pushed her plate away and propped her elbows on the table. "Can I ask you about something else?"

The look he returned had the breath catching in her throat. Because just like that, she caught the same vulnerability she'd seen in his eyes earlier in the week.

"What do you want to know?" he said, and for a second, she couldn't remember her own question. She just wanted to sit there, maybe reach over and take his hand. Tell him that everything would be okay.

But she didn't honestly know if everything would be okay. His dad had a long road to recovery; the farm was decimated.

"Are you still planning on leaving after you get everything done?"

And just like that, a curtain dropped over his vulnerability.

"The house"—she didn't let his silent "back off" deter her—"cleaning up the trees that don't make it . . . you're really just going to finish everything and go?"

"Yes."

"But . . . why? How? Your dad has Parkinson's, Nate. He's—"

"I know what the deal is with my dad. But the fact is, I'm not going to stay forever, no matter what. So, what's the difference in leaving now or leaving later?"

She could repeat that same question back to him. Why not stay longer?

Why not stick around and be there for his dad for a while longer?

"Is it money?" The question crossed the line into too

personal, but she couldn't stop herself. "Do you need to get back to a paying job somewhere?" She was aware he'd previously worked in Alaska for chunks out of the year, and Jaden had always implied he traveled around wherever a job took him the remaining months.

Nate sliced into the last chunk of his steak. "I have plenty of money."

"Then . . ." She let her words trail off, astutely reading in his expression that this topic of discussion had come to an end, so she searched for something else. "Fine," she mumbled. She caught sight of the dark trousers and black loafers of the manager again, but the man didn't stop at their table. "Then let's talk about trees. How are the trees at the farm doing?"

Nate popped a bite into his mouth. "Dead."

She stared at him until he finished chewing, refusing to get riled by his antics. *This* was typical Nate. Shut down and providing short, to-the-point answers. Not the pleasant conversationalist who'd initially shown up.

"What about the fifteen percent?" she pushed. "Is it still only fifteen?"

"It is." He forked another bite.

"Have you started cutting down any of the dead ones yet?"

"I have."

She sighed. "Are you intentionally trying to get on my nerves, or are you just obtuse?"

His hand paused with his fork at his mouth again, the last bite of steak lingering, and his eyes drilled a hole into her. But she could see that he was faking his annoyance. He had a smile tucked away, just daring her to pull it out of him, and she became determined to see it.

"Did you miss my expert help while finishing the ramp this week?"

The fork slipped past his teeth, but the corners of his lips twitched as he chewed. "I managed to finish the ramp, cut down a pile of trees, demo the bathroom, *and* cook dinner for myself every night." He held out his empty fork. "Tonight notwithstanding. So, no." He shook his head. "I didn't miss your help."

"*Expert* help," she corrected, and the corners of his mouth twitched again.

"That either." His eyes held hers.

"Then how about my lovely personality?" She widened her eyes and gave him a smile before blinking several times. "Did you miss that?"

"And if I said I had?"

The question caught her off guard. Especially since it was delivered in his straightforward, no-nonsense way. Before she could form any sort of snappy retort, however, their waiter appeared at the table.

"Thank you," Nate said as he accepted the bill.

"No," Megan said. "Tonight's on me." She grabbed the cross-body backpack she used instead of a purse, pulling out a small notebook as she dug for her wallet, and by the time she'd come up with her debit card, Nate had not only passed off his card to the retreating waiter, but he'd also picked up a loose piece of paper that had apparently come out with the notebook.

"Hey." She reached for the paper. "Don't lose that. It has the shopping list for my apartment on there."

The list she still hadn't gotten around to.

"It also has another list on it." Nate eyed her over the paper, confusion marking his brow, and she remembered the other list she'd scribbled on the paper, as well.

Dang.

Instead of answering his unasked question, though, she decided that he deserved a bit of his own medicine. So she kept her mouth shut and merely stared. Her inaction didn't get her the paper back, but it did finally give her that smile she'd been after.

Her insides swooned. Because dang, he had a killer curve to the most luscious set of lips.

"Mike Jackson," he said, his gaze reverting to the paper, and Megan mentally smacked herself for thinking his smile cute. It wasn't cute. It was *evil*.

Just like him.

"Casey Campbell. Justin Angelo."

"Stop it," she whispered. "My lists are none of your business." She held out her hand again.

"Like you asking me if I need to leave Birch Bay because I'm out of money is yours." He ignored her hand and didn't take his eyes off the paper. "Colin Rogers."

"*Fine*. You're right, and I apologize for overstepping." She wiggled her fingers to get his attention, but he only leaned back in his seat.

"No apology needed." He kept reading. "Crews Stevens. Dustin Crowder. Mark Gr—" His eyes shot to hers halfway through Mark's last name, and with his free hand, he pointed to the paper. "That's loafer guy. The guy who stood you up tonight. Mark Gray."

He looked back at the names, and Megan could feel the heat creeping up her neck.

She could also see him putting two and two together.

She still didn't say anything, but she knew he would. And she didn't have long to wait for it to happen.

"These guys are all single." His statement came out sounding like an accusation.

"They are."

"And Mark Gray . . ."

He looked back at the list, and his eyes narrowed in contemplation. When the waiter unobtrusively placed the padded folder back down on the table, Nate signed the receipt, almost without giving it a second look, and then he pinned his eyes on hers. He shook his head.

"Mark Gray isn't good enough for you. Nor is Mike Jackson." He marked through both names with the pen he still held. "And Casey Campbell is questionable."

"Duly noted." She yanked the paper from his hands after he marked Casey with a question mark, and she shoved both paper and her notebook back into her bag. She then stood to leave.

"I'm not joking." He rose to follow her out.

"And I'm not asking."

Several pairs of eyes watched them as she hurried through the crowd several feet ahead of Nate, but she didn't slow to wait for him to catch up. The second she pushed through the outside door and the cool air whipped across her face, though, she stalled to shrug into her jacket.

Her movements stilled when Nate's hands moved to the collar of her coat, and she held her breath as he settled the material onto her shoulders.

"Thank you," she murmured. Then she stepped out of the path of incoming patrons.

"You're welcome." He slipped into his own coat, his gaze sliding to her backpack as he did.

"Don't," she warned.

But he didn't listen. "Why do you have a list of single men in your bag, Megan?"

She looked out into the parking lot instead of into his questioning gaze. "I have lots of lists in there. I happen to like lists."

"I like lists, too, but I don't have a full catalog of all the women I want to date."

Mortification enveloped her, and she brought her gaze back to his. "I don't want to date *all* of them."

"Then what do you want to do with them?"

She stared at him, her intention to correct his presumed assumption that she wanted to go down the list one by one, marking notches on her bed post. But before she could open her mouth, she recognized an honest lack of understanding peering back at her. *Not* a look of judgment.

What she wanted to do with the men on her list was her business, and hers alone. And she *should* tell him so. Instead, because something about his expression made him look as alone as she so often felt, she offered the truth.

"I want a fiancé." She didn't look away as she spoke. "So, I've made a list of potential men, and I'm going through them until I find a contender."

Chapter Five

S he wanted a fiancé.

Nate took another swing at the tree that was proving harder to bring down than he'd anticipated, and he grunted through the movement. That time, his axe finished the job.

So she'd made a list of potential *options*.

He shoved the tree out of the way with his foot and moved to the next. Who did that?

He swung again, recognizing the feel of a blister forming under the protective layer of his right glove, but he didn't let that slow things. He'd been out since daylight, just him and his mighty axe, and he wasn't yet ready to go back in.

Nor was he ready to switch out to the chainsaw, which would be one hundred percent easier.

He finished off that tree, grunted again for no reason other than because he was a man and sometimes men needed to grunt, and then he moved on down the line.

Who looked at finding a husband so matter-of-factly?

He swung. He'd hightailed it out of the parking lot after Megan's announcement the night before, thrown so off balance by her proclamation that he hadn't stopped to ask what kind of hallucinogenic drugs she must have been taking. But that thought had played through his mind all night long. Because who decided they wanted a fiancé and simply went down a list? That wasn't how things were done.

Dating was what a normal person did.

Two people met, hung out, decided if there was the potential for more.

Well . . . other people did that. *He* just hooked up.

But Megan was a normal—*reasonable*—individual. She wasn't the hook-up kind of girl. Nor the clinical-fiancé-finding kind. She was the dating kind. And sure, maybe she was super smart and sometimes overly methodical. And because of that, he could totally see her using lists for the majority of the priorities in her life. Hell, *he* did that. But for a fiancé?

This time he kicked at the trunk of the tree when it was down to the final few chops, and the resounding crack of wood had him puffing up his chest. He kicked one last time, expecting the tree to tumble over, but instead, a burst of pain radiated up his ankle. The resulting throbbing not only deflated his pride but also had his mind shifting from Megan to Jaden.

It had been Jaden's broken ankle that had started *him* down the path of falling for Arsula. Not some damned list.

And, of course, his broken ankle had happened the very night that *Megan* had broken up with him. Nate growled under his breath at the memory. Jaden hadn't taken the breakup well and had instead drunk himself into oblivion at Gabe's wedding reception. Then he'd ended up going home with Arsula, who'd been one of the bridesmaids. And, of course, he'd regretted his actions the next morning, had run from the room like the baby that he could be, and he'd subsequently fallen down the icy outside stairs.

Nate rolled his eyes. His brother was such a cliché.

He glanced toward the house, where baby cliché had been when Nate had come out at sunrise. Though the family home had six bedrooms and it was only the two of them living there at the moment, it had felt far too claustrophobic that morning.

He'd have to go back when Nick arrived, of course. They planned to start the bathroom remodel today. But he did hope that Jaden would be gone by then. And maybe he'd spend the rest of the weekend with Arsula.

Nate rested the axe on its head, ground his teeth together as he lifted his still-throbbing ankle, then he twisted his foot in circles to work out the soreness. He hadn't done any real damage, of course, but he'd apparently put more force behind the kick than he'd realized.

Calming the pain back to a twitch, he lifted the axe and set back to destroying things.

How about my lovely personality? Did you miss that?

He swung a little too hard at the next tree and this time rattled his shoulders. He could practically hear Megan's voice as she'd teased him the night before.

And if I said I had?

He stopped himself before kicking the trunk again—especially since there was barely more than a small chunk knocked out of this one—but he *did* call himself fifty kinds of moron. Because of course he hadn't missed her last week. And what an absurd thing to say just to try to get a rise out of her.

It had been just as absurd as him being jealous when he'd first seen her waiting at the restaurant for a date.

As absurd as the flare of excitement when he realized the date wasn't showing.

He was an idiot. He was *not* attracted to Megan.

He stared down the line of trees he'd just taken down. Megan was nobody to him. She was less than nobody because she was Jaden's ex.

But damn. He *had* enjoyed having dinner with her the night before. She'd made him laugh. She'd eased his burdens for the evening.

He pulled his phone from his back pocket, ostensibly to check the time, but he also knew it was to make sure he hadn't missed any more texts. Because there'd been one waiting for him when he'd woken up that morning.

Thanks again for "rescuing" me last
night and not making me do the stood-up
walk of shame. I owe you one.

He hadn't let himself reply earlier that morning, but he did now.

No return payment needed. Just being a
friend.

He then shoved his phone back into his pocket before he did something stupid like stand there and wait for a reply. He picked up his axe again, but as he lifted it, the muscles in his shoulders protested. Which made him wonder how long he'd been out there. He hadn't even looked at the time while he'd had his phone out.

Reaching for his phone again, he didn't have to call himself an idiot again to know he was one, but before he could slide the device from his pocket, he caught sight of Nick's long strides crossing the field. Nate hadn't even seen his brother pull up.

He waited, less than anxious to head toward the house, and it didn't take long for Nick to reach his side. As he did, he took in both the line of trees that had come down that morning, as well at the section Nate had removed over the last week. Quite a few of the designated "bad" trees were still questionable so they wouldn't come down for another week or two, but not a single tree in the field where they stood had produced so much as a hint of a leaf.

"It sure is sad to see this many gone," Nick said. He braced both hands on his hips.

"I don't disagree." Nate shoved at the trunk of the last one he'd downed. He'd come back out with the tractor in the morning and move everything into piles. "And it's still not looking like more than expected will survive." And those were so scattered, he wasn't sure it would make sense to keep any of them.

"You still don't think that'll be enough to support the store, right?"

"I know it isn't. Not if we want to continue selling items year-round made with Wilde cherries."

They both went quiet, both looking around at the expanse of land that butted up to Flathead Lake, and Nate felt a chunk of his earlier foul mood seep out of him. The land had that ability. As did the water. It was part of the reason he'd stuck around so long this time. He'd missed it.

Nick eyed the axe in Nate's hand but didn't comment on his tool of choice. "You done anything concerning looking for a manager yet?"

"I've written up an initial description of what I think we'll be looking for." His phone buzzed in his back pocket.

"And what do you think that'll be?"

Nate knew that Nick asked because the group of them still had yet to discuss the reality of the situation. Do they sell? Do they replant?

Do they let the place grow over with weeds and leave it for someone else to deal with?

The last option wasn't a valid one, of course. No one wanted to see that. But somedays that's exactly what Nate wanted to do with the place. Because far too often, Wilde Cherry Orchard had felt more a thorn in their sides than a source of pride to be handed down to the next generation. With a narcissistic mother and a father who'd struggled to even attempt to stand up to her, the six of them had been forced to live with the befuddlement of often being played off one another for the sole purpose of their mother having control. Of her having *attention*.

Thankfully, she'd died in a car crash when Nick and he had been ten, but those ten years had been formative. Not to mention, when Dani had come home from college to help finish raising them, nothing had ever been brought up about the mental abuse handed out in their own home. At least not until things had come to a head three years before.

Nate turned, not wanting to relive thoughts of how his family had once been on the precipice of fully shattering, and after grabbing his jacket where he'd earlier tossed it to the ground, he headed for the house. "I wrote the position up as one to manage and replant."

"Is that what you want to do?" Surprise filled his brother's voice.

"I don't know what I want to do. I just . . ."

He trailed off, because it was easier than trying to explain his feelings. And because the whole thing had weighed on his mind far too often over the last few weeks. What he needed to be doing was getting the place in order and making plans to leave. Period. End of story. Which he *was* working on. But other thoughts had plagued him over the last week, as well. Other ideas of how they could use the land and still turn a profit.

"Send it to me if you want me to take a look," Nick offered. "There are a couple of placement agencies who work with the town now. I can get you their names, and once we . . ."

This time it was Nick whose words trailed off. And that was due to the sight of Gabe's SUV turning into the driveway. The drive was long, and the main road couldn't be seen from the house, but from where they were, still a couple hundred feet from the front porch, they could catch glimpses of the turn-off through the pines. And what they saw next was Dani pulling in behind Gabe.

And then Cord.

"What the hell." Nate jerked his eyes over to Nick's. "What's going on?"

"Not a clue."

After the setup at the store the week before, Nate didn't know whether to believe his twin or not, but he also didn't stand around and dwell on it. He took off. Cord was in his own vehicle, which meant he'd driven all the way from Billings. Therefore, this wasn't a surprise visit. Something was up.

He and Nick reached the house at the same time as everyone else, and as they all piled out of their vehicles, Jaden poked his head out the back door.

"Everyone's here?" He scooped up a bite of cereal from an oversized bowl, and Nate took note that his tone hadn't come across as surprised to see everyone.

His temper spiked. "What the hell is going on? What's the ambush about this time?"

Cord held his hands up, a wad of papers clutched in one fist. "No ambush," he said, but his voice brooked no argument. "I started calling as soon as I pulled into town." He nodded toward Jaden. "Jay said you and Nick were in the fields, so we all just came on over. There's something we need to talk about."

Nate looked around at everyone else, still doubting they weren't there to come at him for something, but from the looks on their faces, his siblings had no more of a clue than he did.

"Fine," he said. "Then let's go in."

He didn't wait for everyone else. He took the stairs two at a time, following Jaden back into the oversized living room, and as Dani came up behind him, he heard her say, "Nice ramp."

"Thanks," he mumbled, but he didn't look back.

They all filed into the room, where everyone sat except Cord. Cord positioned himself in front of the floor-to-ceiling windows that faced the lake, held up the papers for the second time, and jumped right into it. "We have an offer to buy the property."

"An offer?" The question came from Dani, and she immediately jumped back up. "We haven't even decided if we want to sell or not."

"Nor have we listed it," Nate added. He watched his other brothers. The entire room had gone on edge.

"It's from a developer in Billings," Cord explained. "I

mentioned the situation, in passing, to a couple of buddies—who apparently mentioned it to a couple of *their* buddies—and what we have is a man looking to not only buy our place, but also the Wyndhams' property next door." The Wyndhams had also lost the majority of their trees, and they'd not been quiet about being ready to get out. "This guy wants to level both houses," Cord went on, "and turn the entire thing into an upscale resort."

It was Jaden who popped up from his seat next. "A resort?" He swung an arm out, motioning toward the windows. "This is a cherry orchard."

"Not anymore," Nate muttered.

"And it *is* in the perfect location to *be* a resort," Gabe tossed out, and Nate could see the wheels turning in his oldest brother's head. "Lakefront," Gabe went on. "Close to hiking, skiing, water sports. I could see it pulling in some cash."

"But it's not a resort!" Jaden yelled, and at his explosion, Dani studied their youngest sibling.

"Since when do you even care that much?" she asked, her words spoken carefully. "You were always the first to want to sell."

"Yeah, well . . . I don't want to sell anymore, okay?" Jaden moved to the windows, his booted foot making a hollow sound with each step across the wood-planked floor. He crossed his arms over his chest and turned back to the room. "This is our home. Have we all forgotten that?"

When silence only greeted his question, he pinned their sister with a look. "And anyway, since when do you *want* to sell?"

"I don't know that I do." She followed Jaden's path, moving slowly as if in deep thought at the same time, until she ended up standing beside their youngest brother. Nate watched as she stared out at the land. At the arriving green from the spring warm-up and at the revamped deck with the new ramp waiting for their dad. "I'd definitely still prefer to save the place," Dani mused. She glanced back over her shoulder. "We're getting it all set up for Dad. But since there *is* an offer on the table, we should at least consider it, I'd think."

Nate didn't say anything, but what surprised him was the desire to respond similarly to Jaden. Because he didn't want to sell, either. And he hadn't realized that until just this moment.

This was *their* house. *Their* orchard.

If some company came through and leveled not only the trees, but the home the six of them had grown up in, it would almost be like they'd never existed.

And it would be far too easy to never be together again.

"The place won't be profitable as is." Nate made himself think logically, but he also let the other ideas he'd been harboring percolate. "Even if we replant, it'll take years to get back to where we were."

"None of us are dependent on the money on a daily basis anyway," Cord pointed out. Which was true. They all *liked* the money, but ever since Gabe and Dani had given up running the place and taken other jobs, it had served only as a side income stream for everyone.

"So, if money isn't the issue, why be in a hurry to do anything with it?" Nick asked, and five sets of eyes shifted to him. "I mean, we don't have to sell just because there's an offer. We could replant. Keep going."

"And who's going to run it?" Gabe asked.

"Whoever we hire," Nick returned.

"And what about the house?" Jaden jumped back in. "And Dad?"

Nate had the answer to that one. "Dad lived in town for several years before he took back over out here. If we hired a manager and included the stipulation that he or she could live in the house while they ran the place, Dad could move back to town."

"But—"

"They make handicapped accessible places, Jaden," Dani pointed out, and Nate could see the anguish on her face. She loved the idea of them keeping this place. Of making it be something other than the house of bad memories their mom had once controlled.

He closed his eyes, blocking out the panoramic view he'd grown so used to over the last weeks. Trying to picture never being able to see it again.

The place held memories, bad *and* good. Would he be okay walking away from it?

"What's the offer?" Gabe asked. He crossed to Cord to look at the papers.

"To be honest," Cord answered, "I think we could do better."

"Better?" Jaden jumped at the opportunity. "Then it's a no. We're not going to give the place away."

"It's not a no or a yes," Gabe replied. "Not yet." He flipped through the pages, his brow furrowing as he read. "But Dani's right. We have to consider it."

"I agree." Cord cupped his hands together in front of him. He stated the dollar amount. "The offer holds only if they can get the Wyndham's place, as well," he said. "But they went to them already. It's a yes."

"They're just going to sell out?" Dani looked crestfallen. "Just like that?"

"It's not just like that," Gabe told her. They'd all been friends with the Wyndhams for years. "They're ready to retire. I ran into Lou in town last week. They want to move to Texas to be closer to their grandkids." He finished with the contract and passed it off to Dani.

"It's not the best offer, for sure," Cord went on, "but we could get out. Quit fighting the place that more than once has tried to take us down."

"Quit fighting for us, you mean?" Nick voiced the exact words Nate had been thinking.

"No." Dani turned to Nick. "If we sell, we don't quit fighting for us. Ever. We're good these days." She took in all of them. "We stay that way."

"Agreed," Gabe confirmed, and though Nate thought Gabe and Dani might actually believe the sentiment, Nate didn't know that he did.

This house—the orchard, for all that it was—had also been the thing that held them together over the years. Even when the only time they saw each other was at harvest. And whether he was here with them or not, Nate didn't want his family to lose that. And *he* could give them that.

He *wanted* to give them that.

"We don't sell," he announced, and everyone turned to look at him.

"Why not?" Cord asked, but he seemed more curious than disagreeing.

"First of all"—Nate pointed toward the papers—"because that's a shit offer. The guy is trying to steal our land right out from under us."

"Agreed," Nick added.

"But if none of us wants to run it," Gabe started, but Nate held up a hand to cut him off.

"We *don't* sell," he reiterated. "At least not yet. Hear me out first."

He rose from the position he'd taken on the arm of the couch and paced to the fireplace.

"I've had a few ideas over the last week," he explained. "Ones I think we could not only make work but that could bring a breath of fresh air to the whole town. It could even help with tourism."

Surprise flashed in Nick's eyes "You want to turn the place into some sort of resort, too?"

"Not a resort. Not exactly. And I don't want to change the house. Dad can stay." Nate looked around at all of them before picking up the notepad he'd left on the mantle the day before. "What I'm proposing we do is add cabins around the property." He flipped to the sketch he'd drawn out and passed the pad off to Nick. "Clear out the dead trees and build individual one- and two-bedroom cabins. We can partner with companies that do hiking, fishing, skiing, that sort of thing. Then we add in a couple of fire pits, picnic tables. Make it a rustic—yet comfortable—place to get away."

"Tours to Glacier National Park," Nick added as he handed the notepad to Gabe.

"Exactly. We're right in the middle of so much that nature has to offer. Why not make it available for others?" When no one said anything else, Nate went on. "And I've figured out how to get it done in a hurry." He rubbed his hands together as excitement built. The conditions Cord had mentioned in the contract had settled the last of the pieces of the puzzle into place. "First of all, if we don't sell, the developer likely won't want the Wyndham's place either. But they still want to go to Texas. So, we offer to rent the house from them."

Gabe looked up from the notebook. "Why would we want to rent their house?"

"To use it for lodging for a construction crew."

"For a . . ." Dani's brows pulled together. "What?"

"To build the cabins." Cord clued in.

"Right." Nate pointed at him. "Along with whoever we can hire locally, I've worked with enough guys in the off-seasons over the years that I'm confident I could have a group here asap. The Wyndham place only has four bedrooms, but it has plenty of square footage. We can bring in enough bunk beds to make room for everyone, then I can start work on the permits and a loan from the bank, and we could potentially break ground as early as next week."

He caught a look of contemplation on Nick, and knew it wasn't so much about the idea as it was for the level of thought Nate had put into this. This wasn't a flash-in-the-pan idea.

"And you'd be willing to stay long enough to see these built?" Cord hedged.

Nate's logical side screamed for him to consider the question further, to think about how staying longer would make it even harder for him to leave later. But he nodded without hesitation. "To keep us from being undercut on a sales price? Absolutely." And also, just because he wanted to. He loved the idea of revamping the place. Of making it still theirs . . . but better.

"And if we do this," Nick added, "when would we have anything ready to rent?"

Nate turned to his twin. "Depending on how many guys I can bring in, I'm looking at ten cabins completed by July fourth. I could hire a manager to run things by then, as well."

Shock filled the room.

"That's only ten weeks from now," Jaden pointed out. "How could you possibly accomplish that?"

"And is that really what we want to do?" Dani added. Nate could see her nerves at the idea of changing the orchard in such a large fashion, but he'd thought about this a lot over the last week.

Actually, the idea had first come to him several years ago.

"I don't know that going forward as we always have is an option these days," Nate answered in all sincerity, and he saw the nods of his brothers' agreement. "It would take too long to regroup. To be the orchard we once were."

"And honestly," Nick added, "I don't know that any of us *want* to be what we once were."

Again, there were multiple nods. Everyone knew Nick wasn't talking about the orchard itself so much as the memories associated with their childhoods.

"But the cherry trees . . ." Dani spoke softly, and then she turned once again and stared out at the land. Nate saw her throat rise and fall with a swallow. "It's who we are," she said, and Nate crossed to put an arm around her.

"It's where we began," he corrected. "But we could build our own future."

"I'm in," Jaden abruptly announced. "Why hand over our blood, sweat, and tears for nothing?"

"Exactly." Nate paused before adding, "We create something

that would bring the kind of price we know we're worth . . . we prove that it's viable . . . and *then* we decide if we want to sell or not."

His sister looked up. "We might still sell?"

"We reevaluate afterward," he confirmed. But in truth, he hoped it wouldn't come to that. He'd love for the place to stay in the family. "Let's see how this season goes first. You put your marketing skills to use filling the cabins with guests, and we see if it's worth staying in the vacation business." He gave his sister's shoulder a squeeze. "And if we do keep it, we replant some of the trees this fall."

"But we won't have the space with the cabins," she argued.

"We don't need a lot. Maybe just the pick-your-own field."

"Or simply enough to support the store," Gabe interjected.

"Right." Nate nodded. "And if that's what we decide, then we tweak things there until we have a big enough crop to fully support our cherry-supplied products again. But wherever we land, the important thing is that we have options." And for the first time in a long time, he found himself wanting options, as well. He wanted to do more than wander the world, looking for the next place to rent a room.

He just wished that coming home could be one of them.

Chapter Six

"I'll see you next weekend, Mrs. Tamry. Have a great day." Megan handed the bagged items over the counter to one of her best customers, and she smiled at the woman's husband as he touched his wife's elbow, and they turned for the door.

"You be sure to save us some of that new jam," Mr. Tamry reminded her.

"One for you and one for your son." She tapped the piece of paper where she'd written the note. "Don't worry. I won't forget."

After the door closed behind the seventy-something couple, the store was—for the first time that morning—empty of customers. She turned to look for Brooke, who'd arrived thirty minutes before.

"Where did you go?" She stretched out her neck, trying to see to the back of the store. She and Brooke planned to go shopping after the store closed at noon to pick out things for her apartment.

"Looking for a Father's Day present," came the reply. "My dad has already decided on baking as his next hobby."

"But Father's Day is still two months away." Megan straightened the stack of business cards that held the store's website address. "Mother's Day comes first."

Brooke's face appeared from behind the cookbook section. "You think I don't know that? I purchased Mom's gift back in February."

"Of course you did," Megan muttered. She sprayed cleaner onto the countertop and reached for the roll of paper towels. "If I ever start thinking I have a habit of being too prepared, all I need to do is take a look at you."

"There's no such thing as being too prepared." Brooke's words were muffled since she'd once again dropped behind the aisle, and a couple of seconds later Megan heard a soft "Ah-ha!"

She grinned. "I take it you found something."

"I found the perfect something." Brooke's face appeared again, and she held up two softbound books. One that used cherries or cherry flavoring for each recipe it contained, and one filled with tips and tricks for baking breads.

"Two perfect somethings," Megan agreed. "Tell me again why you shop for gifts two months early."

"So I never forget."

Megan tapped the notepad that could always be found beside the register. "Lists," she said as Brooke headed for the front counter. "You'd never forget anything if you'd start making lists."

"Ah." Brooke plopped her selections onto the counter. "But if I don't have lists, then I don't run the risk of the wrong people seeing what's on them."

She gave Megan a knowing look, and Megan had to concede her point. They'd texted briefly after Megan had gotten home the night before, and she'd filled her friend in on the "highlights" of dinner.

"I still can't believe he read out all the names like that," Megan mumbled.

"And I still can't believe you carry around that list on a day-to-day basis."

"Of course I do. What if I meet someone I want to add to it?"

Brooke rolled her eyes. "There are other ways to keep lists, you know?" She held her phone over the digital pay symbol to pay for her charges, then waved the device in front of Meg's face. "*Digital* ways."

"Yeah. But I just . . ." Meg sighed. It made no sense to most people. She knew that. Especially given her degrees and previous job in computer programming. "I like the feel of writing with a lead pencil, okay?" She often even transferred items from apps on her phone to paper. "I get that from my aunt."

"Your aunt?" Puzzlement had Brooke tilting her head. "You've never mentioned an aunt."

Megan didn't make a practice of mentioning any of her family members all that often. It had become habit over the years. She shrugged as if thinking about her aunt was no big deal. "Aunt June was my mom's sister. I spent a lot of time with her and Uncle Ray before I went away to college."

"Was?" Brooke reached out and patted Megan's hand. "I'm sorry. Did she live in San Francisco, too?"

That's where Megan was from. "About thirty minutes away."

"What did you do when—"

The front door opened, interrupting the conversation, and Brooke stepped to the side of the counter to be out of the way. After Megan greeted the two teens who'd entered and told them to let her know if they needed anything, she took a quick peek at her phone. It had buzzed with a text.

A smile curved her lips as she read the message. Nate had finally replied.

Stay away from loafer guy. He's no good for you.

She'd texted Nate earlier, thanking him again for the rescue the night before and saying she owed him one, and when he'd replied that there was no return payment needed, she'd pointed out she at least owed him dinner since Mark was supposed to pay last night. Nate hadn't replied in over an hour, though, so she'd assumed he wasn't going to.

She went to work tapping out a response. `You don't have to tell me twice. Loafer guy is permanently off the list.` Her thumbs hovered over the screen for two seconds before she quickly added, `I did find someone new I'm thinking about adding, though. He came into the store this morning.`

She had *not* found anyone new to add to the list. And she wasn't sure why she'd said so.

But her grin widened at his reply.

`Who is it?`

`Why do you want to know?`

`So I can tell you if he's good enough for you or not.`

She nibbled on her lip as she contemplated what to say next, then she realized that Brooke had put her own phone down and was staring at her.

"What?" Megan said.

"Why are you smiling like that?" Brooke leaned toward her, trying to see the face of her phone. "Who are you texting with?"

"Nobody." Megan turned her hand away and offered the flippant reply before she could stop herself, and Brooke's eyebrows shot up.

"Is it *him*?"

"Is it who?"

The teens left the store, giving a wave goodbye on their way out, and Brooke rounded on Megan. She jabbed a finger at her. "That's Nate, isn't it? I knew there was more to last night than you let on."

"There was *not* more to last night." She'd told Brooke everything. "He's just a friend."

"Yeah. A friend who makes you smile like he's the man currently sitting at the top of your list."

"What?" Megan shook her head. "*No.* He does not." But she had been smiling. A lot. "He's just . . ."

Her phone buzzed again, and she looked down.

You know you want my advice. I mean . . . you thought Mark Gray was potential. You *need* help with this.

She bit down on her grin.

"He's just what, Meg?" Brooke's voice came out softer that time, and the sincerity in it had Megan's heart pounding. Brooke was a good friend. They'd met after the first of the year, not long after Megan had offered to stay in Birch Bay to help with the store. And they'd only grown closer since.

She looked up from her cell, guilt winning out in the play for most prominent emotion, and she gave her friend a tiny shrug. "He's hot, okay." Lord, was he hot. "I'll admit that. He's hot. And he's funny. And he's . . . *kind.*"

And she'd had far too enjoyable a time with him the night before . . . which she'd thought about all morning.

Brooke's expression didn't alter. "He's also the brother of your ex."

"Yes. He's that, too."

"And you're okay with that?"

She knew her friend's concern was only because she didn't want to see Megan get hurt. But really, thinking the man was hot and doing anything about it were two totally different things.

"There's not anything going on with us, Brooke. I swear to you. Last night truly was just two friends having dinner." She held the phone up in the air. "And he's asking about my list now, okay? That's all. He's offering to tell me if anyone I might add is good enough."

"Like he did last night?"

Megan had told Brooke about Nate marking through a couple of the names the night before. "Right."

"And you think that's just because he wants to be your friend?"

"Well, I'm pretty sure he doesn't want to be anything else."

But was she? He had come to her rescue last night. And he was sort of—*kind of*—text flirting with her right now.

Or did she just *want* him to *want* to be something more?

And was she just going to drive herself mad if she didn't stop thinking about him like this?

Brooke wrapped her hand around Megan's, which still clasped her phone, and lowered both to the countertop. "And I'm pretty sure that you might be sliding close to the edge," she suggested. "So, I'm just saying be careful, Meg. Know what you're doing . . . *before* you do something you might regret."

Megan stared back at her friend, and she couldn't help but wonder. *Would* she regret it?

She didn't have to think long for an answer. *Most likely.*

Because Nate didn't fit anywhere within her new plan. He wouldn't be staying in Birch Bay once he got things cleaned up at the orchard, and unless all other options failed her, she had no intentions of leaving.

"He's just my friend, Brooke. As are all of the Wildes." She loosened her fingers, letting go of her phone, and slid her hand out from underneath Brooke's. "A friend who means no more to me than his brother, who is also my ex."

MEGAN SAT IN HER CAR, the engine turned off, and stared out through the windshield. A tractor with attached wood chipper sat quiet and unmoving in the back field of the Wilde orchard, several piles of downed trees dotting the space around them, but she didn't see Nate anywhere in the vicinity. His truck sat in the driveway, though, so chances were good that he was here.

She glanced over at the deck and up to the back door. Was he in the house?

The inside door stood open, but the glass of the screen door reflected in the sun, providing a shield against whatever or whomever might be inside. And the idea of getting out of her car suddenly had her nerves humming. She shouldn't have come.

It was Monday afternoon, and given she'd never replied to his last text on Saturday—the one where he'd suggested she needed his help culling her list—she hadn't heard a thing from Nate since. Which wasn't unusual. There was no reason she *should* hear from him. Only . . . she'd hoped to. As stupid as it may be, she'd picked up her phone several times throughout the weekend, her thumbs skimming over the keypad, wanting nothing more than to just say hi.

How ridiculous was that?

At the end of the shopping trip on Saturday, Brooke had reminded her yet again that pushing the envelope with Nate was not a good idea. Being friends was one thing, but flirting with the idea of more?

Bad thing.

And Megan knew she was right. The man was Jaden's brother. He was a loner, in all aspects of the word, and he seemed to want to stay that way. Seeking him out . . . thinking about him in any way that was *anything* but friendly . . . would do nothing but sidetrack her ultimate goal.

Yet, here she was.

After thinking about him all weekend.

She sighed at the absurdity of it all, then she grabbed the just-cooked chicken and broccoli casserole off the passenger seat and told herself he wouldn't be in the house. He was most likely in the barn. Or maybe in another field that she couldn't see from there. And when he *wasn't* in the house, she'd simply sneak inside and leave the meal on the kitchen table. The food was repayment for him buying dinner the other night, and once her debt was paid, she could get back to focusing on her mission. Back to looking for a potential future husband.

A message appeared on her phone screen before she managed to get out of the car, and it was as if the device had synced up with her brain and was listening to her every thought. It let her know that she had two new matches waiting in her dating app. Two new possibilities that *were* the type of man she wanted.

Two men who *weren't* Nate Wilde.

She lifted her head and stared out through the windshield again, this time skipping over the cherry trees and taking in the beauty of the lake. And she called herself a fool for coming out there. Two minutes in and out, she reminded herself. That's all it would take.

Then she'd check out her latest matches.

Chapter Seven

Nate shucked his jeans for an older pair then tugged on his work boots. So far it had been a busy, but productive Monday, but he still had hours of work ahead of him. He'd been to city hall, working on the needed permits for the cabins, along with ordering supplies, filling out an application for a loan, and making a couple of equipment purchases for additional attachments for the tractor.

He'd also talked to several people over the weekend, and so far, he had five guys who would be heading his way tomorrow, with another six coming in early next week. Dani had spoken to the Wyndhams about renting their place for the summer—and they'd then spent the weekend excitedly packing for their upcoming trip to Texas—and Cord, Nick, and Jaden had gone out to the rehab facility and filled their dad in on the new plans. Their dad held a lot of pride in how well the orchard had done over the years, but to hear his brothers tell it, he was excited at the turn of events. And Nate truly hoped he was.

At the same time, he also didn't care if his dad liked the idea or not. The man had almost killed himself because of the damned cherry trees, so it was time for plan B.

Grabbing a T-shirt off the back of a chair, he headed for the stairs, and when he was halfway down, a noise came from the direction of the living room. "Jay?" He rounded the bottom of the stairs, pulling his shirt down over his abs, and started down the hallway toward the back of the house. He'd thought Jaden had a meeting in town today and then planned to stay with Arsula again tonight. "I thought you—"

But it wasn't his brother who stood inside the back door.

"Megan?" A spark of excitement flared inside him. "What are you doing here?"

He hadn't expected to see her today . . . and he shouldn't be glad to have been wrong.

"I brought you dinner for tonight." She lifted the foil-covered dish she held in her hands. "It's payback."

"Payback?" A chuckle rolled through him. "That sounds ominous."

The thrill of seeing her was ludicrous.

"You planning to kill me or something?"

"Something like that." She made a face at his teasing and moved toward the connected kitchen. "How about a favor returned instead of payback, then? I told you I owed you one."

She had told him that—to which he'd suggested she didn't. He didn't want her buying him dinner.

But a homemade dish?

His stomach rumbled at the thought, and he remembered that he hadn't stopped for lunch.

"What's in it?" He also realized he hadn't moved from the hallway since he'd first seen her.

"Chicken and broccoli casserole." She reached the kitchen table, then she looked over at him with a not-so-patient tilt of her head—as if waiting for him to quit standing ten feet away like he was afraid to come near her.

His feet started moving.

"I assume you like chicken?" she asked.

"I like anything someone else cooks for me."

"Good."

When he made it over to her, she held the dish out, but instead of taking it, he lifted a corner of the foil. The smells that assaulted him had his stomach growling once more. "I'm starving." He eyed the chunks of chicken bathed in cheese and breadcrumbs. "Would it hurt your feelings if I made this lunch instead of dinner?"

A smile finally found her lips. "You can make it anything you want, Nate. It's all yours."

"Perfect." Without letting himself think about his actions, he turned and pulled two forks from a drawer. "Then I want it to be my *and* your lunch."

This made her laugh, and she finally set the dish on the table. "It's two o'clock in the afternoon, in case you haven't noticed. I've already had lunch."

"Not me. I somehow managed to forget to eat today." He pulled out a seat for her. "And no problem if you aren't hungry. You can just talk to me while *I* eat."

He gave her a big smile, and when she hesitated, he knew he should let her go. He enjoyed her company too much to suggest she hang around. But ever since the decision had been made for the changes to the farm, he'd found himself being a bit more relaxed about things. A bit more interested in having company instead of always being alone.

He lifted a finger and pointed toward the back window to where the tractor could be seen. "Talk to me while I eat," he repeated, "and I'll let you help me with the wood chipper when I'm done."

The excitement that flashed in her eyes had the muscles low in his gut tightening. But other than that one flicker of emotion, she showed no other sign of joy. Instead, as if annoyed, the line of her lips went flat. "Tell me the truth first." Even standing a foot shorter, she somehow managed to look down her nose at him. "You *want* my help, don't you? Because I was so *extremely* helpful with the ramp last week?"

Her words were a reference to their conversation from Friday night, and though he wanted to smile at the memory, he made sure his expression matched hers. "Your *expert* help, you mean?"

She didn't hesitate. "That's the only kind I offer."

"Then, absolutely I do."

When she laughed, the unabashedly gleeful sound pinging off every pleasure zone in his body, a warning sign the size of Montana flashed inside his head. This woman was danger. And not the kind that would intentionally use a man for her own personal games . . . nor the kind to land him in jail after too many beers or an ill-timed joyride or two.

No. Megan Manning was the type of danger that would leave him wanting. For all the things he could never have.

If he had even half a brain cell, he'd heed the sign and send her cute little tush packing. Instead, he nodded to the chair. "Sit, oh expert helper of mine. And regale me with stories as I enjoy this grand feast."

She sat, but she also sent him a side-eye. "What's different about you today?"

"Nothing is different about me." He took the chair at a ninety-degree angle from hers then ripped off the foil covering the dish. *"Mmmm . . ."*

"Yeah . . . there is." She said nothing else after that, and the mood in the room seemed to hesitate, just hanging in the air, waiting. The moment stretched out, along with her silence, until he finally pulled his gaze off the forkful of food he'd just scooped up.

"What?" he asked.

"You're"—a wrinkle appeared between her brow—"*happier?*" She crinkled her nose as if the word smelled bad. "Is that it?"

He shook his head. "I'm not an unhappy person, Manning. I'm often grumpy, yes. And I like to scowl." He scowled at her as if to prove his point. "But I'm not unhappy." Which wasn't fully true, but it was close enough.

"Okay. Then you're chirpier."

At this, he paused again, this time with his fork halfway to his mouth. He offered another scowl. "Men are not chirpy. That's a girl thing." And the idea was almost enough to make him lose his appetite.

"I don't know . . . have you looked in the mirror lately? Because there's definitely something 'chirpy' about you today."

This wasn't what he'd had in mind when he'd invited her to stay.

"You're smiling more, Wilde. You're easygoing. Teasing me like you may not get another chance to do it anytime soon." She leaned forward and narrowed laughing eyes at him. "I mean, you're *practically* glowing."

He found himself leaning in, as well, and when he inhaled through his nose, he could smell the light scent of pears. "Maybe the glow is from the sun." He didn't look away from her. "Did you think of that? I did spend a lot of last week working outdoors."

"Maybe," she considered. "Or maybe something happened to lighten your mood. Something . . . *good?*" She pulled back, as if she knew she'd landed on the answer, and at the separation, it was as if he'd been cut loose from an invisible connection holding them together.

He focused back on the food. He didn't want to keep peering into eyes that saw too much.

"That's it, isn't it?" she continued talking as he closed his mouth around the first heavenly bite. "What happened, Nate? Who made you chirpy?"

The fact that she kept using the word chirpy wasn't lost on him. She was teasing him, too.

And he liked it.

But she wasn't wrong. Well, he wasn't *chirpy*. But he definitely felt happier than usual. Lighter. And he knew exactly what had done it for him.

"It's not a who." He forked up another bite, then poked it into her mouth instead of his own. Her eyes rounded in surprise, but she didn't protest. "It's a what," he said. "Have you talked to Jaden lately?"

As she chewed, she shot him a disgusted look. "You have to let the Jaden thing go."

He mimicked her look. "I'm not talking about that. I just mean, have you talked to him? Or to Dani?" Even though she officially reported to Dani, he knew that the two of them were also good friends. He popped another bite into her mouth, watching her chew. "Has anyone told you about the new direction we're taking for the farm?"

As his words sunk in, her eyes went wide again. "New direction?" she said around the bite. She quickly swallowed. "What new direction? Do you mean you're not going to sell?"

"No. We're not selling."

He didn't know why he'd put it that way, because they very well might still sell the farm. But given the way her eyes had lit up, he didn't correct himself.

"What are you going to do then?" She turned in her chair so she faced him, and one side of the V-neck of her T-shirt gaped. "How can you take a cherry farm in a new direction?"

He forced himself not to look down her shirt, and he found himself excited at the idea of sharing this with her. Glad that no one else had yet. He just hoped she liked the idea. "By building cabins to turn the property into a rustic retreat . . . that *also* has cherry trees."

He spent the next few minutes filling her in on the details, and the more he talked, the more excited he got. She'd been spot on in her estimation of him. He was happier. And the change wasn't simply him being more relaxed due to a decision being made about their childhood home. He was honestly thrilled with the path they were taking.

Thrilled that it had been *his* idea. And that his family needed *him* to make it happen.

As he wound down, he had the thought to point out that she suddenly looked happier, too. He didn't know why them not selling mattered so much to her, but it gave him a sense of pride to see it. He'd put that look on her face.

"I love that you aren't going to sell." She made a pleased sound. "I absolutely love it."

"Why does that make you happy?" He watched her closely. "I mean, surely it's not just because of your job? After all, you've got a lifetime of basement-coding ahead of you if the store falls through, right?" He scooped up another bite. "*Not* that I intend to let that happen."

"Good to know. And you're right. I could always fall back on coding." She picked up the second fork and joined him, thus taking away his excuse to feed her himself. "I'd just need to find the right basement, and I could make it happen."

"Maybe your new fiancé will have one."

The mood in the room shifted again. Or maybe it was just his own disposition that had changed—since he'd been the one to bring up her ridiculous plan.

"With any luck, he will." She poked at the casserole, and he took the moment to grab a couple of bottles of water from the fridge. The table suddenly seemed too small for the two of them.

He handed her a bottle, but instead of returning to his seat, he leaned back against the countertop. "So why does it?" He unscrewed the cap. "Why does us keeping the farm matter?"

She looked over her shoulder at him. "I don't know. I guess . . ." She shrugged after a long pause, and a bit of the light paled in her eyes. "I just don't want to see you all splinter. I know you had some rough years before, and I'd hate for anything like that to happen again. Your family deserves to be happy. And together."

He sometimes forgot how much she knew about their family.

"We did have some rough years," he agreed. There'd been a time when he'd seen this very place as nothing that he'd ever wanted to come back to. When several of them had. "And I agree. Splintering would be bad." It would be the worst possible scenario.

"You say that even though you still plan to leave as soon as you finish the cabins?"

"I do."

He stared into her eyes for a few seconds, thinking about the day when he would leave again, and how it wouldn't be quite as easy to do this time. He'd gotten used to being home. But without a doubt, that day would come. Bad followed him, and it always had. It also had a way of showing up just when he started to want more. Not to mention, there was still the matter of his secret hanging over his head.

A secret that could bring his family to their knees if it ever got out.

"Did you have any more dates over the weekend?" He changed the subject, needing to ensure he stayed firmly rooted in reality.

"I didn't."

"And is that because you were waiting on me to okay someone first?" He smiled with the words and was rewarded with one in return. She turned back to the food, though.

"I don't *need* you to okay people for me, you know. I'm confident that my list is solid. However, I *will* admit that I messed up thinking that Mark had potential." She peeked back at him, and a sparkle shone in her eyes. "I'll be sure to let you know if someone comes along that I need a second opinion on, though."

He chuckled. "You do that."

Feeling suddenly too far away, he rejoined her at the table. This time he sat in the chair directly beside her, and after she slid the dish closer, he dug back in. They both ate in silence for a few minutes, her doing more picking at the food than devouring it like he was, until finally, he said, "So what, exactly, is it you're looking for in a fiancé?"

When she glanced over at him, he almost wished he'd kept the question to himself. He could see her trying to figure out *why* he'd asked. While at the same time, he was doing his best to make sure she didn't read anything into his asking. The truth was, though, that he didn't *know* why. He just knew that ever since she'd declared finding a fiancé as her intention, he hadn't been able to keep from wondering what that man looked like for her. And why Jaden hadn't been it.

His brother might annoy the piss out of him at any given moment, but he was also a good guy. So, if not Jaden . . . then what *was* she after?

"Do you really want to know, or are you teasing me again?" She nibbled on another bite of food as she waited for his answer, and he told himself to back off. To end the conversation with "just teasing."

He didn't want to end it, though. And he really did want to know. "I'm not teasing," he said, and his voice came out as a half-croak. He cleared his throat.

"Then why do you want to know?"

Geez, the woman couldn't just answer a question. She had to probe.

"Why?" He stalled, and when she immediately nodded, he decided to go back to teasing. That would be safest. So, he leaned in and bumped her shoulder. "Because maybe I've met the perfect guy already and can send him your way. I know plenty of people. And I'd never steer you wrong."

His tone lost its teasing before he finished speaking, but he gave her a goofy grin at the end. She rolled her eyes at his antics.

"Fine," she muttered. She put her fork down and looked at him. "First of all, I want someone who can make me laugh."

"Well, that shouldn't be hard. You're easily amused."

She smirked at that and held up two fingers. "I want someone who doesn't take himself too seriously."

"Naturally." He nodded. "Why would you want someone boring? Like loafer guy?"

She elbowed him in the ribs. "I want someone who wants kids."

"Reasonable."

She lifted a fourth finger. "And I want someone who doesn't have a job that takes him out of town."

That one stopped him. That was very specific. "You mean . . . never?"

"Well, not regularly. I want a husband who wants to stay home with me as much as I want to be with him."

Nate turned in his chair, but she kept her gaze on the chicken casserole. "What's the problem of him coming *back* home to you if he has a job he really loves?"

"What's the problem of him *not* wanting to leave me if he loves me enough?" she rebutted. She picked up her fork again, but it seemed to be as more of a thing to do opposed to wanting food.

"Nothing, I suppose. I just—"

"Exactly. Nothing would be wrong with it." She jabbed her fork into the dish, leaving it standing there, then went back to silence. Except, her fingers filled the void. The pointer finger on her right hand started tapping rhythmically against the top of the table.

"Can I ask you something personal, Megan?"

She didn't answer immediately, her gaze now glued to the windows that spanned the wall at the back of the living room, and he had the thought that she might just get up and leave. This was supposed to have been a couple of friends enjoying a few bites of food and hanging out being smartasses. But it suddenly felt like more.

She *didn't* get up, though, and when the jut of her chin eased slightly and her eyelids briefly flickered, it took every ounce of strength inside of him not to pull her close. She looked so hurt.

She looked so much like she expected to be hurt again.

"You can if you want to," she finally answered, and her words came out too soft.

"I do want to." He reached out a hand to lay over hers, stopping the mad tapping, and at the touch, she jerked her gaze back to his. He kept his hand over hers, though, and before he asked his question, he gave her fingers a light squeeze. "Why did you break up with Jaden?"

The question seemed to surprise her. And honestly, whatever had gone on between her and his brother was none of his business. But there had been something hauntingly sad about the last couple of moments. About the idea of her wanting a man who'd never leave her.

She shook her head and pulled in a breath before answering. "It's not because he left me on some regular basis, if that's what you're thinking. Your brother is as stick-to-his-woman as they come."

He nodded. "That would have been my opinion, too." But *someone* had left her. He narrowed his eyes. "But did he make you laugh?"

At the lighter tone he'd forced out, the corners of her lips twitched. "He did. Believe it or not, your brother can be one heck of a funny guy."

"I can believe it. He would have learned that from me." At her eye-roll, he gave her another wink. "Then how about taking himself too seriously? Did he do that?" But Nate could answer that question himself. His brother definitely had a habit of being overly serious at times. At least he had in the past. He seemed to be working on that.

When she gave a knowing look that matched his own thoughts, he tipped his head in acknowledgment.

"One more personal question," he said, "and then I'll let it go." He realized that his hand still rested over hers, but instead of releasing hers, he picked it up and clasped it between both of his. This forced her to physically turn in his direction. "Why do you want a fiancé so badly?" He watched her carefully as he spoke. "You're still young. Why not just let things happen naturally?"

"But what's not natural about what I'm doing?" She sounded so earnest. "I'm just going on dates."

"True. But typically, dating is just that. You meet someone, have some fun, get to know each other. Sometimes that's all it is. Fun. And sometimes you decide it's not worth continuing, so you start dating someone new." He wanted to stop right there, because he wasn't sure he truly believed in the idea that dating could grow into anything more. But his siblings seemed to have things figured out. "And then *occasionally*," he went on, "if all the stars align—and probably some magical potion is thrown in, as well—things progress far enough that *both* people in the relationship start thinking about the future. *Both* people decide on the bigger picture being what they want. But most people don't set out specifically looking for a fiancé."

She stared back at him, her eyes seeming larger than he'd noticed before, and he took in the many colors flecked in with the dark brown. "I would argue that they do," she countered. But she also had that look again. The one that said she expected to be hurt.

"Megan . . ." He didn't know what else to say. He didn't know how to fix whatever her hurt was. How to assure her that he'd keep her pain from being repeated.

A phone started ringing before either of them said anything else, and after she pulled it from her pocket, her gaze shot back to his.

"I have to take this."

MEGAN WAITED until she'd stepped outside to answer the call, though everything about her had screamed for her to answer the second she'd seen who the caller was. Before he changed his mind and hung up. She'd made herself wait, though, because she not only needed distance from Nate and the conversation they'd been having, but she didn't want him watching her with those penetrating eyes while she talked.

The instant the door closed behind her, she pushed the button to make the connection.

"Dad." She couldn't hold back either the smile or the eruption of joy at getting to talk to him. "How are you? *Where* are you?"

He chuckled as if her excitement humored him. He'd always done that.

"I'm good," he said when the laughter faded off. She used her thumb to lower the volume on her phone. His voice had always been strong and booming, and it came through loud and clear today. "And I'm in the States right now. Got back a couple of weeks ago, actually."

"A couple of weeks?" She'd sent him several text messages over that span of time. That he'd never answered. "Are you working somewhere?"

Her dad was a biophysicist consultant who traveled more than half of each year out of the country. It had been that way for years.

"No." He sounded relaxed. "Haven't been for about a month now. Took some time off. Went to see your brother. He's doing good."

"Good. I'm glad to hear it." She talked to her brother even less often than she talked to her dad.

Her brother had followed in their father's footsteps. He'd gone into the sciences and was also a much-sought-after consultant.

"So, where are you?" she asked again, and when she realized she was still standing directly outside the back door, she forced herself to move away. She made it to the top of the ramp, and then she stood there, staring off toward the lake and its gorgeously clear waters.

"You're going to find this funny," her dad said. "But I'm practically at your back door. I met a few buddies in Snow King to get in some last-minute skiing before the season closes."

"You're in Jackson Hole?" Just south of the Grand Teton National Park wasn't exactly "at her back door" given that it was several hundred miles away, but since he was often on another continent, it did feel like it. And it was also close enough to get in a visit.

"Just until tomorrow," he answered. "Then I have to be in Seattle."

She turned and leaned against the railing and tilted her face up to the sky. A breeze whispered over the bare skin of her neck, and the blue above her was as picture-perfect as the first time she'd seen it. "So where do you go after that?" Her father's job was based in Seattle, so it was as close to a home base as he got. She pinched the bridge of her nose. "Do you have time to come here for a visit before you leave again? I've got the cutest apartment, and I'd love to show it to you."

Her dad didn't immediately answer, and when she realized she was holding her breath, she silently blew it out. She kept staring at the sky and started counting the clouds. She'd counted a lot of things in her twenty-five years.

"I'm not sure I can make it to Montana. It's too bad you're not in Seattle anymore."

"Yeah. I know." She didn't know what else to say. She'd been in Seattle for six and a half years, and she'd seen her father five times.

"Will Jaden be finishing his master's this semester?" At his question, she remembered that she hadn't told her dad about their breakup.

She sighed inwardly. He liked Jaden. "He'll be receiving it in three weeks. But, Dad—"

"Maybe I can make graduation then. I missed yours, but I could see his."

She closed her eyes against the beauty of the world. As far as she knew, Jaden *did* plan to go back to Seattle for graduation. He'd be out of his boot by then, and he'd probably take Arsula with him. If her dad did show up, he might not even notice that she wasn't the one there with him.

"Dad." She pulled in a deep breath and prepared to confess.

She could already imagine his reaction. "Jaden and I aren't together anymore. We broke up a couple of months ago."

A rattle of keys and the sound of a car door closing came from the other end of the connection. "You what?"

"We broke things off. We're still friends, but we decided to leave it at that."

There was a pause of a full five seconds. "Then why are you still there?"

That was the reaction she'd expected. He'd never approved of their plans to move to Birch Bay. He wanted her to do more with her life. "I'm here because I love the town, Dad. I've made good friends. I have a job I love. And I intend to stay."

"But you can do that job anywhere. Or better yet, one of the companies I sit on the board for has an opening in its artificial intelligence department. It's a great position. I'll get you an interview. It could be the start of a great career for you."

She also hadn't told him that she'd given up her technology job. He had no idea she was managing The Cherry Basket permanently. "I've already got the start of a great career, Dad." Just not in the field he expected her to work in.

"Your job is good, yes. But that's a starter job. With your brain, you could do so much more."

With her brain, she could "touch the world." Exactly as he, her brother, *and* her oldest sister were doing. Too bad she and Mica hadn't followed suit. Or their mother.

A car started on his end, and she knew the conversation would soon be ending. Her dad was a stickler for not driving while talking. All eyes on the road, all senses honed for safety.

"I'm going to have to cut this—" Her dad's words stopped, and she heard the engine of the vehicle shut down, as well. "Don't tell me you're still in Montana because you've already found some other man, Megan. I'm sorry that you and Jaden didn't work out, but you're not your mother."

The harshness of his words stung. She'd never been particularly pleased with some of her mother's choices, either, but it wasn't like not being like *him* made the woman a horrible person.

"Of course I'm not *like* her," she started. "But that doesn't—"

"You've always been more like me. Don't make the mistake of thinking otherwise. You have purpose in this life, Megan. You shouldn't squander it."

The way he steamrolled over her made the muscles in her neck tighten. It had always bothered her that he saw only two options for her. One, be like him and try to "save the world" one continent at a time. Or two, follow in her mother's footsteps and let life take her wherever the next man she met wanted to go. But she saw a third option. And that was simply making her own statement about what was important in her life.

She just hoped she could achieve what she actually wanted. That it wasn't *her* that caused all the people who were supposed to be there for her to always leave.

"I'm not squandering anything." She could barely get the words out. "I just—"

"Then send me your resume. I'll pass it along to my contact." The car started up again. "I need to go, Meg. It was good talking to you."

He disconnected before she could even tell him goodbye, and when she looked back at the Wilde house, to the home that had housed a family she'd once thought as lonely as hers, tears threatened at her eyes. The Wildes had so much more going for them. Maybe they weren't perfect, but at least they were trying. While she had a dad who couldn't even be bothered to return a text.

She pocketed her phone and made the decision to head home. She shouldn't have stayed as long as she had, anyway. This was supposed to have been a two-minute drop-off. Not hanging out for the rest of the afternoon with someone else whose life plan basically mimicked her father's.

Chapter Eight

Nate turned up the heater in the truck and slowed as he approached a red light. The morning was cold and gray but given that the guys who'd showed up the day before had spent the last several winters out on crab boats, working in chilly weather was nothing new for any of them. The five who'd arrived had looked over his initial plans the night before, and this morning, they'd started early, clearing out the remainder of the trees where the cabins would be built. While they did that, Nate had agreed to run Jaden to the rehab facility so he could relieve Gloria for a few hours and spend that time hanging out with their dad. He'd done that several times since his dad had been hurt.

"Thanks for the lift," Jaden said. Due to his booted right foot, he remained unable to drive himself, but his day of freedom would be coming soon.

"No problem."

"I mean, I know you got tired of driving me around."

If he hadn't still been rolling to a stop, Nate would have closed his eyes in irritation. He was not in the mood to talk. And he absolutely wasn't in the mood to deal with passive aggressive comments referring to the ambush at the store from nearly two weeks before. "I didn't get *tired* of driving you," he pointed out, same as he had that day. "I got tired of *only* doing that."

They hadn't talked about the argument since it had happened —likely because either Jaden hadn't been at the house all that much or Nate had been busy working when he had been around —but Nate was of the opinion there was nothing to discuss. Families had arguments; people went on. There was nothing earth-shattering in that. His brother, though . . . *the up-and-coming counselor-to-be* . . . had other ideas.

"Well, I do appreciate it," Jaden said. "And though I stand by my prior decision to not stay at the house while I initially recuperated, I've been thinking about how it must have felt to you. And I apologize for making you feel unneeded."

Nate *did* close his eyes then—but he was also stopped. "I'm a big boy, Jay. I promise you. I've already gotten over it."

"Are you sure about that?"

The light turned green, and Nate accelerated. "I assure you that my feelings are intact, and I've suffered no long-term damage due to your unacceptance of the full level of help I was prepared to give."

Him stringing that number of words together at one time should shut his brother up, if only for a few minutes. Unfortunately, it didn't even last that long.

"Then if not me, what had you so upset at the store that day? And the days before. And most every day since." As he finished, his words tapering to a level of seriousness that came as a surprise, Nate glanced over at him.

"What are you talking about?"

"I'm talking about whatever is going on under the surface with you." Jaden waved a hand toward him, and Nate went back to paying attention to the road. "I know the idea of overhauling the farm has given you a thrill these last few days. That's been obvious. And understandable. But still," Jay went on, "there's something simmering. I'm not sure if it's anger or what, but it's been there for several weeks."

"Nothing is simmering. And getting upset because my family ambushes me is to be expected."

"Maybe." Jay studied him to the point that the back of Nate's neck started to itch. "But it feels different than that," he went on. "It feels unhealthy. And whatever it is, it had you ready to pull out of town and never look back."

Nate started to argue. He'd never said he didn't plan on looking back. He always looked back. He just didn't stay long when he did.

"It worries me even more because it was only a few weeks before all this happened with the orchard and with dad that you'd admitted you were ready to come home for good."

That was bullshit. "I never admitted any such thing."

"But you also didn't deny it when I brought it up."

Nate frowned and pushed his foot down harder on the gas pedal. His brother really had put on his counselor suit this morning. But he also had it wrong. The conversation he was referring to had been one where Jaden had once again been trying to play counselor. He and their sister had felt that Nate being home for so long had been due to him avoiding someone or something. But he'd been home because he wanted to be home, damn it. And *not* necessarily because he wanted to *stay* there.

But none of that mattered now anyway because he'd failed his dad. And he'd almost died because of it.

If only the man would have—

Nate shut down that train of thought as soon as it began. It didn't matter what their dad had or hadn't done that morning. What he'd *not* allowed Nate to do.

None of it fucking mattered now. Their dad's life was forever changed by that one act; the orchard was no longer a working orchard, and Nate would make the necessary changes, and then he'd get the hell out. And he wasn't fucking angry!

The road to the rehab center came upon him faster than he'd anticipated, and he had to stomp on the brakes in order to make the turn. Still, the tires squealed as he swung wide onto the connecting two-lane road, and Jaden, wisely, chose not to comment. The remaining five minutes of the trip were made in silence, but when Nate pulled up to the front sliding doors, he knew he couldn't be so lucky as to have the drop-off go the same. Instead, Jaden turned to face him.

"Get out, Jay." Nate tried to cut his brother off before more "well-meaning" bullshit could be spewed.

"I will get out. But I could also walk from the parking lot. I'm not that damaged. Why don't you go ahead and park, and we'll walk in together?"

"I don't have time to come in. I have a crew at the house that I have to get back to."

"I met your guys last night." It had actually been a fun evening with him and his brother hanging out with all his friends. "They're a good bunch. And they're more than capable of waiting ten extra minutes while you come in and say hello to Dad."

Nate frowned at his brother, wondering why this was going to be a thing today. "Tell you what. You say hello for me." He leaned over and pulled on the latch to open the passenger door. "Now get out so I can go."

But of course, Jaden *didn't* get out. Instead, he gave Nate one of his "insightful" looks. The kind that implied he thought he'd landed onto something deep and personal. "Does it have to do with Dad?"

Nate sat back in his seat. "What are you talking about? Does what have to do with Dad?"

"You haven't come by to see Dad since the day we got him set up here. Are you avoiding seeing him for some reason?"

The observation reminded him of Megan pointing out his lack of a visit the week before.

And then thinking about Megan made him think about the fact that she'd hightailed it away from the house right after taking that phone call the other day. She'd barely stuck her head back in long enough to tell him she had to run.

"I've been busy, Jay." Too busy to even follow up with Megan and see if she was okay. Something about that call had upset her. "Have you forgotten that? It's the reason you all asked me to stay. And now I've committed to getting the cabins done by midsummer, so I have even less time for anything else."

"But no one expects you to work around the clock. No one wants you to feel like you can't take the time to do anything else." He looked over at the multi-grain-cracker-colored one-story building before turning back. And this time he shifted on his seat to face Nate. "Did something happen between you and Dad before the accident?"

Why did his brother have to try to make something out of nothing? "No, Jay. Nothing happened between me and Dad before the accident. He went out that morning, same as he'd been doing every day for weeks. He went out, and I drove into town for breakfast. End of story."

"Are you angry because you weren't there when it happened?"

"Are you?" he fired back. Arsula—even though she and Jaden had been broken up at the time—had tried to get ahold of Jaden that morning before she'd finally reached out to the rest of them. She had a gift that sometimes allowed her to sense things via her dreams, and she'd awoken that morning certain something terrible had happened to their father. Nate had rushed back home the second he'd gotten the text, but thankfully, Dani had already been there and called for an ambulance.

Jaden chose not to answer Nate's question, and Nate took that as the discussion being over. He reached across the seat once again and pushed at the still-open door. "We're all upset over that morning, Jay. We all wish we'd have talked him into stopping his early-morning checks. We all feel like we should have realized that he wasn't as healthy as he'd been before. And if that in some way manifests into anger, then fine, I'm angry. At *myself*."

~

"I'll take a cup of roasted tomato basil soup and . . ." Megan scanned the menu hanging on the wall once more as the café worker waited on her to finish her order. "A grilled cheese sandwich." She should probably have a salad since she hadn't made it to her exercise class last night, but she planned to walk over to the lake to eat her lunch, so she wanted something warm. Plus, she liked dunking a grilled cheese into the soup.

"Any croutons for your soup?"

"No need. But make it to go, please." She scooted down the line to make room for additional customers filing in, and then noticed the way the three female workers on the other side of the counter were now casting glances to someone standing behind her.

The girl who'd waited on her plastered a bright smile on her face and turned to the next person in line, and as she asked to take their order, Megan snuck a peek herself. If whoever stood there was that good looking, then . . .

It was Nate.

And yeah, he was that good-looking.

"Hey." He grinned at her as if sneaking up behind her had taken some great amount of effort.

"Hey." She hadn't seen him since hightailing it out of his place Monday afternoon after taking that call from her dad. "You grabbing lunch for your guys?"

His eyes registered surprise. Apparently, he wasn't aware that a couple of the men he'd brought in to help with the cabins had been at the bar last night—which was also where she'd been instead of at the gym working out.

"Just lunch for me," Nate corrected. He ordered a baked potato topped with meatballs and marinara, as well as three chocolate chip cookies—also to go—and then he turned back to her. "You've met the guys?"

"I met Cade and Dre." She wiggled her brows but held back the *"yummm"* she'd uttered to Brooke as the two men had first entered the bar. She did offer the kind of smile that might make a person wonder if that was exactly what she was thinking, though. "Cade's a good dancer."

"Is that so?" He nudged her shoulder to get her to slide farther down the line. "He's also a total player. He wouldn't be in it for the long haul."

"Good to know." And she'd already figured that out herself. But the boy could still dance. "How about, Dre, then?" Dre had been the more interesting one anyway. And the better-looking one, though only marginally. He was originally from a small town in Pennsylvania and had said he'd fallen for this area several years ago when he'd taken a summer job in Glacier National Park. He'd been looking for a good excuse to come back ever since.

"Dre is—" Nate reached for Megan's bagged food before she could get it, and she slapped at his hand.

"Don't even think about it, Wilde."

A heart-stopping half-smile made her weak at the knees. "I was just getting it for you." He set the bag on the counter in front of her and motioned toward the register. "Have at it, Manning. No one here is trying to pay for your food. I promise."

"Good." She passed over her debit card, her gaze tracking his hands as he reached out once again and accepted the bag that held his food, and she wanted to kick herself for even noticing anything about him. That's the whole reason she'd gone to the bar the night before. Because ever since she'd last seen him, even though reminding herself that he 1) would be leaving Birch Bay within a couple of months, and 2) was still Jaden's brother, he kept popping into her head at the oddest of times.

Like when she'd been eating dinner Monday night and had thought about him feeding her own casserole to her.

Or when she'd almost texted him Wednesday afternoon after spotting loafer-guy-Mark as she'd been entering the grocery store.

And every time she'd thought about him, her mood had taken a bit more of a nosedive.

"I should pay for yours just to teach you a lesson," she

muttered, and as he passed over his own debit card, his eyes twinkled down at her as if to say that he liked "lessons," both giving and receiving. And, of course, her stupid mind came up with half a dozen on the spot that she'd be willing to offer for free.

She blew out a breath. What in the world was wrong with her?

She snatched her lunch off the counter and took a step away. She needed to get away from him. Or maybe what she needed was to hunt Cade up and take him up on the one-night stand he'd so boldly offered. And *then* her mind could get back to what was important.

"I'm actually glad I ran into you," Nate said as he pocketed his receipt and debit card and followed her with his food. "I have a proposition for you."

Again, her mind went to a place it shouldn't. "And what's that?" She grabbed a handful of napkins and shoved them in her bag.

"It's actually something I'd rather not talk about in public."

At his more somber tone, her dirty mind got punted to the backburner, and she studied the lines of his face. He didn't look upset. More like he'd suddenly gone all business. "Sure. I planned to walk over to the lake to eat my lunch. Do you want to go with me? There might be people around, but surely we can find a quiet spot."

"That sounds good." He held the door for her and nodded toward his truck. "Let's ride over, though. I have an appointment to get to, and I don't want to be late. Plus, your casserole dish is in the truck. I can drop you and it off at the store afterward if you want."

"No need." She headed for the truck. "I parked over by the lake this morning because I don't plan to return to work this afternoon. My assistant manager will handle things."

As she climbed into the vehicle, she retrieved the dish from the passenger seat and set her bag of food down in it while he went around the back of the truck. She didn't ask what he wanted to talk about, but since the picnic area in the downtown part of town was only a few blocks away, she'd find out soon enough.

"I also wanted to thank you for the meal itself," he said as he settled behind the steering wheel. "*And* to tell you how good it was." He looked over at her and smiled. "I was so busy inhaling it Monday afternoon that I don't think I stopped to say either of those things."

She laughed. "You said you'd missed lunch. I'm guessing that doesn't happen often?"

"Basically never." He pulled out into the traffic, and she settled back against the seat.

"I don't usually cook a lot," she told him. "But what I brought over is one of my favorite dishes to make. So, I'm glad you liked it."

"No. I *loved* it. Feel free to cook for me anytime."

Her dirty mind returned with the idea of cooking for him wearing nothing but an apron, and she shook her head in disgust. Honestly, she just needed to get laid. She was going through a bit of a dry spell lately, and apparently everything was doing it for her.

He turned at the corner office where his sister ran her marketing business, then made his way to Second Avenue. As he drove, Megan searched for something to talk about, if for no other reason than to keep from thinking inappropriate thoughts. She rolled down her window and propped her elbow over the doorframe and brought up a subject that should totally get her mind off Nate.

"So tell me about Dre." She tilted her face into the wind and let the cool breeze wash over her cheeks. "I interrupted you in the café before you could finish whatever you were going to say."

"What do you want to know?"

She peeked at him. "Good guy?"

"One of the best."

"Marriage material?"

A muscle in his jaw twitched, and he kept his eyes on the road. "I would guess that he is. And he's not necessarily tied to any place, either." He glanced at her then, his eyes unreadable. "Nor does he care whether he returns for another season of crab fishing."

"So, he could potentially settle in Birch Bay?"

"I'd say it wouldn't be completely out of the question."

"Good to know." She scoped out the picnic tables as he pulled into the small parking lot and immediately saw that at least two were empty. "What about the guys I haven't met? Anyone with potential?"

He cut a look over at her the way he might a little sister asking if any of his friends were cute, but he also followed up the look with an answer. "Chris, no. Dustin, no. Jordan?" He lifted a shoulder. "Maybe. And then there are the ones who aren't here yet."

"Wait." She paused in the act of opening her door. "More men are coming?" She was going to have to bring Brooke in on this. "Are they all as hot as Dre?" Dre was six three, skin the toasty color of Dwayne Johnson's, cut with muscle, and he had a shaved head and close-cropped beard that reminded her of Taye Diggs. And as she'd said before . . . *yummm*.

Nate eyed her as he reached behind his seat and retrieved a handful of rolled-up papers. "You certainly have the hots for Dre."

"Well, duh. Have you looked at him? He's hot."

He laughed as he followed her out, the sound coming across more as shock and astonishment than all-around humor, and as they met back up in front of his truck, he peered down at her. His eyes weren't laughing, but as usual, she couldn't tell what thoughts ran behind them. "Should I put in a good word with him for you?"

She thought of how odd it was to have one man whom her subconscious wanted to think about at the top and bottom of every hour telling her about other men and offering to put in a good word for her. Life was strange sometimes.

"Absolutely." She pointed toward the nearest table. "Now let's eat while the food is still warm, and then you can get busy propositioning me."

Chapter Nine

The idea of propositioning Megan had floated through his mind several times over the last few days, and only one of those ways had involved business. And *that* was the only one he could entertain. If he hadn't already assured himself of that fact, her infatuation with one of his best friends would have sealed that fate for him today. Or, at least, it should have.

What it *had* done, however, was make him want to drive back to the house and tell Dre that his time here was over. Which was just ridiculous. He knew Megan was dating. Hell, he wanted her to date. He wanted her to find a good man, and Dre definitely was that. And if she *did* find a good man, then hopefully the ridiculously lustful thoughts that had made a hobby of taking root in his head would stop.

But did he want her dating his friends?

Honestly, he wasn't so sure about that. Nor did he know why the thought bothered him.

"This table okay with you?" she asked, and Nate agreed without even paying attention to where they'd ended up. It didn't matter, anyway, as long as there weren't clumps of people standing nearby. And at a quick glance, that didn't appear to be the case.

"Sit." He nodded toward the table, letting her choose a side before he circled around and lowered himself so that he faced her.

What he wanted to talk about was business-related, and given he'd decided to keep the changes to the farm quiet for as long as possible, he'd rather this conversation remain private. And he wanted to keep things quiet because with their tight timeline, he could afford no delay with distractions. No time for everyone in town to decide they needed to stop by just to see how things were going. The number of people who'd likely visit once his dad got home would already be bad enough, so he had to get as much work done as possible before that happened.

He sliced a meatball in half and forked up it, as well as a mouthful of potato. "Do you come over here to eat often?" He hadn't intended to grab lunch at the café today. He'd planned to hit a drive-thru and down a couple of burgers while on the road. But given he'd been heading to The Cherry Basket for the specific purpose of speaking with Megan, when he'd seen her entering the café down the street, he'd quickly readjusted his plans.

"I hope to now that the store is downtown and the weather is warming up." She dipped a corner of her sandwich into her soup. "I love the lake."

"Yeah?" To many people he knew, the mid-sixties wouldn't yet be considered "warming up." But then, to others he'd been around over the years, it would practically be summertime. "What do you love about it? The sound of the lapping water, the quiet?" He studied her, wondering if Jaden had ever taken her out on the lake. If not here, then in Seattle. "Or are you more of a get-out-there-in-the-middle-of-it, water-activities person?"

A light flashed in her eyes, and she swallowed her bite of food. "I'm a get-out-in-the-middle-of-it, read-a-book, and take-a-nap kind of person."

"Ah." He should have guessed. "The introvert."

She lifted a shoulder. "Not totally. But enough of one to enjoy the quiet of sitting alone with a good book."

"And what about if someone were sitting in the boat with you while you read your book?" He didn't know why he'd asked that. It sounded like an invitation.

It wasn't, though.

At least, he didn't think so.

But the idea of buying a boat suddenly held appeal.

"As long as that someone was worth being on a boat with, I suppose." She concentrated on her food, her eyes seeming to be intentionally downcast, and Nate couldn't help but wonder if she was thinking of a specific person. Or if he'd like her answer if she told him who it was.

"Like Dre?" he asked. And then he put his fork down. He wasn't hungry anymore.

"Like"—her gaze lifted back to his—"whoever I might date, I suppose. Or maybe friends."

He'd like to take her out on a boat. "How about fishing? Do you enjoy that?"

"I enjoy *watching* people fish." Her gaze seemed to go hazy then, and she peered off toward the lake. He held his breath as he waited, giving her a moment with whatever memory the idea of fishing had dragged out, but his brow furrowed when she bit down on her lower lip.

She hadn't yet turned back, so he whispered her name.

"What?" she whispered back. But she still didn't look his way. He could tell that her breaths had grown shallow. Her chest rose and fell with her quickened breaths.

"What's wrong, Meg?" He almost reached over to cover her hand like he had at the house, but he stopped himself at the last minute. They might be friends, but touching her should be kept to a minimum. "You look sad," he added.

"I am sad."

She didn't say anything else, and he couldn't find any other words to fill the void. So, he just waited. Like him, she'd quit eating. But unlike him, she remained far off and in some other place and time.

Finally, she closed her eyes and shook her head slightly, and when those brown orbs once again turned to him, his fingers slid to the middle of the table.

"You're still sad," he pointed out. But he did manage to keep himself from closing the distance.

"I was remembering my aunt. She used to love going out on her boat."

He picked up on the past tense of the word and assumed that was telling. "Did she take you out with her?"

Megan nodded. "Any time I asked."

"Do you want to tell me about her?" The request surprised him, but at the same time, it also felt right. And he wasn't merely offering a venue for her to express memories that obviously still caused a lot of pain. He was hoping she'd share that pain. With *him*.

But once again she shook her head, this time in a distinct negative motion, then she pointed to the blueprints he'd pulled from the back seat of the truck. "What are those?"

Oh, yeah. He'd almost forgotten why they were here.

Reaching over, he slid the rolls of paper in front of him and moved the remains of his lunch to the side. But before he spread out the ideas that until today he'd only seen in his head or roughly drawn onto a piece of paper, he pressed his forearms against the edge of the wood table and leaned in. "These have to do with the proposition that I wanted to talk to you about."

She nodded, her eyes flickering between him and the papers. "What's the proposition?"

He began unrolling the first blueprint. "I don't have a basement for you to work in, but I'll gladly add to the savings account that'll someday hopefully buy you one. I'm hoping you'll put your skills to use for us and create the website for our new venture."

"The website?" She nodded. "Of course. I've actually already started thinking about it."

He chuckled. He should have known she would have.

"And you don't have to pay me to do it."

"We'll pay you, Megan. It's what *you* get out of the proposition."

As he finished unfurling the document between them, he watched as her excitement built, and when he had it fully spread out, her mouth dropped open. "These are blueprints for the cabins!" Pure thrill registered on her face. "So soon?"

"It has to be soon." He weighted the edges of the paper down with the remnants of their lunches. "I only have a matter of weeks to get these done." He tapped the others still tucked against him. "I have three different designs, one smaller and with only one bedroom, and the other with a larger gathering space for people who want to rent more than one at a time but then all congregate together in one space. I talked an old friend into putting a rush on these. I just picked them up today."

"Oh my God, Nate." She lifted up off the bench and bent one leg under her so she could rest back down at a higher position. "This is terrific." Her fingers traced over the outline of the walls.

"I didn't know if you'd find this part of the process as exciting as me, but I wanted to show them to somebody." And he'd wanted to show them to her.

"Of course I find this part exciting. It's the beginning."

And it *wasn't* the end. He didn't say the words, but it felt as if they'd run through both of their minds. She'd seemed as invested as he in revamping the orchard and keeping the place in the family, so that was probably why he'd thought of showing it to her first. But then, it's possible he'd just wanted to see this kind of reaction firsthand. Because no matter what he'd said, he'd had a feeling she'd be as excited as him.

"So, what do you think?" He waited for her to look up at him. "We have ten weeks to get the cabins finished and signed off for occupancy. Any chance we could have a functioning website done before then, too?"

"I can have a prototype done by next week. I'll check with Dani on marketing ideas that I can work into the site as well." She hadn't looked up, as he'd hoped, but the joy that remained on her face when she reached over and unrolled another blueprint thrilled him. "But I have an addendum to the proposition," she said.

"Name it." For some reason, he suspected he'd give her anything. Just to have her involved.

This time, she did look up. And he was lost in the pull of her enthusiasm. "I want to help design the interiors." She tapped on the master bedroom in the second blueprint. "Each cabin needs its own design, though similarities should run throughout all to tie them together. I've already been thinking about that, too. How each one can be different but unique."

Surprise had him sitting like a stone on the bench. "You've been thinking about the design of the cabins?"

"I told you, I have too much free time on my hands." She reached for the third blueprint and spread it out, and he could see the wheels in her head turning. "And I know I'm not an actual designer, but—"

"You did a good job designing the new store."

She looked up at him. And then her smile lit up her face. "So, it's a deal, then? You'll let me help?"

"A website *and* a woman's touch on the interiors?" He'd be a fool to say no. Reaching across the span of the picnic table, he finally did what he'd been itching to do since the moment they'd sat down. He wrapped his fingers around hers, and he silently savored the feel of her softer skin against his. "It's a deal."

"And then there was that time with Meleah. Remember her?"

"We *all* remember her."

"Well, I remembered her first."

Laughter rang out around Nate as the eleven guys he'd brought in for this job joked about women of years past. Listening, he slumped farther into his seat and angled his head back. Exhaustion bore down on him—on *all* of them, no doubt—but the day wouldn't be complete without a toast around a fire.

They'd spent the weekend before getting the foundations poured, then after successful inspections had given them approval to move forward, they'd worked from dawn until dusk the last few days. And as of six o'clock that evening, frames on all ten of the cabins were officially up. The sheathing still had to be applied tomorrow and then the plumbing and electrical could be roughed in, but as far as projects went, this one had started off strong.

They'd called it a day a couple of hours ago, then after showers, all of them had met back up at the house. Burgers had been grilled. Someone had plopped a fire pit in the middle of the deck, and flames were rolling. And they were all now busy getting shit-faced.

At least, several of them were. Nate had drunk only one beer —he rarely had more since his stint in rehab a year after he'd left home—and another of the guys who was originally from Salt Lake City also always made it a point never to drink more than one. Dre remained mostly sober, as well, as did Conner, who didn't partake at all.

The rest of them, though? They were heading down the path of a bad morning headache. But they deserved it. They'd worked hard.

Chris stood, beer held out, and offered a salute to all the houses—and all the women—any of them had ever driven nails into. Raucous laughter followed. And then so did the sight of a little red car.

Before everyone quieted from Chris's "joke," Nate had his gaze trained on the Prius that he found himself constantly keeping a watch for anytime he drove through town. He hadn't seen Megan in almost a week and wondered what she was doing there now. Then he wondered how in the world he'd manage to keep this bunch from turning their conversation to her.

Dre noticed her next, and Nate watched as he sat up in his seat. He rubbed a hand down over his jaw, put his beer on the ground, and was on his feet even before Nate could do the same.

"What is it?" Conner asked as both Nate and Dre stood, then he swung his gaze around in time to catch Megan climbing out of her car.

"*Who* is it?" someone else said.

Nate heard another voice reply, "Someone who's now next on my list of women to get to know," as Megan came around the front of her car, and then all sounds from the other men ceased. Megan wore some sort of garment tossed over her shoulders that looked like a small blanket, its ends hanging in angles past her hips, along with what looked similar to a pair of military-style black boots. Dark-washed jeans showcased her trim figure, and a form-fitting long-sleeved black T-shirt had been tucked in at her waist. She might be small in stature, but the woman definitely packed a punch.

"Meg," Nate called out before anyone else spoke and headed toward the stairs.

"Hey." She turned her one-hundred-watt smile on him, giving him the satisfaction of knowing that with eleven other men there, all hoping for her attention, he'd snagged it first. "I hope I'm not interrupting."

"Of course not. We're just having a beer." He paused before tossing out the obligatory "come on up," then clenched his jaw to keep from taking it back. He didn't want her up there in the middle of the guys.

"Thanks," she said. And then she turned the same smile she'd offered to him to every other man waiting behind him.

His stomach sank at the sight, but he ignored the implication. It shouldn't matter that she hadn't come out there just to see him. And clearly, she hadn't. She'd dressed up. She smelled like heaven as she passed him on the stairs. And the assessing way her eyes took in each of the other men told him that, though he might be the one whose house she'd come to, he wasn't where her interest lay.

"Hey, beautiful." Dre eyed her from where he'd stood. "What brings you out tonight?"

"The better question is, who will she be taking *home* with her tonight." That came from Cade, and one of the other guys elbowed the idiot in the gut.

"*Oof,*" Cade said, bending forward from the hit, but Nate noticed that he never lost his smile—nor took his eyes off Megan.

"Give it up, Tuttle," Nate said. He shot the other man a look that couldn't be misinterpreted. "You're nowhere near good enough for her."

"Can't blame a guy for trying." Cade winked at Megan and finished with, "Nice boots."

"Thanks." She literally preened in front of them. One leg bent at the knee, heel coming off the ground, showing off the side of one boot that, given the snubbed chunky heel, *should* come across as more work-ready than sex-kitten. It didn't, though. Then she rewarded Cade with another grin. "They belong to my friend Brooke."

"Brooke, huh?" Cade's interest piqued even more. "The one who was with you last week?"

"That's her."

He shook his head back and forth and tsked. "You should have brought her with you tonight."

She laughed, the sound strong and clear, and it shot straight to Nate's dick. "Maybe I'll do that next time."

Irritation—and a bit of astonishment—had kept Nate silent longer than it should have. Whatever the hell this was going on right in front of him, he was ready for it to end. "Meg," he said again, and once again headed her way. Only this time he didn't stop until he reached her. He put a hand to the small of her back. "Let me introduce you."

Going around the group, Nate introduced the men one by one, all the while watching Megan's reaction, attempting to figure out what she thought of them. Knowing her, she'd text him later to get his thoughts on the lot of them, but at this point he couldn't say that he'd recommend even one. *Nor* had he put in a good word for her with Dre.

He didn't know why he'd offered in the first place. The bunch of them were hoodlums and not good enough.

Of course, that hadn't stopped Dre from asking about *her.* He'd brought her up in conversation one day, and once he'd discovered that she'd once dated Jaden, he'd not only grilled Nate for more information, but the couple of times Jaden had been around, he'd laid into him, as well.

After the introductions were over, Nate wasn't sure what to do. In any other situation, he'd invite her to have a seat and join them. But with these guys . . .

"Do you have any plans for tomorrow night, Megan?" That came from Stefano, the half-Italian half-Mexican "pretty boy" of the group. He was also overly ballsy. "I could wheedle a car out of one of these losers and take you out. Wherever you want to go."

"I . . .uh—" Megan looked at Nate.

Then she cast a furtive glance over at Dre.

"I'm actually already busy tomorrow night." The softened smile she tossed Stefano's way would help ease any letdown. "But maybe another time?"

Hoots went up from every corner of the deck, and a pretty flush heated Megan's cheeks. Nate's irritation grew.

"Can I get you a beer, Megan?" He pulled her attention back to him, deciding that if these guys didn't rein it in, he would end up having to kick more than one of them in the head. "Or something else?" He angled his head toward the back door, his eyes remaining on hers, hoping she'd take him up on his silent offer and follow him inside. He needed to get her away from the men.

"Actually"—her gaze flickered over several of the others again —"I was hoping to get a quick peek at the area where the cabins are being built." She finally pulled her gaze back to Nate's. "I wanted to talk to you about some initial ideas I've had. But . . . I could come back another time? Or you could drop by to see me in town someday?"

Another couple of childish hoots went up, and Nate scalded the offenders with harsh glares.

Silence fell.

"I'd be glad to show you the area. We can go out now and talk through your ideas." He branded the remaining guys with more shut-the-fuck-up glares, but few of them paid attention. Instead, they only had eyes for Meg.

"Would you like some help?" The question came from Dre. "I could go with you."

"I've got it, Haskins. You get yourself another beer." With that, Nate turned away from the rest of the group and motioned toward his truck. "Let's ride out. It'll be dark soon."

Chapter Ten

As Megan settled into Nate's truck for the second time in a week, she couldn't help but sneak another glance his way. She hadn't known if showing up out of the blue would be a good idea or a bad one, and from his grumpiness, she was guessing bad. She supposed that attitude answered her other question, as well. He *definitely* wasn't interested in her. Not that she'd really thought he might be.

Still, she hadn't been able to quit thinking about him. Especially while she'd been out on a date over the weekend. The guy had bored her to tears, and all she'd been able to think about was how she appreciated Nate's sense of humor far better than anyone she'd gone out with over the last couple of months.

She even liked his grumpiness. Sometimes. Mostly when she could see the "cute" Nate behind it.

And yes, she knew she had it bad. And that it clearly had to stop. Because apparently, *she* brought out his grumpy. Which wasn't a good sign at all.

At least she'd gotten to lay eyes on the rest of the guys, though. That had been a bit of a bonus for putting in the effort to spruce up for the evening. And there were some good-looking men currently sitting on Nate's deck—if looks were all she was looking for. She'd pass the info along to Brooke, though. That had been the excuse she'd given for needing to come out tonight anyway.

She snuck another peek to the other side of the seat, and this time, a pair of blue eyes peered back at hers. Her heart thumped.

"Looked like you were having a nice evening back there," she offered. "I apologize for interrupting it. I should have called first."

"It's not a problem." The truck bumped over a rut in the path. "But yeah, we kicked back tonight. The guys deserved it. They've worked hard this week."

She studied him in the orange glow cast by the lowering sun. That was another thing she liked about him. He gave credit away before taking it. "You probably worked hard, too, didn't you?"

He glanced her way again. "The boss is expected to work hard."

"And do you like being the boss?"

"Huh?"

She motioned out in front of her, her hand sweeping toward the overlook she knew they were heading toward, and she voiced some of the thoughts that had run through her mind since seeing the blueprints the week before. "The boss," she repeated. "Do you like it? You brought in all those guys. You had this whole idea. *And* you pulled it together and got things kicked off insanely fast. Clearly, you're good at it. So, I'm just wondering . . . do you like doing it?"

The truck came to a stop in the middle of the field, and Nate shifted into park. His upper body twisted toward her, one arm stretching out across the back of the seat, and Megan held her breath. She didn't know why he'd stopped or what he was thinking.

But then he nodded, his gaze sincere. "Yeah. I do like it. I like seeing things get done."

She licked her lips, her mouth having gone dry. "It seems like the guys like working for you, too."

One dark eyebrow quirked up. "You got that from tonight's catcalls and inappropriate behavior?"

She laughed, the sound feeling almost lonely in the space. "I got that from the relaxed attitude everyone had around you. *And from the simple fact that they all apparently dropped whatever they were doing and showed up here to begin with.*"

He shrugged. "They're friends. That's what friends do."

"Maybe. But I also sense respect."

When she couldn't take the intensity of his stare any longer, she pulled her eyes off his and looked around at where they'd stopped. And then she gasped. *"Oh my."* She took in the barren field they sat in, her heart aching for the missing trees. "It looks so different," she whispered. "So *wrong.*"

She'd loved this orchard from the first minute she'd laid eyes on it. It had felt like home.

"It's definitely different," Nate agreed. "But it's going to be good in the end."

"I'm sure it will be." If anyone else had said that to her, she couldn't say that her reply would have been anything more than a platitude. But given the thrill she'd seen in Nate's eyes, both when he'd first told her about the plans and when he'd laid out the blueprints in front of her, she suspected that whatever final form the new "Wilde Cherry Orchard" ended up as, it *would* be good. Something told her that he wouldn't have it any other way.

"I stopped here for another reason, though." He leaned toward her then, his arm coming off the back of the seat, and he pointed to a spot on the other side of her.

Turning her head, she didn't find what he wanted her to see at first. Instead, all she saw was the occasional remaining clump of cherry trees. Or the pines that lined the outer edges of the property. But then her gaze landed on what he'd pointed to, and her heart lodged in her throat.

"That's the tree?" she asked.

"Where dad had his accident, yeah." Nate's voice had gone

even deeper than normal, as well as a bit of a scratchiness being added to it.

The tree was massive. It wasn't a pine, but she wasn't sure what kind it was, and it had a trunk as wide as Nate's shoulders. But what was so distinct about it was the missing chunks of bark from about shoulder height down to knee height and the obvious gouges that had been crudely dug into the newly bared wood.

"He was so lucky." She whispered the words. "It could have turned out so much worse."

"It definitely could have."

The gravity of the situation wasn't lost on Megan. Nor was the pain rolling off of Nate.

He'd lowered his hand to the seat between them, and as he'd done for her a couple of times in the past, she covered his long fingers with hers. The muscles under her hand tensed, but soon relaxed, and she found herself wrapping her fingers more solidly around his. His hand was warm and strong, and she wished he'd flip it over so she could twine their fingers together.

"How is he?" she asked, and at her question, his eyes once again found hers.

He didn't say anything at first, and when he shifted his gaze back to the tree in the distance, she felt tension vibrating off him. "I can't bring myself to visit him."

He'd uttered the words so softly she almost hadn't heard. And the admission floored her.

"Nate . . ."

He shrugged off her concern, quickly pulling his hand out from under hers, then put the truck back into gear. "It's no biggie. Everyone else goes out all the time." He brushed off his comment. "They hassle him every day, so I'm staying busy here. Staying out of his face. And also getting as much done as possible before he comes home."

"Nate." She said his name again, and when he ignored her, she wanted to reach over and put the truck back into park. To turn his face to hers, and to make him deal with what he'd just said.

She also knew that the mere fact he'd said anything was far more than the norm, so she let it sit. She would bring it up at another time, though. And maybe by then he'd be ready to talk about it.

As they bounced on down the path, no cherry trees anywhere near, Nate jabbed a thumb back the way they'd come. "For the record, I had to get those yahoos back there to help me with the wood chipper last week." He tossed her a quick grin, clearly trying to lighten the mood. "It sure would have been a lot more entertaining doing it with you."

She laughed. "My apologies for running off like that. I do know how terrible it can be to suddenly lose such expert help." She had a full-blown smile on her lips now. "If it makes you feel any better, though, I really *did* want to help."

He stared straight ahead, but the size of his smile stretched to match hers. "It helps—*a little*." He tossed her a wink. "But I'll be expecting you to put in some time in the future to make up for it."

"Deal."

They fell quiet, and she wondered if he was thinking at all about *why* she'd left so suddenly that night. Of course, she hadn't shared with him who'd been on that phone call, nor that it had upset her. But the man was astute. She was quite certain he hadn't just assumed she'd changed her mind.

As they curved around the path and reached the top of a small crest, the shells of the ten cabins came into view. And as she'd done when she'd taken in the barren field, she gasped. This location—as she'd known it would be—was perfect.

The lake glistened just beyond the property, and the Salish Mountains were clearly defined on the far side of the water. The positioning of the cabins was near a drop-off, which added to the drama of the setting, but she knew there was a nearby path that would lead visitors down to the small beach, pier, and the lake frontage owned by the Wildes.

"If you had to lose trees in order for those who don't live in the area to get to experience this, you picked the most beautiful spot on the land to make that happen."

"Thank you." He pressed the gas and kept moving them forward. "I've always loved this location."

After they parked, they got out and took their time walking through each building. As she'd seen with the blueprints the week before, there were three distinct layouts. None of the cabins were spaced terribly close together, but two groupings of three cabins each sat on both ends, both with the two-bedroom with the extra living space positioned in the middle. The other four cabins, two two-bedroom and two one-bedroom, were staggered in between.

"You'll need to plant some fast-growing trees," she said. "To provide future privacy."

"I've already got a guy scouting for good-sized ones that can be transplanted this year."

"Perfect." She stepped inside one of the larger cabins and tilted her head back. The ceiling in these would be vaulted. "Rustic," she murmured, "but not with taxidermy placed everywhere." She'd seen that in some of the local hotel lobbies. The area was abundant with wildlife, and tourists often liked to see them up close. "Something more understated."

"Originally, I was leaning toward using artwork to bring the outdoors in," Nate said, and Megan immediately nodded.

"Each cabin could be centered around a different animal. Black bear, big-horn sheep, bison, eagles." She looked up again. "Tongue-in-groove ceilings for the vaulted rooms, and not too cutesy with the décor." Listing out several more of the thoughts she'd had over the past few days, she continued to talk. She changed up a few of her previous ideas as she took in each space and pulled out her phone to share several of the screenshots she'd saved while looking for ideas.

"It sounds like you've already got a great start on things."

"It's all I can think about." She grinned. She couldn't help it. She loved this kind of stuff. She turned back to the lake and noted the first inkling of color painting the sunset. "I always wanted to build my own home someday."

"Yeah? And if you were to build one today, where would you want to put it?"

The evening breeze wafted over her, and she tugged her blanket wrap closed in front of her. Then she shot Nate a grin. "I suppose it would be too forward of me to say I'd like to build one right here, huh?"

He laughed at that. "Well, seeing as this spot is currently taken . . ."

She eyed the grooves that lined his cheeks when he smiled. He could best any man sitting on his back deck with that smile.

"There is a similar spot on the property next door, though." He turned away and pointed south. "We're renting the Wyndhams house for the summer as we do the work here, but I've been over there several times throughout the years. There's a gorgeous perch very similar to this one. Beautiful view, a handful of fifty-year-old birch trees providing plenty of shade, and at a nice private distance from the road. It would be perfect for a house."

As he finished the sentence, his words softening the longer he spoke and the spot he'd described painted vividly in her mind, she couldn't help but wonder if he'd imagined the same before tonight. "Too bad they already have a house on their property," she pointed out.

"True. But I also know that they plan to eventually sell." He looked over his shoulder at her. "So, who knows? Maybe the land could be split, and you could talk them into a great deal?"

The idea was the best one of the night. Too bad she couldn't jump on it.

She sighed. "I don't think the timing is right for that." Nor did she likely have enough for a down payment on lakefront property.

"Why not?" he asked as they stepped out of the cabin and headed back the way they'd come. When she didn't answer, he looked over at her, then tilted his head as if to see even closer. "Is it because you don't want to build a house just for yourself?"

His ability to know what she was thinking astounded her. "It's just one of those things, you know?" Hopping onto the porch of the next cabin, she wrapped a hand around one of the 4x4s supporting the roof overhang, and leaning out, she walked in a circle around it. "I've always dreamed about building a house *with* my husband." It was easier to talk without looking directly into his all-knowing face. "Not in the hopes that I'd someday find one who'd move into it with me."

Nate didn't respond immediately. Instead, he hopped onto the same space as her and leaned back against another post. "So you and Jaden were going to build?"

"What?" She stopped moving and looked over at him.

He shrugged. "I know you'd planned to buy a house after he finished school and you both got settled here."

"We did, but . . ." She shook her head. "No. We were just going to buy. We never even talked about building."

"Yet you've always wanted to build."

"I have." And she had no idea why she'd never mentioned that to Jaden. Nor why it had never so much as crossed her mind to do so. "I guess I forgot about that dream for a while." She hopped back down to the ground. "Or maybe I only used to want to build a house because my uncle was a contractor."

"Which uncle?"

She glanced over as he joined her. "The only uncle I had. He was married to Aunt June."

"And Aunt June was the aunt with the boat?"

"A fishing boat, yes. Of which I watched but didn't partici-pate." She offered him a smile, feeling as if they'd gotten back to an easier footing, and as she did, she was stopped by the beauty of the lowering sun. "It's so beautiful out here," she murmured.

"It most definitely is." He turned, legs braced shoulder-width apart, hands on his hips, and took in the scene with her. Long streaks of reds and purples passed behind the mountains, and the remaining snow on the crests seemed to glow with firelight behind it. "Let's go out on the water when we're done," Nate said. "We'll celebrate."

"What?" She wasn't sure what he was suggesting.

A date?

He didn't look at her. "When the cabins are done," he repeated. "We'll have worked hard, so let's celebrate on the water. I'll fish and you can read a book."

So, not a date. *Probably.*

She stared up at him, seeing more of his jawline than anything, and found herself frustrated when he didn't look down. He had to know she was standing there waiting for him to meet her eyes. For him to say why he'd suggest such a thing.

"Just you and me?" she finally asked, and though he didn't nod, she had the idea that he wanted to.

Finally, he did look at her. And his eyes were unreadable. "Whatever you want." He offered with a tight smile. Then he started walking in the direction of the truck again. "Tell me about your uncle. Did you want him to build your house for you?"

She didn't want to talk about her uncle. She wanted to talk about whatever that moment had been.

Or almost had been.

Because she hadn't been imagining that, had she?

But Nate's head faced forward, and his posture said that *this* was the only subject he was willing to discuss.

Fine. She started after him.

"I don't know," she answered. "Maybe?" She thought back to her early teenage years when she'd first had the idea. Uncle Ray used to take her to job sites when she'd visit for the summer. At that point, she hadn't been living with them full-time yet. And he'd answer every question she ever asked. "I at least wanted to talk to him about it, I guess. I always loved the idea of being involved myself. I mean . . . I know I'm no contractor, but the idea of helping to design my own home from the ground up is appealing. I want to picture every room as it's built. Have a hand in all the details from day one."

"Kind of like you're doing here?"

He'd finally looked down at her, and her cheeks heated with embarrassment. "I guess I kind of forced myself into your project, huh?"

He didn't smile, but his eyes did. "Maybe a little. But that's okay. I'm glad you did."

Dang. Were they about to have another quasi-moment?

She waited, her breath held in her throat, but again, he turned for the truck.

"When did you lose your aunt and uncle?"

She blew out a breath. She needed to give up the idea that the man might have even a tiny percentage of the lust for her that she did for him. "Uncle Ray passed when I was sixteen," she said in a monotone. He'd died just two months into the school year the first year she'd moved in with them. "He developed cancer, and there was nothing they could do. And Aunt June"— her voice hitched, but she recovered quickly—"I lost her my sophomore year in college." That one had hurt more. That one wasn't supposed to have happened.

"And what about the rest of your family?"

"What about them?"

They'd reached the truck, but instead of getting in, they both turned toward the lake. Toward the sun that was just about to dip behind the mountains. "What kind of family do you have?" he said. "Big? Small? Close?"

She could feel him watching her instead of the sunset. "I was closest with my aunt and uncle."

"No other family?"

She wanted to tell him to stop. That she didn't want to talk about any of her family.

But at the same time, she *wanted* to tell him. She wanted to have someone to rant to because with her somewhat large immediate family, she often felt so very alone.

Not taking her eyes off the other side of the lake, she said, "I have a mother, a father, two sisters, and one brother. There's twelve years between me and my next-oldest sister. Mica is basically Mom made over. They both live in Boston."

Nate paused before saying anything more, and she finally felt his attention shift back to the sunset. She wanted to lean into him.

"That's a long distance away," he observed. "What about your other siblings? Are they like your mom, too?"

She shook her head "They're like Dad. They're scholars. They have a passion for all things science."

"So, you're more like them, then? A scholar?"

She shrugged, but she didn't say anything. She supposed she was like them—aside from the fact that she'd moved to Birch Bay due to Jaden. That was on the scale of something her mother would do.

She also supposed she should quit ignoring her father's text messages and send him her resume.

The sun dipped behind the mountain, but Nate didn't move to get into the truck. Instead, he asked, "Which one of them was on that phone call last week?"

"What?" She looked at him without meaning to, and when she caught him studying her, his eyes quietly saying that he wanted to help, she couldn't look away. She swallowed. "What are you talking about?"

"I'm talking about that phone call that sent you running from the house."

She knew he'd had to have guessed it upset her. "That phone call wasn't important. I just remembered something I had to do at home, that's all. That's why I left."

"Liar," he murmured. He then leaned in and whispered, "And not a very good one."

Nor had she ever been. "Why haven't *you* gone out to visit your dad since he's been in rehab?"

Surprise flashed across Nate's face at her question, then something resembling appreciation colored his gaze. "So, the lady fights dirty."

"The lady fights to win." She inched up her chin. "Are you going to answer the question or not?"

He held his stance. "Are you?"

She wanted to. She really did.

And that scared her more than the idea of telling him about how much it hurt that her dad was never around for her and that she was the only one it seemed to bother.

She opened the passenger door. "Let's go back. It's too dark to see anything else."

NATE WATCHED MEGAN DRIVE OFF. They'd returned to the house in silence, and when they'd gotten there the guys had been gone. The fire had been snuffed out, and silence greeted them. Nate hadn't pressed again on that phone call, nor on the fact that there was obviously some issue with her family. But he had made the decision that he'd do just that at some point in the future. Just like he suspected she'd made a similar decision concerning him and his dad.

And being "only friends" with Megan or not—and truly that's all they could ever be . . . a brother didn't do that to another brother—deep down, he didn't think either of them were finished pushing.

He turned back to the house, climbing the deck stairs in silence, only to discover Dre sitting in the dark.

"Hey, man." Dre nudged his chin in Nate's direction. "You get everything squared away out there?"

Nate had mentioned before today that Meg would be helping with both the cabins' interiors as well as the website. "She saw what she needed to help fill in the holes."

"Good to know." Dre stood from the Adirondack chair where he'd had his feet stretched out in front of him. "Then I have one more question."

"Shoot." Nate picked up a stick and poked at the smoldering embers.

"Do you have something going on with her?"

At the question, Nate's motions slowed, and he looked over at his friend. He'd known Dre since his first time out in the Bering Sea, and the two of them had been through a lot together. What they'd never done, though, was want the same woman. At least not seriously.

"She's my brother's ex," he said.

"Which doesn't answer the question." Dre stood with his back to the house, the light from inside casting a shadow over half his face, making it impossible to get a read on what he might be thinking.

"No. I don't have anything going on with her."

"Do you want there to be?"

He felt raw from the last forty-five minutes of being near Meg. "Are *you* into her?" he asked instead of answering, and Dre didn't respond at first.

Then he gave a slow nod. "I could be."

And there it was. The gauntlet had been tossed down. Though it wasn't so much a gauntlet, Nate knew, as it was making sure not to step on a friend's toes.

"She's my brother's ex," he repeated, though it pained him to do so. "There isn't and there *won't* be anything going on with us."

Dre nodded, but then Nate added, "But hurt her, and you'll answer to *me*."

Chapter Eleven

"That was an excellent band." Megan tugged at her earlobe as they drove toward her place, mildly worried about hearing loss after she and Dre had found the only empty seats in the bar tonight—which had been right next to the stage. She smiled when he looked her way, though, to show that there were no complaints. It truly had been a fun night.

"They were great," he agreed. "But I'm sorry it left us with so little opportunity to talk. When I asked you out, I had no idea there were so few things to do around here on a Saturday night."

She chuckled at his mock shudder. She'd grown used to the small-town feel of the place. "Just wait until it warms up. I've been in town a few times during the summer months, and there's always someone out on the lake or coming and going from hikes."

"That's what I'd like to do." Dre pulled his car in front of her apartment, parking next to hers, and turned off the ignition. "The summer I spent working in Glacier was the best." He turned toward her. "I'd love to take you hiking someday." His sincerity was palpable.

"That would be fun." She didn't commit to the idea any more than that, but she could totally see hiking in Glacier with Dre.

He was definitely the outdoors type. A man who had energy oozing from his pores. So, sitting in a crowded bar tonight had *not* done their date justice.

Of course, by the time enough snow melted to go on a hike and really get up in altitude, he would probably already be gone.

The reminder put a damper on her mood. Dre had called the store the day before and asked her out, and she'd been excited at the idea. But the more she'd built it up in her mind, the more she'd also wondered if there was any point. Even if they started dating regularly, chances were slim they'd be at a place by the time the cabins were finished where he'd consider sticking around. And she wasn't at all interested in a long-distance relationship.

"Can I see you again?" he asked, and in the darkened front seat, she pushed her worries aside and found that she couldn't quite discount the appeal of him yet. At least not entirely.

"Maybe," she said, and she smiled again when he blew out a dramatic breath at the letdown. But she needed time to think about it. She stretched across the seat and pressed her lips to his cheek. "Call me next week and we can talk about it?"

His eyes, so similar in color to hers, stared back at her when she pulled away, and a shiver ran through her at their intensity. "Is that the best I'm going to get?"

His voice was like warm cream, and she wasn't sure if he meant the question to be as far as a commitment to seeing him again or about a good-night kiss. But the answer remained the same for both. Once more, she touched her lips to the roughened beard covering his firm cheek. Dang, he smelled good. "Next week," she whispered. She needed the distance from tonight to see things more clearly. She needed to figure out if getting tangled up with someone who might not be around for long was worth it.

She got out of the car and had made it within ten feet of her front door when he spoke from behind her. "Next week," he said, and she peeked over her shoulder, flattered at the way he had both arms hanging out the open window and a seriously playful—and super sexy—smile gracing his lips. "I'll call you," he added, then tacked on an air kiss, and she almost said yes right then. What could it hurt to go out with him a second time?

But she'd already made up her mind. "Next week," she agreed, and when he bit his lip before pulling his head back into the car and backing out of her driveway, she laughed out loud.

The man had obviously wanted to kiss her. She'd sensed it while they'd been at the bar and had felt it again in the tension all the way back to her place. But something had held her back. She didn't know if it was due to the doubts that had been plaguing her leading up to the date. Or if it had anything to do with who his friend was.

If the latter was the case, she might be screwed all the way around until Nate finished the work at his place and left town. And if that was so, that would just suck. Because that dry spell was only going to get longer. Not to mention, she'd never been an overly patient person, and she was already frustrated with dating as it was. She'd been with Jaden for so long that she'd forgotten how difficult it could be to find someone you truly clicked with. And as she'd decided when she'd broken up with Jaden . . . she had no intention of settling.

As she approached the small porch, keys in hand, a creaking noise came from the back corner, and the hair on the back of her neck immediately stood up. Jabbing her hand into her bag, she had her pepper spray out and pointed in that direction before her mind registered that someone was saying her name.

A voice she recognized.

"Nate!" Her eyes adjusted, now seeing him standing in front of the rocker, his arms outstretched in front of him, and she flipped on the small LED penlight that hung off her keychain. The beam shined in his eyes. "What in the heck are you doing sitting on my porch?"

The man had scared her to death!

He shielded his eyes with one hand. "Waiting on you."

Twisting his head to the side, he added, "Can you please turn that thing off? I don't want to go blind here."

She switched off the light. "What are you *doing* here?"

It was eleven o'clock on a Saturday night.

"And how long have you been here?"

"Which question do you want me to answer first?" he grumbled, and as he stepped closer, she had the urge to kick him in the shin.

"I want you to answer both of them. Along with"—she turned back to the street to make sure she hadn't missed it before—"where in the world is your truck?"

She unlocked the front door, but instead of stepping inside, she simply reached in and flipped on the porch light. She'd intended to do that before she left, and now, it would certainly be the first thing she did the next time she went out. One scare of a lifetime was enough.

Turning back to him, she crossed her arms, her irritation mounting. "What are you doing here, Nate?"

He held up a spiral-bound notepad. "I wanted to talk about designs for the cabins."

Her bullshit meter went off. That didn't seem a topic worthy of an almost-midnight, Saturday night visit. But on the other hand, from the looks of the thing in his hand, she could at least see that the notepad wasn't brand new. So, it was possible it held design notes.

"And how long have you been here?"

"Not long." His words were followed by a glance across the street to the two-story belonging to Gabe and Erica, and she couldn't help but wonder if they'd give a different answer if she went over and asked. But then, maybe they hadn't even seen him here. Like she hadn't until she'd practically been on top of him.

"*Where* is your *truck?*" She shouldn't be so riled up at finding the man on her porch, but the scare he'd put in her still had her adrenaline flowing.

This time when he answered, it wasn't just a blunt few words. It was a few embarrassed ones.

He nodded toward the darkened dead end stretching beyond her house, the line of his jaw clenched in the glow of the overhead light, and she would swear that his neck turned pink. "I parked at the end of the road," he muttered. His eyes no longer looked directly at hers.

"And then you walked all the way back up here?" Before he could even nod, she added, "To talk about the design of the cabins?"

What a load of crap.

She knew exactly what the man was up to, and she didn't like it one bit.

Crossing to stand in front of him, she jabbed him in the chest. "You knew I was out with Dre, didn't you?"

Again, his jaw clenched. "He might have mentioned it."

"And what? You're just nosy? You wanted to see how it went?"

He opened his mouth to reply, but she slapped a hand over it before he could speak.

"What if I'd invited him in, Nate? Would you have just sat here in the dark and watched us?"

"Of course not."

"Then what would you have done?"

He didn't answer, and from the way his eyes frosted over, she had the feeling that sitting there unnoticed would have been the last thing that would have happened. But why?

If he didn't want her, what would be his issue if his friend was interested?

"Good grief," she muttered. She stepped away from him and pushed the door to her apartment open wide. "Come on." She motioned for him to go before her. "Come in and let's talk about these all-important designs that couldn't wait."

When he looked at the door and then back to her, as if silently saying that *she* needed to go in before *him*, she let the full heat of her anger flare.

"Get. In. My. Apartment."

He went into her apartment.

And then he just stopped.

"Oh, good grief," she mumbled again. She shoved in past him and slammed the door. "It's just a fireman's pole. Have you never seen one before?"

She'd rented the place from Erica, who'd bought it late the year before after renting it when she'd first moved to town. The place had been renovated before that, and what once had been a fire hall was now the cutest little one-bedroom apartment she'd ever seen. And it didn't still just have the pole in the middle of the living room. The hole remained in the floor above, as well. The bedroom was located up there, and some mornings after she got up, just because it was fun to do so, she slid down the pole instead of using the stairs.

"Take off your coat," she said and tossed her own over the back of the couch. "No need to just stand there looking shell-shocked."

Her phone chirped then, and as she watched the muscles in Nate's shoulders tense, she smiled to herself. She seriously hoped it was Dre texting her after just driving away from the place. Just like she knew Nate assumed it would be. And if it was, she just might set up that second date right now. Because darn it, this man shouldn't be here. Not if he didn't want to—

Her thoughts cut off, and her irritation switched focus.

"What is it?" Nate finally moved from just inside the front door and crossed to where she stood in the connecting kitchen. She'd dropped her purse on the island countertop, and she remained there, staring down at her phone.

Son of a—

"Megan?"

"What?" She bit the word out as if the anger caused by the text message was Nate's fault.

"What's wrong?"

"You mean besides my so-called 'friend' checking up on me after my date?"

He stared at her as if trying to figure out what she'd meant with the air quotes around the word "friend," and she rolled her eyes. Men wouldn't have a clue how to function in the world if it weren't for women.

"It's my *dad*." She held the face of her phone out toward him. "He's not coming. *Again*."

Nate reached for her cell phone. "Your dad was coming to visit?"

She snorted at that. "Of course he wasn't. He never planned to. Even though he texted me just yesterday to tell me that he'd stop by tomorrow morning."

She'd known she shouldn't get her hopes up. But darn it, she almost had. She'd even pulled out her resume and considered updating it.

She snorted again, disgust rolling through her, and then realized she'd handed her phone over to Nate. She turned her back to him, not wanting to face anyone at this point, but at the same time, not really caring if he read her father's lies or not. What did it matter?

"What's this about a resume?" he said, and she looked back. He'd apparently scrolled up.

"He wants me to send him one," she told him. "He thinks I should work for some big company based in Chicago."

"A tech company?"

Like she cared what kind of company it was. "It's an Artificial Intelligence Research Scientist position."

"And what? You're now looking to move? I thought you wanted to stay here."

She snatched her phone out of his hand, tired of the questions. "No, Nate. I'm not looking to move. He *wants* me to move. He wants me to live up to my 'full potential.'" She stared down at the phone, tears suddenly trying to get the best of her, and found herself unable to contain her contempt. "And hell.

Maybe I should go. Maybe that would finally score me some points."

"What?" He looked confused, and she turned away again. She hadn't meant to say that.

"Nothing," she muttered.

"It's something. What do you mean, points?"

When she didn't respond, his hands landed on her shoulders. They tugged slightly, trying to turn her around, but she resisted.

"Meg."

She shook her head. "Don't."

"Talk to me."

"I don't want to talk to you, Nate. I don't want to talk to anyone." But without meaning to, she faced him again. She stared at him without saying anything at first, her focus zeroed in on the concern written across his face. She *didn't* want to talk to anyone. That was true.

She didn't want to talk, or think, or give her father yet one more chance to make her feel less.

She didn't want to hurt, dammit.

But Nate stood there, and he looked so concerned for her. And it had been such a long time since someone had truly seemed to see her and the hurts she carried. So, she opened her mouth and let a flood of words come out.

"There are things I don't talk about." The words came out slow at first. "Like how my father couldn't care less if he ever saw me. Or that I also haven't seen my mother in two years, because she's off chasing around what she hopes to be her fourth husband since my parents' divorce. Nor do I share with people that *none* of my three siblings have time to call me. *Ever.*" She shook her head again, the hurt from years past and the pain of years to come rising like bile in the back of her throat, blocking out all reason. "And, of course, *you* don't want me either, do you? You're just fine patting me on the head and being my 'friend.' Sending me off to date *your* friends. You couldn't care less if I—"

His mouth closed over hers, and she stopped breathing.

Her heart seemed to miss a beat before it suddenly took off again, and when Nate's hand slid around the back of her neck, gripping her a little too tight and holding her punishingly to his mouth, she moaned.

This was what she needed.

This heat. This *passion*.

Nate stepped closer, closing the distance between them, and the hard, solid, one hundred percent male that was Nate Wilde, pressed into her from head to toe. His mouth then proceeded to ravage hers, while his other hand came up to hold her chin in place—as if there were *any* chance she might break contact with this—and then *she* managed to get them even closer.

No space existed between them as she stood on her toes and slid her arms around his neck, and when a deep guttural groan rumbled from the back of his throat, she hitched one leg around his thigh.

Nate's hands lowered, gripping her under the bottom curve of her butt, his fingertips digging into the stretchy material of her dress and the tops of her thighs, and she lifted her other leg to wrap both around him. Then everything that had been on the corner of the countertop hit the floor, and he plopped her down in front of him. The cold of the granite against the backs of her bare thighs had her gasping and arching backward, and when her mouth pulled away from his, she could see the full amount of his desire coloring his features. He was mindless with it.

"Nate," she whispered, and his mouth was back on hers.

He yanked her forward until the hard length of him pressed against her, and a whimper escaped her throat.

"Too many clothes," he muttered.

One hand moved to the buttons on the front of her dress, the other grabbing her by the hair and angling her head back, and then his mouth and teeth got busy at her neck. As teeth scraped against the tendons and a quick nip at the base of her throat had her going instantly wet, his fingers never stalled. One by one, the buttons down her chest came free, and by the time cool air whispered across the lace of her bra, everything about her throbbed.

She blindly reached out, desperate to feel him as he was now doing to her, and as her fingers fumbled to shove at his jacket and started with the buttons of his shirt, he removed his hands from her to help. As he did, her lips sought out his, heat and need and urgency all combining to fuse their mouths together as their fingers feverishly worked.

She heard the jangle of his belt buckle, and her breathing became even more rapid. This was the last thing she'd expected when she'd come home tonight, but she wasn't about to look a gift horse in the mouth. It might be crazy, but she wanted Nate. And whether this was a one-night thing or whether they'd have a wild fling until he left for better pastures, she wouldn't complain. She wanted this, and she was going to have it.

Only, his hands stopped moving. And then his eyes opened.

He looked at her, their faces too close to focus, and as he leaned slightly back, she watched a flicker of confusion pass through his eyes—quickly followed by horror.

"Oh, *Christ.*" He jerked away from her, his arms bent at the elbows and his hands going in the air on either side of him. *"Megan."* He panted, trying to catch his breath. "I'm so sorry. I didn't mean to . . ."

His words trailed off as one hand waved toward her exposed body, and her anger from earlier returned. "You didn't mean to what?" she snapped. "Kiss me? Undress me?"

"No. God . . . *no!"* He shook his head. "I didn't mean to do any of it."

She wanted the ground to open up and swallow her whole. He didn't have to sound so damned disgusted by the fact that he'd laid his hands on her. "Then why did you, Nate?"

"Because you . . ." He swallowed compulsively and motioned toward her chest again, then he glanced toward the front door as if regretting ever walking through it. His other hand dragged down over his face, likely hoping it would erase the error of his ways, and she wanted to vomit. How humiliating.

She didn't move to cover herself up, though. He wouldn't get that from her.

"Why did you?" She asked the question again. "Was it only because I went out with your friend and that made you jealous?" She should have known he wasn't really into her.

"Yes!" He nodded, the movement quick and jerky, and then seemed to think better of the answer—or maybe it was the death glare she sent his way. "I mean . . . *no*." He shook his head. "That's not *why* I did it. That was just the impetus for me coming here tonight."

"The impetus?" Well, at least he was honest about that. Though why some men didn't want a woman but didn't want other men to have her either was beyond her. "Then why did you kiss me once you were here? Why did you touch me?"

The way his face crumpled, he looked like a kid pleading for forgiveness, but she wasn't about to let him off the hook. He'd been about to make love to her . . . and now he was horrified. What the fuck?

She continued to glare at him, and he finally uttered, "I kissed you because I wanted to, okay?"

"You wanted to?"

"Yes! I wanted to!" His arms flailed out toward her, and then he seemed to remember that he wasn't fully dressed himself. As his fingers once again fumbled with his own shirt, closing up what they'd previously opened, he seemed to get himself partially under control. His breathing slowed, and the look of horror morphed back to apology. "I also kissed you because I couldn't stand to see you hurting from your dad. And because every damned time I see you, I want to put my mouth on yours, okay? Does hearing that make you happy?" He looked her up and down, his eyes lingering momentarily where her dress gaped. "I want to put my mouth on your lips, Megan. Your neck. Your body." He dragged his eyes back to hers. "I want my hands roaming over every square inch of you. Every damned time I see you."

That wasn't what she'd expected to hear at all.

"Only . . . *that's* not going to happen again." He stepped closer and began buttoning her dress.

"Why isn't it?" She remained ticked—and humiliated—but not enough to never want his hands on her again.

But the look he gave her wasn't promising at all. The heat had disappeared from his eyes. The light inside them dimmed. "Because you're my brother's ex. And I won't do that to him."

She closed her eyes. That's what he was hung up on?

Well, she could set the record straight on that.

Hopping down from the counter, she squared her shoulders, going for confident and not looking nearly as shook up as she was, and she peered up at him. "Listen to me, Nate Wilde. For the record, *I'm* okay with what just happened here. With what *almost* happened here. Clearly you aren't, and that's okay. But Jaden and I broke up months ago. He's wildly happy and in love. And I'm confident he'd want the same for me."

Panic flared in Nate's eyes, and he moved back so quickly that he stumbled, and his elbow hit the pole. "Who said anything about love?"

She let out a half-growl-half-sigh. "That's *not* what I meant. I'm just saying that if kissing you makes me happy . . . if doing *more* with you made me happy . . . then he'd be okay with that."

He rubbed his elbow. "I find that hard to believe."

"And why is that? Do you think *he* wants to be kissing me again?"

"No." He made a face at the idea of that.

"Then why would he care who I'm kissing?"

"Because I'm his brother, Megan! You don't do that to brothers."

Granted, she'd never been overly close to any of her siblings, but still . . . she and Jaden had parted on completely friendly terms. His whole family even still liked her. Was this honestly that taboo? "You wouldn't be *doing* anything to him, Nate. That's my point. He's moved on. Or wait"—she held up a hand, one finger in the air, as she clued in to the likely issue— "is the problem simply that he and I were together to begin with? That you know I've kissed him? That I've done *more* with him?"

The look of distaste on his face would have been comical if she wasn't still ticked off. "I know what happens in a four-year relationship, Megan. I'm not dense."

"Okay, then. So, you just think that your brother still has some sort of tie on me?"

"No. Of course I don't. I just think it's wrong. Brothers don't do that to brothers. End of story." A look of chagrin tightened the lines around his mouth. "Plus, I'm not looking for forever. You know that. I'll be leaving soon. So, what would be the point?"

Sexual satisfaction? But she didn't suggest that. Because he did have a point. She'd just temporarily forgotten the end game.

"I suppose you're correct," she said, her anger deflating. "You and me getting together would be nothing more than a waste of time."

"Right."

"Right," she repeated, and she felt almost as sad in that moment as she had the day she'd come home from college to bury her aunt. She moved to the door. "It's time for you to go, Nate."

She opened the door, and he picked up his coat and the notepad he'd come in with, but before stepping out, he stopped in front of her. She had the idea that he might say something that in some way would make up for what had happened there tonight. Or what *hadn't* happened.

He didn't, though.

What he said instead was, "Don't go out with Dre again."

She blinked up at him. "Excuse me?"

"I said don't—"

"I heard you clearly the first time," she growled out. "But why in the hell not?"

And who did he think he was to say that to her?

He lifted his shoulders halfheartedly, as if he had no real excuse. "Because I don't want you to."

The bark of laughter she bit out could probably be heard all the way to where his truck sat at the farthest end of her street. "Wrong answer, Wilde. Now get out of my house."

He didn't hesitate. He just walked out. And she slammed the door behind him.

Chapter Twelve

"I still can't believe he had you practically naked, and he stopped." Brooke paced across the kitchen in Megan's apartment, stopping to look at the spot on the counter where Megan had sat hot and wanton only twelve hours before. "What kind of man does that?"

"One that has more willpower than I do," Megan muttered.

"Or one that's a moron," Brooke corrected.

"That, too."

"But I still don't understand how it even happened." Brooke spun back to face Megan, who sat on the opposite side of the kitchen at the dining room table. Brooke had come over as soon as Megan texted to offer brunch and mimosas, and though they were on their second drink, brunch hadn't yet happened. Instead, all they'd done was talk about Nate.

"It happened because I went out with Dre, and Nate didn't like it."

"No." Brooke waved off the explanation. "I know that part. You said that already. But *how*? As in, how did *you* let it happen. I thought you were just going to be friends with him?"

"I was. I *am*."

"Then how did last night go from looking at design notes at midnight to stripping each other on the kitchen island?"

Megan took another sip of her mimosa as Brooke returned to the table. "I got a text from my dad that upset me."

"Okay?" The utter perplexity on her friend's face turned her heavy, almond-shaped eyes into narrow slits.

Megan had never told Brooke anything about her parents other than the basics, so she added, "We have an 'unstable' relationship." But that wasn't exactly true. They had the relationship that her dad wanted . . . and she just always let him get away with it.

She'd yet to call him out on never having time for her. It had been bad enough when he and her mother divorced and he'd moved to Seattle, but once she'd finished high school, it was as if he'd washed his hands of her. Like his job had been finished.

Except, he still expected her to live up to her full potential.

"I don't see him often," she explained, "and I guess deep inside, I'm a daddy's girl." At least, as a kid she'd considered herself to be one. She'd once followed him around everywhere. "It's been a while, and I miss him. So, Friday he texted that he would stop by today on his way back out of the country, and last night he changed his mind. I was upset. And . . . I got a little heated."

"And that made Nate kiss you?" Doubt crept into Brooke's voice, but Megan wasn't sure how else to explain it.

"Yes. That made him kiss me. He apparently didn't like seeing me upset."

Brooke nodded. "Okay. I get that. Men don't do well with tears."

"I wasn't crying."

"Still. He knew you were hurting. Maybe he thought he'd kiss you *before* you cried."

Megan gave her friend a contemptuous look. She was *not* a crier. "I wasn't even on the verge of tears. In fact, I was screaming. And I might have also screamed something about how he didn't want me, either. That he'd rather pat me on the head and just be my friend."

"*Ah.*"

"Ah, what?"

"Ah, you goaded him into kissing you."

The statement was an insult. "I did no such thing."

Brooke studied her with a gleam in her eyes. "I think you did. And I also think that you meant to. Just like you meant to get all naked and do the deed in the 'heat of the moment' right there on your counter."

Megan gaped at her friend. Then she looked at her countertop.

Brooke was being ridiculous.

"And *I* think you're reading far more into this than there is," Megan returned.

"Umm-hmm." Brooke fired off a look of superiority. "Like I read more into your dinner out with him a couple of weeks ago, right?"

"You *did* read more into that. It was nothing but two friends."

"A friend you've since cooked a meal for, had lunch with, and then volunteered to help him design the cabins."

"I also flirted with his friends and went out with one of them last night," she retorted.

"And did you kiss *him*?"

Megan was caught red-handed. Brooke knew her too well.

"I'll bet he wanted to," Brooke went on. "I saw the way he looked at you at the club that night, so no way did he not want to lay one on you. *And* he drove you home, so he had the perfect opportunity to do so."

Megan finished off her mimosa, using that as an excuse to ignore her friend a bit longer, but when she set her glass down, Brooke was leaning across the table, her face directly in front of Megan's.

"Dre wanted to kiss you last night, didn't he, Meg?"

Megan stuck out her chin. "Maybe."

"And he's seriously hot, and any other time you would have totally taken him up on that. Because you just *know* he knows how to use those luscious lips, right?"

Brooke could be so dramatic sometimes. But she had a point.

"I have no doubt that he knows how to use those lips." She'd had that very thought on more than one occasion the night before.

"Then why didn't you kiss him?"

"I didn't say that I hadn't."

"You also didn't say that you had." She picked up Megan's empty glass and went to the kitchen to refill it. "You didn't kiss him because you were thinking about Nate. Am I right?"

Megan scratched at a spot on the tabletop. "Not entirely."

Brooke shot her a look.

"*Fine.* That's why I didn't kiss him. Are you happy?"

"Are you going to go out with him again?"

Megan answered by way of a shrug.

"Are you going to kiss Nate again if he decides he wants to?"

Another shrug, and this time she turned her head and looked away.

"Do I need to buy you new batteries for your vibrator to get you through this?"

"What?" She turned back. "*No!* I'm . . ." She let out a heavy sigh, then gritted out, "I have batteries, thankyouverymuch."

Brooke's laughter echoed through the space, and once again, Megan turned her head away. She knew she was acting childish, but Brooke seemed to think the whole situation was hilarious. And Megan didn't see it that way.

Brooke brought another mimosa over to the table, with a freshened one for herself as well, but instead of sitting back down, she moved over toward the windows that lined the garage door. The garage door was actually the original door that had been used when the building was a fire hall, and though it led from the outside directly into the dining area, the man who'd renovated the building had kept it intact as part of the building's charm.

"*Oh!*" Brooke suddenly exclaimed. "There's the awesome threesome."

"Who are you talking about?" Megan stood to look out the windows and made out Erica, Maggie Crowder, and Arsula standing on Erica's front porch. "Oh, yeah. They've become really good friends." Megan had seen Maggie and Arsula next door several times since she'd moved in.

"We should invite them over." Brooke headed toward the door. "Get their take on this thing with Nate."

"What?" Megan whirled to stop her friend. "Brooke! *No.*"

But it was too late. The front door had already been opened. "Hey, ladies!" Brooke waved, and Megan watched through the windows as all three waved back, smiles lighting up their faces. Brooke held up her freshly poured mimosa. "Come over if you're not in a hurry to get somewhere. We're having a girls' morning. With mimosas!"

"Oh!" Arsula was the first to head their way. "I *love* mimosas."

"*Brooke!*" Megan hissed, but the other woman ignored her, and the next thing Megan knew, her place was filled with women. Brooke moved back to the fridge to pull out the champagne and orange juice, and chatter quickly filled the room.

"So, what are you three up to?" Megan crossed to the kitchen, doing her best to shoot daggers at Brooke.

"We're heading out to the orchard," Erica explained, and over the top of her head, Brooke waggled her eyebrows at Megan. "The guys got the updates done to the bedroom and bathroom yesterday, so we're going out to take inventory of things and see what other prettying up we can do. Then we're going shopping."

"Oh, you should come with us." That came from Arsula as she turned to Megan. "Nate said you're helping with the cabins. And from the work you did on my website, I know for a fact how great your eye is for colors and space."

"Did Nate say anything else about her?" Brooke blurted out,

and as she pulled down three more champagne flutes, the other three turned to her.

"Say anything like what?" Arsula seemed confused.

"Like *nothing*," Megan assured them. "Brooke is just being weird today. And she's not at all funny."

She shot her friend a look that promised swift and fast retribution if she brought up Nate's name again, and as Brooke ignored her look and started pouring champagne into the first glass, Erica held up her hand. "Just give me orange juice, if you don't mind."

Brooke paused with the champagne bottle tilted over the second flute. "You're sure?"

Arsula snorted. "No alcohol? You're not pregnant, are you?"

The room went quiet, and all eyes turned to Erica.

"No." She shook her head, her gaze bouncing to each one of them. "Of course not. I'm just driving. *And* I'm a schoolteacher. I can't risk getting pulled over and have someone smell alcohol on me."

"Good point," Maggie agreed. She nodded toward the glasses. "I'll just have orange juice, too. In school-teacher solidarity."

Again, silence prevailed, and this time Arsula looked Maggie up and down. "You're not pregnant, too, are you?"

"Of course I'm not."

"And I didn't say that I *was* pregnant," Erica pointed out.

"Well, you two do what you want." Arsula made a face. "But *I'm* having a mimosa. And I'm certainly not getting pregnant anytime soon, so maybe I'll have the ones for you two, as well."

After the drinks were poured, talk turned to men. Specifically, the men Nate had brought in to help build the cabins. Megan knew he'd been trying to keep the work going on out there quiet, but with a slew of hot guys like that traipsing all over town, word had quickly spread.

"I've met them," she announced with a grin.

"She went out with one of them last night." Brook waggled her brows again.

"Really?" Maggie swiveled on her barstool. "Which one?"

Anticipation peered back from all three of them, and Megan pulled up a mental visual of Dre. "I went to the club with Dre. He's an ex-football player from Penn State who's about as big as he is hot."

"Which is a *lot*," Brooke added, and all three of the other women groaned. Megan laughed, enjoying the moment, and—assuming Brooke continued to keep her mouth shut about Nate—she was glad Brooke had invited the women over.

The conversation eventually made it back to Max. Megan had been out to visit him again the weekend before, and she knew he still hoped to come home at the end of the week. She turned to Erica. "How's his progress been this week?"

"Surprisingly well. I was out there yesterday, and his therapy is really kicking in. They've got him moving around far more than I would have expected by now, but"—her voice softened—"he did have a hallucination while I was there. They still seem to be an issue, but from what I understand, Doctor Hamm and Cord have been in close contact with the specialist, and they still have a couple of other options to investigate. They're thinking it's mostly due to his medication."

Maggie had choked on her orange juice the instant Erica had mentioned Cord, and she now waved a hand in front of herself as she coughed. Once she had herself back under control, she pushed the glass away. "Ummm"—she cleared her throat again before continuing—"Cord isn't going to be at the house today, is he?"

Megan looked at Brooke. Did Maggie have a thing for Cord?

"No," Erica assured her. "I wouldn't be taking you out there if he was."

The three of them laughed, and then Arsula explained that Maggie had long carried the hots for the brother with the reputation as the biggest player.

"I told you before that he has too much baggage for you." Arsula frowned at her friend.

"You've told me a lot of things before," Maggie countered.

"And most of it has come true," Erica pointed out. Which was very accurate. Arsula was the reason Megan had broken up with Jaden in the first place. Megan had been having dreams that left her with strong feelings of unease, and when she'd talked to Arsula about them, the other woman had suggested her dreams expressed worry about the man she was with. Arsula hadn't met Jaden at that point, but she'd been spot on in her reading.

The three of them finished their drinks, and afterward, Megan and Brooke followed them to the door. As they crossed the road, Brooke leaned in and muttered, "Maybe you should get Arsula's advice on you and Nate."

"*Shhh.*" Geez, the last thing she needed was for any of them to overhear.

But it was too late. Arsula had turned back. "You and Nate?"

Chapter Thirteen

❧

"The smell of this pot roast is one of the best things that's happened to me in a long time," Nate's dad announced as he scooped up another bite of the roast and potatoes. "Aside from getting sprung today, that is."

Everyone around the table laughed.

"Your dad sure has missed good home cooking," Gloria added.

"And we've sure missed Dad," Dani said. She reached to her right and gave Gloria a quick side-hug. "We've missed you, too, Gloria."

"Thank you, dear. The feeling is mutual."

It was Saturday evening, four and a half weeks since his dad had transferred from the hospital to the extended-stay patient rehab center, and just getting him out of the car and into the house earlier that afternoon had been like a carefully orchestrated chess match. The entire family had been there waiting when Cord arrived with him and Gloria, and afterward, Nate and his brothers had cooked the meal while their dad napped. The women had jumped into the fray, as well, allowing Gloria to take a much-deserved rest with her feet up. They'd pulled enough extra chairs and card tables together to fit everyone in the kitchen for dinner, while the two seven-year-olds had entertained baby Mia. It had been a busy, chaotic, wonderful afternoon. The kind that Nate would sorely miss when his time here was up.

"We're going to need to buy a larger table before the next time we get together, though."

"Your dad and I have already been talking about that. I plan to start shopping next week."

The sounds of fourteen family members enjoying a meal and time spent together eased some of the tension that had built in Nate's back and shoulders since he'd gotten out of bed that morning, and he pulled in a deep breath before slowly blowing it out. Dani was right. They'd sure missed their dad. *He'd* missed his dad.

And he should have been visiting him these last few weeks.

"Tell me more about these cabins being built," his dad said from the end of the table. "Got any pictures of them yet?"

"Absolutely." Nate pulled out his phone and brought up the latest pictures, then passed the phone down the table. "I'll drive you out there tomorrow and let you see for yourself . . . if you want to."

"If I'm not napping all day, you mean." His dad grunted, the new lines that had carved into his face over the last couple of months pulling his features downward. "I nap like a baby these days," he grumbled.

"You're still healing, Max." Gloria's tone was soft but firm.

"Healing, smealing. I'm ready to get back to work."

There was a brief pause as all the other adults at the table seemed to quit breathing due to surprise at the words that had just come out of his mouth, and then Nate spoke for all of them. "Your working days might be over, Dad. It's time for you to go back into retirement."

"Malarky." His dad waved his fork in the air. "Once I get my prosthetic—"

"Which will be a while," Cord interjected.

"True. But once I get it, I'll be good as new. And speaking of new"—he glanced at Gabe and then on down the table to Nick —"the cherries will start coming in soon. Has anyone sprayed the trees yet?"

It irritated Nate that his dad hadn't asked him since he was the one living at the place. He didn't let that show, though. "I took care of it earlier this week, Dad."

Once a full account had been taken of the trees that hadn't been too damaged or killed outright, what they'd ended up with were three decent-sized fields situated on the front side of their land, with the rest of the remaining viable trees scattered around the rest of the property.

"Good deal." His dad nodded. "We'll wait and replant in the fall, of course."

"Or . . ." Nate drew out the word, and his dad turned his head and looked at him. They'd shared the plans for the cabins, but they'd decided to wait on filling him in on everything else. On the decision to hold off until the changes were completed before reevaluating their next step.

"Or, what?" his dad asked. "The place is going to need more trees. The cabins are an excellent idea, but ten cabins won't take up the space needed for the number of trees that had to come down."

Gabe spoke up from where he sat directly across from Nate. "We'll decide later this year on whether to replant or not."

"I've already decided."

"Okay, Dad," Dani said. She sat two seats down from Gabe with her six-month-old daughter in her lap.

"Don't pacify me, Dani girl. I may be down a leg, but I'm not out of the game yet."

"That's just the thing," Nate spoke up. "We shouldn't have ever asked you to get back *into* the game. You shouldn't have had to take the orchard back over. It was our responsibility."

"Bullshit," his dad spit out, and then looked mollified when Jenna's and Haley's eyes rounded in surprise at the bad word said at the dinner table. "Sorry, girls," his dad mumbled. He then went on, "If you all can remember, none of you asked me to take it back over. I offered."

"*And* we've enjoyed doing it," Gloria added.

"That's right. *And* we've done an excellent job." Their dad wore a mulish expression as he looked at Nate and each of his siblings, but then the lines in his face eased. "And anyway . . ." He lifted his glass of milk for a drink, his throat convulsively swallowing as if trying to down the whole thing. Once finished, he seemed to focus on what remained of the platter of roast sitting in the middle of the table. "It was my own selfishness that forced it to be your responsibilities to begin with."

Nick's fork clattered as it dropped to his plate. "What are you talking about?"

The rest of them wore similar expressions of shock, and their dad slowly lifted his gaze. "Come on," he said. "You know I wasn't that old. I didn't have to retire. I could have—and I *should* have—kept running the farm for years to come."

"But it was an honor for you to deed it to us," Gabe announced.

No one else said anything. Instead, everyone was probably doing the same as Nate and sinking into their own early memories of resentment at being saddled with a place that held such bad memories. Forks poked at the food on plates, eyes shifted, but no one really looked at anyone.

Finally, their dad said, "That the story you're sticking with, son?"

"It *was* an honor," Gabe defended, though the earlier heat from his words had dissipated.

"As well as a burden," their dad added. And still, no one else said anything. "And I get that. And I'm sorry about that. I . . ." When he paused, Gloria reached over and took his hand, and the encouraging nod she gave him made Nate wonder what having that kind of support would be like.

And that made him think of Megan. She'd put her hand over

his in a similar fashion when they'd been looking at the tree his dad ran into. And it had felt good to have her holding his hand like that.

He hadn't spoken with or seen anything from her in seven days now. Not since he'd practically stripped her naked at her place. He'd been too busy with the cabins and spraying the remaining cherry trees. And anyway, he wouldn't have known what to say.

"I didn't want the place anymore," his dad abruptly blurted out, pulling Nate's attention back to the present, and at the statement, everyone gave up pretending to pick at their food. "I had my own bad memories associated with this house," he went on. "With the orchard. Your mother . . ."

"We know what she was like, Dad," Nick said.

"I know you do. And I know she made everyone's life difficult." His dad glanced down at his lap then, seeming to try to pull himself together, and Nate watched as Gloria's hand squeezed his even tighter. "But I added to the problem by not being there for you all the way I should have. By worrying about me first." He forced his chin to lift, and he turned his gaze on Dani. "Dani girl and I have worked out a lot of our issues, and truth be known, we'll probably be working on them for the rest of my life."

"We're good, Dad," Dani assured him.

"We're *better*," he corrected. "But we'll also keep making sure of that." He took in the rest of them. "But I've never fully addressed my shortcomings with you boys." He looked at Gabe. "Gabe had to come home and run the place."

"I was glad to do it, Dad."

"And you did a good job. But I shouldn't have put that on you. You're in a field you love now, and I'm grateful for it. You just should have been able to do that the first go-round in school."

The uncomfortableness in the room intensified. It was as if his dad were giving an I'm-dying speech, and Nate was quite certain none of them wanted to hear it. At the same time, no one attempted to stop him. Because the things he seemed to want to get off his chest probably should have been said years ago.

"You boys were only ten back then." He spanned the length of the tables to Nick. "I'm sure if I'd been a better father—"

"Dad," Nick interrupted him. "You're a great father."

"No. I could have been better. And we all know it."

He turned his attention to Jaden, and Jaden's body language screamed that he wasn't comfortable in the moment at all. Which was odd because this was Jaden's forte. If any of them liked to talk out past hurts and how to soothe them, it was him.

"I should have been there for you after your mother died, Jay." He took in Nick and Nate, as well. "For all three of you. Gabe and Cord were practically grown. They didn't need a heavy hand. But you boys needed a parent. I'll always be thankful that Dani came home and took so much of that on for me, but I do regret my failings there."

Jaden stared back at their dad, as if unsure what to say. And then Arsula reached over and took his hand. "You've never said anything like that before," Jay finally forced out.

"That's the point of this speech, son. To say the things I never have. To clear my conscience." He looked around at all of them again, also taking in the two granddaughters who'd gone quiet along with the rest of them and had been listening with rapt attention. "I almost died a few weeks ago. Right out there on the land I love. And that wasn't lost on me. I almost died because I was too damned proud to let my own family know what was going on with my health. I didn't want any of you to feel like you needed to help out since I'd already dumped it on you once, so I kept my mouth shut. But because of that I almost died. And I would have missed out on seeing my three beautiful granddaughters grow up—and a grandson or two if any of you would ever produce me some." He eyed Gabe, Nick, Dani, and Jaden. "But most of all, I'd have left all of you. My kids that I'm so proud of. And I'm not ready to do that yet."

He finished off his milk, and his hand shook until he set the glass back down.

Before anyone could fill the void of words, he faced Nate, and Nate held his breath. He had no idea what his dad would say to him.

"You left, son. You were here one day and gone the next, and we've hardly seen you since."

Nate glanced across the table at Gabe. He could tell his dad that it certainly wasn't his fault he'd left. Nor was it even their mother's. But his reason for leaving was something he'd held on to for too long to consider letting it come out now. Plus, it still had the huge potential to hurt his family.

"You've been a little wild over the years," his dad went on, "and sometimes a lot ornery. But I've loved having you home these last few months. And I'd *love* if you'd come home for good. If there's anything I can do to make that happen, let me know and I'll do it. I've missed you, son."

Words couldn't have come out of Nate at that point if someone had been holding a gun to his head. He'd enjoyed being home, as well. And he'd like to stay. He'd like to have these kinds of family meals on a regular basis, to have this kind of love in his life.

He'd also like to have what four of his siblings have found. Unconditional love. Support.

Someone to have their backs no matter how many times they screwed up.

He'd like to not always feel like he had to look over his shoulder, waiting for Karma to kick him in the ass.

"Well, personally, I think he needs to stick around and run this new business he's creating," Gloria said, and Nate whipped his gaze over to hers. "He's clearly got a good business head on his shoulders. I think he'd make it a great success."

"I'm just building some cabins, Gloria."

He looked away from her, uncomfortable with the scrutiny, and his dad said, "You're not *just* building some cabins. Gabe brought me a copy of the business plan you laid out to get the loan. It's solid. Thorough and well-thought-out."

"It had far more detail than I'd have ever thought of," Dani added, and at the accompanying nods from around the table, Nate felt a flush of pride.

"The internet is good for figuring out those types of things," he deflected.

"Don't undermine yourself," his dad argued. "I've been thinking. Maybe it should have been you running this farm all those years ago."

Nate made sure to keep a blank face at the comment. Because that's the one thing no one had ever considered. When Gabe and Dani had decided they were ready to step down from handling it, no one had ever thought that he might want to do it in their place. Nor that he *could* do it.

"Cord." Their dad now turned his attention to their last brother, and Nate watched as Cord sat up straighter in his seat. Cord looked as uncomfortable with whatever was to come as Jaden had when it had been his turn. "If I'd been smart enough to get a counselor for any of you kids after your mom died, it should have been for you. And for not doing that, I apologize."

Cord shook his head. "I'm fine, Dad. I didn't need a counselor."

"Are you kidding me?" Jaden jumped in, apparently unable to control himself, and Nate instantly saw his "counselor" face come into play. "*You* found her. You always found her. Of course you needed a counselor."

Their mother had always made sure attention centered on her, and if she *hadn't* had it for some reason, then she'd manufactured it. Several of the times she'd created it herself, she'd done so by situations she'd labeled as "accidents"—the last of which had turned into her causing her own death when the car wreck she'd planned didn't go quite as she'd hoped. And for each of those "accidents," she'd instigated them when she'd known Cord would be there to find her.

He *was* the one who'd needed counseling the most. Likely all of them had, but Cord no doubt had many years of serious issues buried deep.

"And you granddaughters," his dad continued, leaving Jaden's comments to sit like a lump of week-old fruitcake in the pit of all their stomachs. But his tone changed to one of teasing with the girls. Jenna and Haley grinned at him from their seats beside each other, while Mia gurgled happily from her mother's lap.

His dad shook a finger in Jenna's and Haley's direction. "You girls make sure your dads always do right by you, you hear?"

"Yes, Pops," both girls chorused.

"And if they don't, you come see me."

They grinned again, and then Nate watched as Erica gave Jenna a subtle nod. That got the girl out of her chair, with Haley quickly following, and both of them rushed to their grandfather's side, smothering him in hugs.

"We're so glad you're home, Pops."

"I am too, baby girls. I am too."

His dad's eyelids drooped as he held on to the girls, and as if she'd seen the same thing as Nate, Gloria stood from her seat. "Let's get some of these dishes out of the way before you boys show us what's for dessert."

Nate, Nick, and his wife Harper followed her up, insisting that she and everyone else remain seated. And as Nate pulled the strawberry pastry from the fridge, Nick went for clean plates while Harper quickly stacked the dirty dishes in the sink. Conversation stalled as everyone was served and dug in, but it wasn't long until his dad's eyelids drooped once more. Before Gloria could do it herself, Nate rose again and offered to help his dad get settled into bed.

It had been a long day for all of them, so as he rolled his father away from the table and down the hall, everyone else began gathering up the remainder of the dishes. The night was a far cry from where they'd been as a family only three years before, and Nate would always be grateful to have been here for it.

"I missed you coming to visit these last few weeks," his dad said the instant the two of them slipped into the newly renovated room.

"I'm sorry about that." He rolled his dad to the bathroom so he could take care of business before going to bed. "There was a lot to do here."

"I'm sure there has been."

Locking the brakes on the wheelchair, Nate stood at the ready in case his dad needed help getting up. He didn't, though, and once he'd pushed himself to his one remaining good leg and balanced on his crutches, Nate moved the chair out of the way and stood outside the bathroom door waiting in case help were needed.

"I feel like there might have been more to it, though," his dad said from the other side of the door. The toilet flushed, and then half a minute later water splashed into the sink. "Like maybe you were upset with me."

When the door swung open, his dad balancing in front of the wheelchair, Nate shook his head. "Of course I wasn't upset with you. What would I have been upset about?"

"That's what I've been trying to figure out."

Nate helped his dad get back into the chair, and then he got him situated into bed. He didn't comment on the apparent fishing expedition his dad was trying to engage in, because he had nothing to say. Yes, he hadn't visited his dad while he'd been in the rehab center these last few weeks. But no, he wasn't upset with him. He'd just been busy, as he'd said earlier.

Only . . .

"You left mad that morning, if I remember correctly." His dad stared up from his horizontal position in the bed, his eyes barely open. "Though I didn't understand at the time why you were mad."

"I wasn't mad. I just don't always like mornings."

Which wasn't true at all. He had no issues with mornings, and in fact, had been getting up and being down in the kitchen as early as his dad the last few weeks before the accident. He'd thought his dad going out every morning to check on the trees more than unnecessary, but all the same, each day that final week, Nate had been offering to do the check for him. He hadn't liked the idea of his dad being out there before daylight every morning. And though it hadn't fully registered in his mind, deep down he'd begun to suspect there might be something more than worry for the trees going on with him.

Of course, his dad had never taken him up on any of the offers, and that last morning, Nate *had* left out of there mad. He'd gone into town to have breakfast, annoyed that his father apparently didn't think him capable enough of doing something so basic as checking on trees, and he'd been trying to convince himself it was time to wash his hands of the whole thing. No one had ever needed him here, so he hadn't known why he'd bothered.

But then that text from Arsula had come in.

"I need to sleep now, son," his dad mumbled, the words more garbled than distinct. "I'm sorry for whatever I did."

Since heavy breathing immediately followed the words, Nate didn't say anything else. He just got up and quietly left the room. Only, when he stepped out, he found Arsula waiting for him in the hallway.

"Hey," he said. He didn't have a clue what she might want. "What's up?"

He could hear everyone else still in the living room or kitchen, but instead of heading that way, Arsula took his arm and led him in the opposite direction. They slipped into the office, and she closed the door behind them.

His radar lit up. "What's going on?"

Nate took a small step back. Not that he thought Arsula was about to make any sort of pass at him, but he didn't like the idea of being alone in a room with any of his brothers' significant others.

"I just wanted to mention that I saw Megan out with someone last night," she said, and Nate's entire body went tight.

"What's that got to do with me?" he asked.

"I . . ." After pausing, she glanced toward the fireplace, as if searching for whatever words she was after in the long-swept-up ashes, then turned back and offered him a tight smile. "You know that I sometimes sense things."

He'd thought her abilities more involved reading dreams and helping people to connect with their intuition and inner selves, so he remained confused at both the reason for her to seek him out as well as the comment about Megan. But he couldn't let it go without asking. "And what is it that you sense this time?"

"I thought that you might like to know, that's all."

"*Why* would I want to know, Arsula?"

And who had she been out with? That's what he really wanted to ask. Had it been Dre?

He had no idea if she'd gone out with his friend again. He'd avoided being alone with the man as much as possible over the last week, simply because if Dre *was* dating Megan, he didn't want to know about it. But he'd also found himself ashamed of the way *he'd* treated Megan. First, practically shedding her of her clothes on her own countertop. Then, running away as if ashamed that he'd touched her.

Not that he should have stayed and done anything else. She was still his brother's ex.

But he had upset her. And she'd already been upset about her father cancelling his visit. About rarely seeing any of her family.

What was it she'd said? *Maybe that would finally score me some points?*

The phrase had run through his mind several times over the last week, as well as picturing those texts he'd seen on her phone. The ones urging her to send her resume. Was her father unhappy with her choices? Specifically . . . with her working at The Cherry Basket?

It made sense. Retail didn't come close to what she'd studied for.

Another thing that would've made sense that night was if, instead of him putting his mouth on hers when she'd been so upset, he'd dug into the issue. Tried to help resolve it. That's what a friend would have done.

Instead, he'd put a giant roadblock right in the middle of their friendship.

"I guess I was wrong in thinking that," Arsula finally answered. She opened the door, the odd conversation clearly over, but instead of either of them immediately exiting the room, Nate looked at her once more. Her expression was unreadable, but he suspected she thought there was more to him and Megan than there was. Or more than there could be.

"Megan and I are friends, Arsula. Nothing more."

She nodded, though he didn't feel like it was in agreement.

Chapter Fourteen

✦

Megan sat in her store office with her elbow on her desk, her chin propped in her hand, and stared blankly at her computer monitor. It was Saturday night—nearing midnight—and she'd been alone in the office for hours.

She hadn't gone out with Dre a second time the week before, even though he'd called that Sunday, Monday, and Tuesday and asked. She'd *wanted* to go out with him. Even if only because Nate had the balls to tell her not to. But each time she'd talked to or texted with him, all she'd been able to think about was Nate's mouth on her lips and his hands unbuttoning her dress. And that hadn't seemed like a good precedent going into *any* date. Therefore, she'd decided they'd just be friends and she'd moved on.

That's when she'd met Austin. Austin had connected with her through her dating app. He lived in a nearby town and had moved to the area two years before due to work. Smart and with a good sense of humor, Austin was also looking for something serious, as well as wanted kids down the road, a house, everything. In a nutshell, he was top-grade dating material. So, she'd shoved Nate from her mind and given this one her all. And she *liked* him.

She and Austin has gotten together twice in the last ten days —texting several times in between—and during both of those dates, she'd had an excellent time. He was also a decent kisser— though not as good as Nate—and he'd been nice and polite in all the ways that mattered. Simply put, Austin had potential.

But then he'd texted before tonight's date with an "I'm not that into you" message, and though her initial thought had been to be crushed—after all, he had great potential—she'd instead been more *meh* about the whole thing. But refusing to sit home alone just because she didn't have a date, she'd changed into jeans and a sweatshirt . . . and she'd come into the office.

She had a laptop at home, of course. But somehow sitting here on a Saturday night had originally seemed less depressing.

Sighing, she clicked around on the orchard's new website, which was what she'd been working on for the last hour. She'd made a lot of progress in the last couple of weeks—thanks to feedback from Dani, since Megan had been too annoyed after Nate's kiss-and-run to include him in any of her questions. But she was missing Nate tonight. Honestly, she'd missed him most nights. And that annoyed her even more than his kiss-and-run. Because she *shouldn't* be missing him. He was her friend . . . *only*.

And he'd made that painfully clear the last time she'd seen him.

He also hadn't so much as reached out to her in the last two weeks while she'd been avoiding him, so she was beginning to wonder if they were even still friends.

Lifting her chin out of her hand, she shut down the work on the website and reloaded the online room designer app. That's what she'd spent the majority of the evening messing with. That, and ordering furniture for the cabins. Nick had reached out to her a couple of weeks ago. He did the accounting for the Wilde's businesses, so he'd reviewed her suggested budget for the cabin designs then made arrangements for her to have a line of credit for ordering whatever was needed. And she'd ordered a lot tonight.

It had all been required, of course, but she'd taken pleasure in the hope that Nate would see the expenditures and know that his rejection of her hadn't slowed her enthusiasm. She could compartmentalize with the best of them, and she wasn't about to let the man sidetrack her from a project that she was finding she truly did enjoy. It was different than when she'd laid out and designed the new space for the store, but it was just as rewarding. Maybe more so, in fact.

Knowing her brain was too tired and her mood wasn't likely to improve, she finally shut down the computer and headed for her car. It didn't take long to get to her apartment since she lived only a few blocks from the square, and as she parked in front of her place, the first thing she noticed was that her porch light had burned out. Now she would either have to scrounge up a stepladder—or she could just go across the street and get Gabe to do it for her tomorrow.

But either way, it wasn't something she was willing to deal with tonight.

In fact, she didn't want to deal with anything. Maybe not for a long time. Not burned out lights, not men she didn't click with. Not Nate Wilde, who she wanted to strangle with her own two hands. Couldn't the man see that they had chemistry?

That's *who* she wanted to spend time with. Not Dre or Austin or any of the other guys who were still on her much-ignored list.

Climbing out of the car, she slammed the door behind her and, with a press of her key fob, trudged up the sidewalk to her apartment. And right as her foot landed on her porch, she had the first inkling that the darkened light might not be due to a burned-out filament at all.

The hair on the back of her neck stood up, and a split second later, a soft creak came from the same corner as it had two weeks before. Fear was quickly replaced with competing emotions of irritation and giddiness when a bright light flicked on and shined directly in her face.

"I swear, if that's you again, Nate Wilde . . ."

"You'll do what?" came the voice from the dark.

Irritation and giddiness slid into relief, and she wanted to tell him that she was glad he was there.

She didn't, though.

"You didn't answer my question," he said.

And she wouldn't answer his question. Instead, she found herself suddenly unsure of what to do. Why was he there? And could she be trusted to behave if she got close to him again?

She turned her head to block the light from being in her eyes, and she remained silent.

"I heard you were seen out on a date with someone last week," Nate said, and then the creak of the rocking chair started up.

Seriously? He was there to pester her about dating again? "Which night?" she tossed back, and he let out a rough chuckle.

"Friday, I suppose. Arsula mentioned it to me at the house last Saturday."

At the news of Arsula discussing *her* dating status, Megan recalled her quickly fabricated explanation while standing in the middle of the road the day of the mimosas. Arsula had overheard Brooke mention Nate and had immediately zeroed in on the possibility of there being more to the story, at which time Megan explained that Brooke had only been talking about a supposed disagreement in their discussion of cabin plans. She'd sworn to the other woman there wasn't a thing more going on between them, and she'd thought she'd convinced Arsula she'd been telling the truth. But if that were the case, then why would Arsula have mentioned seeing her out on a date to Nate?

"So you're big friends with Arsula these days?" she prodded. Nate and Arsula had had a rough start due to him being an initial nonbeliever in the power of her gift.

"She's going to be my sister-in-law," he explained. "No need having discord where there doesn't need to be any."

It seemed like a made-up excuse to her. "And in the name of civility, you two talk about *me?*"

The light in her face turned off, and she saw nothing but black spots.

He didn't say anything else for a moment, and once her vision cleared, she could make out the silhouette of his body sitting in her chair.

"What did you mean about earning points if you took that job in Chicago?" he asked, and she couldn't have been more surprised at the question.

"Where did that question come from?"

"It's what I should have asked instead of kissing you the last time I was here. So, I'm asking it now. What did you mean?"

"I didn't mean anything."

Her heart rate picked up, and she looked at her front door and considered going inside, leaving him out there alone to do as he pleased. She suspected he might try to follow, though. And she certainly didn't want him in her place again.

"Can I come in?" he asked.

"No."

"Then will you sit down out here and talk to me?"

She had another chair on the porch, and she *could* sit down. And it shouldn't matter if she did.

But her flight-or-fight response had kicked in, and she didn't know if it would be safe to stay.

"Was that your father on the phone at the house that day?"

At his pushing of all her buttons, she let out an unladylike snort. She dropped into the other seat. "Fine. You win," she grumbled. "I'll sit. But I don't want to talk about my family."

"Why not?"

"Because I just don't want to. I never talk about them."

"You did the other night. You told me that your father rarely visits, that your mother and next oldest sister live in Boston, and that—"

"Your point is made, Wilde. I *rarely* talk about them. And I shouldn't have the other night."

"When did your parents divorce?"

"Why are you doing this? And for that matter, why are you even here? I assume you parked down the street again." She smirked.

He leaned forward, coming partially up out of the chair, only to lift the rocker by the arms and put it down again once he'd turned it so he could face her. "I'm doing this because I'm your friend."

Of course that was all he wanted from her.

"And I'm *here* because I might want to be more."

At that, she considered turning on her own pen light just so she could see his face. "What did you say?"

"*Maybe,*" he cautioned. "But I would like to talk about the possibility."

He wanted to talk about the possibility of them being more? How much more?

NATE WATCHED Megan from his position in his chair, and though her face remained partially in the dark, light from up the street cast enough of a glow into her yard that he could see the shell-shocked look on her face. He'd caught her off guard.

"Is that something you'd be willing to talk about?" he asked. The last time he'd been here, she'd said that she was okay with what had happened between them. That she'd be okay with more. And that had gotten him to thinking.

"It depends," she responded.

"Okay. What does it depend on?"

"Are we talking about a one-night stand?"

The mere idea of talking about more terrified him. He didn't know what he could possibly do with more. But a one-night stand wasn't why he was here. He was here because he'd watched his father and Gloria all week. And he'd watched his siblings with his dad. And his siblings with their spouses. And with their kids. He'd really watched . . . and he'd admitted that he wanted for himself the kind of love they all shared.

He had zero reason to believe he could pull it off. And even less chance of thinking that he deserved it. But he wanted it, all the same.

And he wanted to consider giving it a shot with Megan.

There was still the issue that she was Jaden's ex, but he couldn't get the woman out of his mind. And the more she ignored him—and he ignored her—the more he wanted her. So, what he had to figure out first was if he wanted her only because he couldn't have her.

If that was the case, then the deal was off. He would never do that to her *or* to Jaden.

But if he wanted her because he couldn't stop thinking about her and dreaming about her and having the urge to beat to a pulp every single man who got the opportunity to ever spend any time with her, then he wanted to see what this was. Could it be something like so many of his family members had found?

Could it be something that didn't hurt in the end?

"Not a one-night stand," he clarified. "That isn't an option."

She slowly nodded. "Then I'm willing to talk about it."

Relief rushed through him at her words, and he realized that he'd feared she would turn him away before he could even say that much. "Then my theory for figuring out if we should attempt to be more is to get to know each other a little better first." He scooted the rocker even closer, so that their knees now bumped. "To share personal things with each other."

"Personal things?" She stared back at him. "Like my family history?"

"Or mine?" he suggested, and she nodded at that.

"You go first," she said, and at her request, he laughed. Not the nervous chuckle he'd squeaked out earlier when she'd implied she'd gone out on so many dates over the last two weeks

that he needed to narrow them all down by the week, the night
—and possibly the time. This laugh was filled with relief and joy
and the first ever inkling to the possibility of a brighter future all
rolled into one. And it felt good to feel all those things.

"Can I scoot my chair around to sit closer to you?" he asked
before starting any deep conversation.

"You're practically in my lap already," she pointed out.

"Then maybe you should be in *my* lap," he suggested, but
before she could respond, he held up both hands. "Sorry. I
retract that. We aren't there yet, nor have we decided if we even
want to go there." He reached over and grazed his knuckles over
the back of her hand. "But I would *really* like to sit beside you
while we talk . . . if that's okay with you. Or maybe even go into
the house?"

Her gaze darted to the home on the other side of the street,
and he knew she was thinking similarly to him. Would Gabe and
Erica happen to look out any windows and see them over here?
Or step outside with the dog and hear them talking?

It was nearly midnight, so likely not. But it was also chilly
outside. He didn't want her getting too cold.

He'd do whatever she wanted, though. He didn't want to
push, and he didn't want to be pushed away. So, he waited for her
reply.

In the end, they stayed on the porch. But she did let him
move his chair so that it sat directly beside hers, and she let him
drape his coat over her lap. He smiled at the improvements that
had already happened in their relationship and fought the urge
to reach over and take her hand.

"My family history," he started.

She shot him a sideways look. "I already know a lot of it, so
skip the generic parts."

God, he could fall for this woman. She wouldn't allow him to
get away with anything. "Got it. My family history," he started
again, "the ungeneric parts."

She elbowed him in the arm.

He smiled again.

"How about mine and my mother's relationship?" he asked, and when she nodded, her expression going solemn, he laid it out for her in the barest format. "It's simple. I hated her."

"Nate." She half turned in her seat, and he was close enough now that he could make out each dip and curve of her features.

"It's no biggie," he told her. "She hated me, too."

"I know she didn't have the capacity to care like most mothers."

"She was a selfish narcissistic witch whose sole purpose in this world was to make sure a light was always shined on her every minute of every day, and to see to it that everyone else's life was complete misery. And she excelled at both of those things."

"Okay," she said, the word coming out slow. "That's more blunt than my version, but I know all of that, too. I just hate that any child would feel that way toward a parent."

"Me too. But my first memories of her are hate. And of that feeling going both ways."

At that, she took his hand instead of him taking hers, and she laced their fingers together.

"And the funny thing is," he went on, his heart now thumping erratically in his chest, "she always told Nick that she loved me more than him."

Megan watched him in the dark.

"I heard her tell him that on more than one occasion. It didn't make sense at the time, because I *knew* she didn't love me. And there's no way to love a person *more* when there was no love to begin with. But still . . . she was dead before I bothered to tell my own twin that she'd been lying to him all that time. That she'd hated me as much as I'd hated her."

Her fingers squeezed around his. "What was your life with her like? Did you mostly avoid her?"

"As much as I could. But it didn't matter if I was in her sights or not. Everything that went wrong in our family ended up being my fault. She would seek me out just to make sure I knew it. Her car didn't start one morning . . . I'd ridden in it with Gabe the day before, and clearly, my bad aura messed it up. One summer's worth of cherries she'd brought into the house got eaten by my dog, and that's because I'd stayed at a friend's house too long."

Her eyes narrowed. "What were you doing at your friend's house?"

"Not being around Mom mostly." He shook his head, trying to slough off the sarcasm, and thought back to that day. "It had been a really good day," he explained. "Nick and I both got invited. It was with a kid we went to school with, but since it was summertime, school was out. We'd just finished harvesting the cherries for the season, and we spent the entire day with our friend and his mother at a nearby water park. We ended up staying for dinner at their place before she brought us back home, and then the next morning, all the cherries in the house were gone."

The hand in his tensed. "I don't understand. Were you supposed to be taking care of the dog that morning or something? How was it your fault because you'd been with your friend the day before?"

Nate tried to sort it out in his head, but all he got was the same incomprehension echoed from Megan. "I don't really know," he finally said. "I'm probably leaving out something that I don't remember. I'm sure it made sense at the time, though."

"Manipulation like that often does."

"Possibly." He stared back at her. Had that been nothing more than manipulation on his mother's part the whole time?

And then he wanted to kick himself. Of course it had. When had anything with her *not* been manipulation? And how had he never put that together with the cherry incident?

"I didn't know you'd had a dog while growing up," Megan said, bringing him back from the past. "I don't remember Jaden ever mentioning one."

"That's probably because we only had him for about five months. The dog died not long after the cherry incident."

She looked so sad for an animal she'd never known. "What happened to him?"

This one Nate did remember clearly. And this one had definitely been his fault. Because he should have never begged to get the dog to begin with.

"I won a spelling bee," he explained as simply he could.

Megan sat up straight in her chair. "What?"

"Yeah." He knew it was as ridiculous as it sounded. "After school started back up, I learned that there would be a district spelling bee in the fall. My mother constantly told me what a loser I was, so I worked hard on that one. *So* hard. Just to show her, but also because I wanted it. I wanted to prove to myself that I *wasn't* a loser, you know?"

She nodded, her eyes never leaving his.

"I even beat out a kid a couple of years older than me," he went on. "And then when we got home"—he shrugged, the pain of that day still raw inside him—"the dog was gone."

"Gone?" Again, her eyes narrowed. "Not dead?"

He shook his head, but he didn't look at her anymore. "Mom claimed she got a call later that night that a neighbor had found him. He'd been hit by a car."

"And how did she explain this one being your fault?"

"She didn't." He turned back to her. "But she also didn't have to. Bad things tend to happen to me right after anything good."

"Nate . . ." She let go of his hand, and he immediately missed it. "What are you saying, exactly?" She shook her head in confusion. "Because that sounds crazy."

"That's my reality, Megan. It's one of the reasons I don't typically do relationships."

She eyed him carefully before easing back into her chair. "And you don't think that your mom may have just gotten rid of your dog to 'punish' you for doing something good?"

He knew she'd get it. "I very much think that's what she did.

I didn't at the time, of course. But since learning about narcissism, I've seen that I was often in the role of scapegoat of the family. Good things happen, the narcissist often makes bad things be the consequence." What he didn't add was that being the scapegoat had often made him feel like an outsider. He'd always been the brother on the outside looking in at the rest of them.

"So then, you can't make the kind of statement you just did. That *isn't* your reality."

"But it is."

"But how? She's gone. She's been gone for years."

He wished he could make her understand. Maybe then she'd push him away before he had a chance to do anything that couldn't be undone. "Because maybe some of the things that happened *hadn't* always been her fault," he explained. "Maybe *I* screwed up too much. *Still* screw up too much."

"But you just explained that you understand why she blamed you. Why she hurt you if you started to get ahead in life."

He closed his eyes, not wanting to see her need to believe in him. Because that belief, in itself, could be her downfall. "I also know that I've messed up plenty of times." He reopened his eyes. "And my mistakes have caused other people to get hurt, Megan. Or they *would* get hurt if they knew about them."

She studied him as if she could see the full truth of who he was, and when she spoke again, he wasn't surprised to hear she'd hit the nail on the head. "Does that play into why you left so suddenly when you turned eighteen? Why you rarely come home?"

The conversation had taken a much deeper turn than he'd intended it to tonight. And he wasn't sure he could go any further.

He wet his lips, suddenly wishing for a glass of water.

"I think that might be enough for tonight." He made the statement almost as a question, not wanting to scare her off with any harshness that he knew remained inside him on the subject.

But he also wasn't ready to talk about anything more right now. "Will that be okay with you?"

Her hand slipped back into his. "That's fine with me," she said softly, and he covered their clasped hands with his other one.

"Thank you." He almost leaned forward and pressed a kiss to her lips, but he stopped himself just in time. Instead, he just looked at her, a light smile on his mouth. He was glad he'd made the decision to come over tonight. And so glad she'd given him more than the quick brush-off he'd probably deserved. "And now for the important part," he teased, giving her a quick wink. "Do we continue thinking about this—about *us*—beyond tonight? Do we spend a few days talking? Seeing if we want to push this thing further?"

She didn't hesitate, and that warmed his heart. "Definitely," she whispered.

He nodded. He liked her answer. "Then there's something I have to know." He swallowed before bringing up his next question, knowing she might not like it. But it was one he had to put out there. "While we're deciding," he began, then had to clear the croak out of his voice, "are you still going to be dating my friends?"

The idea that he could hurt Dre as much as he could hurt Jaden had crossed his mind, and he didn't like that scenario any more than the first one. But at the same time, he also knew Dre would understand if he leveled with him.

"Would it make you feel any better to know that I only went out with Dre that one time?" she asked, and a breath of air rushed out of him.

"It does." He nodded.

"Then how about you assume I won't go out with *anyone* until we decide if we're going to try this or not. Will that work?"

He wanted to kiss her again. "That'll work perfectly. Fair warning, though." He paused before finishing his thought and touched one finger to the underside of her chin. Tilting her face to his and making sure she didn't turn away, he leveled with her the best he could. "My record is one hundred percent at screwing things up. And the last thing I want to do is hurt you."

She stared back at him, seeming to be holding her breath. "Then whatever we do, we approach it with our eyes wide open."

"Deal." He leaned in then, and just barely brushed his mouth across hers. "Sealed with a kiss," he whispered.

Chapter Fifteen

"The site is amazing, Megan."

Megan sat back in the chair in Dani's office, watching as Dani continued clicking around on the new Wilde Cabins and Adventures website, and at the same time, she scribbled down notes as she saw a few tweaks that still needed to be made.

She'd been working on the website at full speed every night this past week—when she hadn't been texting or talking with Nate—and other than lining up a few final details with the provider who'd make sure to keep the site live twenty-four seven, everything was pretty much good to go.

"We'll do our soft launch in a week," Dani said. She looked over at Megan. "Does that still work for you?"

"Absolutely. That'll give me plenty of time to work out any kinks with the system."

"Great. Then we'll go hardcore in two," Dani added. She had promo lined up to start on that date, and since they'd only be four weeks out from the potential first reservations, Megan had agreed to oversee traffic from the website until a full-time person could be hired.

"You're sure we're not asking too much of you?" Dani asked.

"Absolutely not. My assistant manager is working out great,

so I can make sure to run up to the office and check on things multiple times throughout the day, and I can set it to text me if there are issues."

Nate had also finalized the list of local companies that would be involved in handling adventures any of the guests could request, and at the moment, those requests would be sent directly to them automatically via the website. Then once a full-time person had been hired to oversee the daily management and reservations of the business, they'd take over handling that side of things as well.

"Great." Dani clicked the *X* to close the website and turned away from the computer. "And from what I hear, the guys are already lining up interview potentials?" She looked to Arsula with the question, who sat in the chair beside Dani. Arsula still worked for Dani for the time being, and since she was essentially already part of the family, she'd offered to help out with this in any way she could. She'd monitored the job posting and had provided a first set of eyes on the submitted resumes.

"They are," Arsula answered. "Jaden has the first one lined up for early next week, and I think he and Nate will be talking to a couple of others later in the week."

"That's awesome." Dani tapped a pen against a printed list on her desk. "And Cord has already been planting seeds in Billings with several friends and colleagues. We'll send him promo copy as soon as things are finalized, and before we know it, this whole thing will be off the ground."

The idea of being in the middle of this kind of whirlwind project thrilled Megan. This was the type of work, she was learning, that thrilled her. Seeing a project go from start to finish. Making things happen.

Not merely sitting in front of a computer all day.

Arsula took in both Dani and Megan. "Are we certain the cabins will be ready in time?"

Megan was the one to answer. "I was out there yesterday after work, and Nate says the work is progressing on time, if not ahead of schedule. Assuming no bad weather gets in the way when it comes time to pour the new entrance into the property, he seems confident they'll be ready."

"I'm still amazed at how precisely he's pulling this off," Dani murmured, and Arsula agreed. That had seemed the consensus with most everyone any time Megan had heard it mentioned.

Well, not with the guys he worked with. She'd been out there a couple of times this week, both to take measurements, as well as just to get a few minutes with Nate, and those men not only worked their butts off for the man, they also seemed completely confident in his ability to manage the project.

And due to that, and to seeing Nate in action herself, Megan had grown confident as well. She didn't know what all he'd been involved in over the years, but he'd certainly developed some upper level skills.

"Then ladies"—Dani put down her pen—"it looks like we're about to launch a new business!"

After the meeting ended, Megan hung around the lobby of the office, wanting to catch up with Arsula. It was Friday, and since she'd made a habit of leaving the store to her assistant manager every Friday afternoon, she was in no hurry to get anywhere.

"How's the new place working out?" she asked as the other woman settled back in behind the front desk.

"It's fantastic," Arsula gushed. She and Jaden had found an apartment to rent that had more space than the one she currently lived in above the office and had signed the lease on it earlier in the week. "Jay still feels guilty for not staying at the house with Max any longer than he has, but he and Gloria were insistent that they'd be fine."

"They did look fine when I saw them yesterday," Megan agreed. That had been another reason she'd wanted to stop by the farm. She cared a lot about the older Wilde, as well as his wife, so it was always good to see them. "Nate is still there, too, of course. I think that gives Gloria a sense of relief at having a backup if they were to need it."

"I'm sure it does." Arsula pulled up her email on the monitor in front of her. "So . . . any dreams lately?"

"Dreams?" Megan shook her head, unsure where Arsula was going with the question. "Not really. Nothing out of the ordinary anyway."

"Nothing involving an ex-crab fisherman who seems to have finally found his place in the family business?"

"What?" Her brows shot up. "*No*. Nothing like that at all. I told you nothing was going on there." *Crap*. Had Arsula said something to Jaden?

"I know what you told me."

"Then you should believe it." Except, it wasn't exactly the truth. Nothing was *necessarily* going on, true. Other than talking and texting, and him walking her to her car the two times she'd been out to the farm that week.

But they still hadn't decided whether they were going to take things anywhere or not. Like she'd said at her place, they had to approach this with their eyes wide open. And though she definitely liked him and was more than attracted to him, she still wasn't sure she wanted to go there. Because what if she fell hard and he turned around and left?

"I'm just saying," Arsula began, but when Megan's phone buzzed, she looked down at the screen.

It was a text from Nate.

I've rented a boat for tomorrow . . .
want to go out on it with me?

A boat?

Her entire body went instantly jittery, and that reaction told her that she was more than ready to take things to the next level. She tapped out a response.

```
I thought the boat idea was going to be
a celebration thing.
```

She bit her lip as she waited for his reply.

```
Isn't the website basically ready to go
live?
```

```
Well . . . *yes*
```

```
Then it seems to me that it's something
to celebrate.
```

She grinned at his subtleness, but she wasn't about to let him off the hook.

```
So what would this be, Wilde? Two
friends going out on a boat? Or . . .
```

Two messages came in back to back.

```
Or.
```

```
Definitely.
```

She grinned from ear to ear. She had a date with Nate Wilde.

```
I'll bring along a book to read while
you fish.
```

```
No need. Bring hiking boots instead. I'm
taking you over to Wild Horse Island.
```

Neither of them sent anything else, and when she looked back up, realizing that she'd zoned out of her conversation with

Arsula right in the middle of it, Arsula's smile was as wide as hers.

Busted.

"It's nothing, huh?" Arsula said, and Megan couldn't stop the flush that crept across her cheeks.

"It's . . ." She didn't know what to say. This may or may not go anywhere. And even if it did, she knew that Nate wouldn't be ready for it to become public knowledge. Especially within his family.

"Don't worry." Arsula stood and reached over the counter to give Megan a quick hug. "I won't say a thing," she whispered in her ear. "But I wish you all the luck."

SHE'D HEARD of Wild Horse Island, of course. And she'd seen it from a distance plenty of times. It was a state park sitting within Flathead Lake. And with more than twenty-two hundred undeveloped acres, with all wildlife running free, it was a place she'd intended to make sure she visited in the coming months. But speeding across the water today, she knew that months away wasn't what was meant to be. This moment was. With Nate.

He looked over at her from where he sat behind the steering wheel, a baseball cap pulled low over his brow and the scruffiness of several days' growth of beard covering his jaw, and he shot her an award-winning smile. "You ready to see what we can find out here?"

"I've never been more ready for anything in my life."

Her reply, double meaning and all, didn't go unnoticed, and she watched as his eyes heated and then dropped briefly to her lips. That had happened several times during the course of the trip over, but he had yet to touch her in any way other than a simple hand hold to help her into the boat.

She'd gotten out to the orchard right after closing the store at noon, and Nate had been ready and waiting. He'd had the boat loaded with backpacks filled with food, extra coats and hoodies, and plenty of water for a long day of hiking. Max and Gloria hadn't been at the house. They'd gone into town to visit with friends who'd sent cards and made calls during Max's recovery. So, it had been just her and Nate. And they'd wasted no time heading out.

"Did I mention that I'm glad you said yes to today?" Nate's voice had taken on the same kind of heaviness she'd been feeling ever since receiving his text the day before.

"I think you might have said that a time or ten."

He winked at her, took one more peek at her lips, then went back to paying attention to the boat. Throttling the motor down, he approached the small public beach area that was most accessible by visitors, and she saw that they weren't on the island alone. Two kayaks had also been pulled ashore, as well as another small boat. No one was anywhere in sight, though. Nor could she hear any voices.

"Thank you for inviting me today," she spoke softly as the quiet, calm feel of the island immediately took hold, and when blue eyes glanced over at hers, she added, "I already know I'm going to have a wonderful time."

His look said the same thing . . . as well as that, once again, he desperately wanted to kiss her.

Once he got them up to the beach—which was nothing but the gorgeous colorful rocks that could also be seen in the bottom of the lake—he killed the motor and hopped out to tie off. While he did that, she gathered the backpacks, removed and tied the extra windbreaker she'd worn around her waist, then accepted his hand to help her out.

Once out, though, he didn't release her. Instead, he pulled her in close. "I know I'm going to have a wonderful time, too," he told her, the heat from his body seeming to be reaching out to hers. "And whether the answer to my forthcoming question is a yes or a no, I'll still have a great time." He shifted his hand so they were palm to palm, and he twined their fingers together.

"But there's something I need to ask you before we head up that hill, Meg."

She breathed through her mouth as she peered up at him. "What is it?"

He leaned in a little, his mouth inching closer, and she held her breath. She was *so* ready for this man to kiss her again. That's all she'd been thinking about since he'd given her that tiny peck a week ago.

His mouth bypassed hers and went to her ear. "Do you need sunscreen?" he whispered.

"What?" She jerked back and slapped at his arm. "You're a tease, Nate Wilde."

Laughter rolled out of him, and the tension that had been building since they'd first stepped onto the boat finally eased a little. They both wanted to get their lips on each other, no doubt. But Nate's little joke said that it wasn't going to happen just yet.

Why it wasn't happening yet, she didn't know, but at the same time, she kind of liked the added anticipation.

"I put some on in my car before I got out," she informed him. "So, I guess that's a no."

"Too bad," he murmured. Then he turned, her hand still in his, and they started up the hill.

It didn't take long to get high enough for an excellent view back over the lake and the surrounding land beyond it, and Megan simply stopped and stared. This part of the world was truly magnificent. "I could stay right here all day," she told him. The silence of the place was hypnotic.

He stepped behind her, sliding both arms around her stomach, and she shivered as his hands clasped together at her waist. She leaned back into his arms. "Just wait," he murmured. "This is simply the appetizer." His breath skimmed over her neck, and she shivered again. Her breasts also begged to be touched. But the man simply whispered in her ear once more. "I'm going to show you heaven before we leave here today, Meg."

The man was evil.

And sexy as hell. She could feel the bunched muscles of his thighs pressing into the bottom of her rear, and whatever cologne he'd splashed on that morning circled her and made her heady. "You wait too long to show me anything," she breathed out, "and I'm going to start thinking you're all talk."

She angled her head back and looked up at him, and she could see that it took everything he had not to close the distance between them. But still, he succeeded.

They headed off along the trail again—while she inwardly groaned with mounting frustration—and it wasn't long before they came upon a herd of something off in the distance. Nate stopped and shrugged out of his backpack, and when he pulled out a pair of binoculars, he handed them over.

Putting the glasses to her eyes, she quickly realized they were some seriously high-powered lenses, and when she managed to locate the herd, she saw that the animals were bighorn sheep.

"Wow." Her mouth dropped open in surprise. "This alone makes the trip worthwhile."

"I know." He waited until she offered the binoculars, then he took a look himself. Once he lowered them, he pointed toward the animals. "I guess this means we're heading that way."

Chapter Sixteen

A fter three hours of hiking, seeing many other animals—and absolutely no kissing—they'd found a nice spot on the top of a wide ridge and spread out the thin blanket Nate brought along for a picnic. The day had gone exactly as he'd hoped so far. A lot of laughs, plenty of sharing stories and just talking in general . . . and their time together reinforcing his need to be around Meg.

He'd told himself the week before that he wouldn't ask her out until he was certain it wasn't due merely to her being off limits. And as the week had progressed, he could definitely say that wasn't the case. He'd looked forward to every text that had come from her, and his heart had fluttered each time he'd heard her voice through the phone. Whatever this was, it wasn't simply lust.

But that was okay. He'd shoved the thought of her being Jaden's ex *mostly* to the back of his mind. As well as the likelihood that this whole thing stood a massive chance of ending in a giant ball of flames. And he'd decided to go for it. He wanted to see what this could be.

And if it could be something?

Well . . . he'd cross that bridge when he came to it.

"Would you like something to eat?" he asked. He'd pulled the blanket out of his backpack when they'd stopped earlier, but other than bottles of water and extra sunscreen, he hadn't dug anything else out.

Megan shook her head as she looked over at him. "It isn't food that I want, Nate."

His mouth went immediately dry. "No?"

"*No.*"

Sitting on the blanket with her legs stretched out in front of her, the crystal-clear waters of Flathead Lake surrounding her in the backdrop, she put one hand flat on the ground and leaned into his space. The smell of pears mingled with the outdoors, and hot needy eyes stared up at him.

"This is a date, right?" she asked.

"It is."

"And do you hope to get a second date after this one?"

"I absolutely do."

She nodded, and her gaze slowly trailed down to his mouth. "Then you need to figure out how to make sure *this* date says *yes* a second time."

He absolutely did.

Deciding he'd made the two of them wait long enough, he lifted a hand and gently cupped her face. He didn't immediately kiss her though. He wanted to take a moment to look at her first. He adored everything about her. Her eyes, the plump, high cheeks, her nose. But mostly he couldn't get enough of the curve of her lips. Whether she was angry, sad, happy, or driven half mad with need, her lips constantly drew his attention. And the first time he'd kissed her, he hadn't taken his time and showered them with the attention they deserved. So, this time he planned to.

Pressing forward, he touched her mouth as lightly as he had the week before. He simply breathed her in, and he waited to see if she would push him to hurry. She didn't, though. She let him set the pace. But he could feel that her body was coiled tight, simply through the single touch of his hand to her cheek.

He put a breath of space between them, and then he touched her lips again. This time as more of a nudge.

She nudged back—and his dick came to life.

"Megan," he whispered against her. Everything inside of him had coiled tight, too.

"What?" she breathed back.

"Don't let me try to take your clothes off of you on top of this hill, okay?"

When her lips smiled against his, and a little puff of air slipped out from between them, he gave up any pretense, and he went to work. He slanted his mouth over hers, loving the heat and the feel and the taste of her, and then he used his thumb to tug at her bottom lip. She opened wider, and he slipped deeper inside on a long, grateful groan. And then he couldn't get enough.

Keeping his other hand on the blanket next to hers, he held her with only the one hand, and he continued to feast. He slid his fingers from her cheek to the back of her head. Held her close. And he nipped and sucked and savored for the next several minutes. And then he did it again.

And when he finally forced himself to pull back in order to take in a much-needed breath, he was rewarded by the fact that she seemed as completely fucking lost in the moment as he.

He didn't turn her loose, but he put enough space between their mouths so that both of them could breathe. So that her glazed eyes could focus. And then he silently reminded himself *not* to take her clothes off. He not only didn't want to put on a show for whoever else might be on the island with their own pair of binoculars, but he'd sworn to himself that he'd take things with her slow.

At least as slow as he could.

But that was darned harder than he would have ever thought.

"Did that do enough to tide you over until I can get some

food into you?" He noticed the shake to his own voice, but he didn't find himself embarrassed about it. Instead, he was amazed. No woman had ever made him practically unable to function after nothing more than a kiss.

"Did it tide you over enough?" she rebutted.

"Not nearly." So he closed the distance and kissed her again.

THE WIND WHIPPED around them as they remained stretched out on the blanket. After Nate had finished showing her how unbelievably amazing he could kiss, she'd finally let him feed her. And then she'd fallen asleep. She hadn't been out for long, but she'd awoken to find Nate stretched out on his side beside her, propped on one elbow and watching her, seeming as content as she.

"When's the last time you were over here?" she asked now, rolling to her side to match him.

"I have no idea." He shook his head as he obviously tried to think back. "Not since before I left home, at least. But I used to come out here several times a summer. We had a boat, and I liked nothing better than driving over and sitting right here in this spot."

She looked at him instead of at the gorgeous view spread out before them. "It's a beautiful sight."

"It is." He looked at her, too. "And I'm a lucky man for getting to see it today."

She offered him a small smile and told herself not to be stupid and fall for this man on the first date. But geez, he knew how to do a date right. "You're a charmer," she accused.

"You make that easy."

And then she laughed. But when she went to push herself up, he put a hand on her shoulder. "Don't get up, yet. I'm going to kiss you again in a minute, and I want to test my restraints by doing it in this position."

Well, how could a girl turn down that?

So, she stayed where she was. "What do we do until you decide it's time to run your test?"

"We could talk some more?"

They'd talked the entire time they'd been walking. And she'd thoroughly enjoyed it. "Do you have more what-you-did-in-Alaska-that-one-time stories to share?" She grinned as she teased him, and then she noticed the seriousness in his eyes.

"I could come up with some, I'm sure. But I didn't want to talk about that."

"Okay." She nodded, and she almost started to push herself up again, sensing that this wasn't going to be a laying down type of talk, but since he'd requested her to stay where she was, that's what she did. "What did you want to talk about?"

"My dad?" he suggested. "Maybe your dad, too?"

Ah. She'd wondered when he'd push that direction again. She had bad news for him, though. The issue with her dad wasn't all that big of a thing. The man was a hard-working, upstanding, respected guy. She just wished she got more of his attention.

"I want to know who you are, Megan." Nate touched a finger to the middle of her lip, his eyes both apologizing and pleading. "And to do that, I need to understand where you came from. What made you how you are."

She got that. It's why she wanted to know why he'd left home at eighteen.

She nodded, and then she rolled to her back. "What do you want to know?" she asked. The bright blue above her stretched as far as her eyes could see, and she could almost imagine she was floating in it.

"I want to know why your dad cancelled his trip to see you."

She looked over at him. "Because that's his MO. Ever since he divorced my mom and started traveling more, he somehow thinks it does as much good to *say* he's going to visit and then cancel, as it would if he actually showed up."

"And when's the last time he showed up?"

She had to think back. "Probably a year ago in Seattle. Wait . . . no. I went to see him that time. His base office is in Seattle, and I caught him in town."

"And when before that?"

"I don't know, Nate. And the when isn't what's important. It's that the man has a way of making me want to beg for his attention, and yet that still wouldn't be good enough." She pushed up to both elbows. "And I *hate* to beg. Especially for love."

Steady eyes watched her. "I can see where that would be an uncomfortable thing."

"Yeah?" She dropped back down. "Well, it's so uncomfortable that I haven't once begged for anything since he left me when I was ten. Not like that. And I won't."

"Like what?"

She looked at him again, and she knew that she could trust him with her pain. "Like my life wouldn't be complete if someone walked out the door and forgot me."

Understanding showed in his eyes. "People other than your dad have done that?"

She counted off the names on her fingers. "My dad, my mom, my brother, and both of my sisters."

"I'm sorry." The words were simple and said without inflection. But the weight of feeling carried within them touched her.

"Thank you. But there's no need for you to be sorry." She offered him a small smile. "It's just the way it is. Yet, stupidly, I continue to hope. To try to please him." She let out a sad sounding laugh then and looked back at the sky. "I've got news that isn't going to please him, though. And I'm eventually going to have to share it."

"About your job?" he guessed, and his understanding didn't surprise her.

"He thinks I'm still programming full time."

"And why did you quit?" She looked over at him, surprised at the question. She'd been working full time for the Wildes for almost three months now, of which the two of them had spent a lot of time around each other. And he'd never once asked about her career change.

She answered honestly. "Because it's not my passion. It doesn't make me excited to get up and start every day. And don't get me wrong, I'm good at it. But I can be good at anything I do."

A soft smile touched his lips. "I have no doubt."

"I also quit because I got the degrees in the first place purely for him."

She'd known her dad wouldn't like her quitting long before she'd done it. But once she'd broken up with Jaden, she couldn't see continuing on the same course she'd been on. She'd needed to be more *her* than she'd been in years. And *she* didn't want to sit at a computer all day. *She* didn't want a job where she was as alone during the daytime hours as she'd so often been the rest of her life.

Nate picked up her hand. "And if you took the job in Chicago . . ."

She knew he got it. "Then maybe my dad would 'care' more. Visit more." It wouldn't happen, though. She hadn't been a priority in years, and if she couldn't get him to come see her when she lived in the same city as he, he wouldn't be likely to make the trek to Chicago. "Points," she muttered, knowing Nate would continue to follow her train of thought. Maybe she could score points if she took the job. And maybe someday those points would add up enough that it would make her worth her dad's time.

"You don't need those kinds of points." Nate's words came out rough, and the sound sent a shiver through her body. But he was right. She didn't need them. And she was finished trying to score any.

"I've got all I need in Birch Bay," she told him. "I know that I originally moved here because of Jaden, but the truth is, my heart never left the place after my first trip to the area."

He brought her fingertips to his lips. The soft touch of his mouth grazing her skin filled her with the kind of pleasure she'd always sought. It was comfort, trust, and support. All rolled into one. It was saying that he was listening. And that he cared.

"Enough about him," he said as he pressed one last kiss to her knuckles. Then he offered her another smile. "Let's talk about something happier. Tell me more about your aunt and uncle."

The request was innocent enough, but dang if tears didn't immediately appear in her eyes.

"*Meg.*"

He started to push up, and she shook her head, unable to speak and silently asking him to give her a moment, while the tears that had appeared quickly slipped from the corners of her eyes. They tracked toward her hairline, but she didn't bother to swipe them away. Because he was right. Her aunt and uncle were a far happier topic.

"My aunt and uncle took me in when I was sixteen and my mom was moving to Oregon with Number Two." She could still remember that day. She'd been so excited to move in . . . while at the same time, so broken over why it was happening. "Aunt June was Mom's sister, but they were complete opposites. She was warm and caring. With everyone she met. And *I* came first with her."

"They took good care of you, then?"

"They took *great* care of me. They were more than happy to let me finish out high school under their roof. Uncle Ray was already sick by the time I moved in, so we knew we were going to lose him soon. But Aunt June and I had each other. And we would *always* have each other. Only—"

Her throat threatened to close, so she stared back at the sky and willed her tears away.

"She got into an accident my sophomore year," she finally managed. "Coming to see me during family day. She died instantly."

"Oh, Meg." He clung tightly to her hand. "I'm so sorry."

Megan nodded without looking back over. "At least she didn't have to lie there in pain." She swallowed. "I got the call an hour after most other families had arrived. I was just sitting in my room waiting. And the phone rang."

She could remember that day like it was yesterday. For the first time, she'd thought Aunt June had decided she had better things to do, too.

His thumb stroked over the back of her hand. "Are you mad at her for leaving, too?"

"What?" She jerked her gaze to his. "No. Of course not. I'm . . ." More tears slipped out, and the knot in her throat grew. "I'm not supposed to be mad at a dead woman, Nate," she whispered, and then Nate's arms closed around her. "I'm not supposed to be mad at the only person who said she'd never leave me."

A flood of tears came out then, and she let Nate hold her as they did. He rocked them back and forth on the blanket, murmuring soothing words and stroking her hair as he did, and when she'd cried herself out and had to look one hundred percent a mess, he lifted his head and smiled gently down at her.

"Can I test out my restraint now?" he asked, and it took her a minute to figure out what he was talking about.

She let out a single hiccupy sob. "You made me cry like a baby, and then you want to kiss me?"

He nodded, his eyes smiling, and her grip on keeping him at a distance slipped.

"Fine, Wilde. Kiss me. See if you can do it without trying to take my clothes off."

Chapter Seventeen

✦❦✦

He'd kissed her. And he hadn't taken her clothes off. He'd wanted to, though.

And now they were docking back at the house, and all he could do was think that he wasn't ready to let her go yet. If she didn't want to have sex, he'd respect that. He'd ask to do no more than be with her a while longer. But he'd never had the kind of day he'd had today. One he didn't want to end.

He tied the boat to the pier, deciding he'd wait until tomorrow to return it, then he hopped onto the dock where Megan waited. He took both her hands in his and planted another kiss on her gorgeous mouth. The guys who were staying next door wouldn't be able to see them from there, and the house was too far up the hill for his dad and Gloria to see, as well. So, he took his time. And he made love to Megan's mouth.

When he pulled back, he kept his arms around her waist and peered down at her. Her cheeks were pink from too much time in the sun, and her hair was a mess. Also, any makeup she might have put on earlier in the day had been destroyed by her earlier crying jag. But she'd never looked more beautiful.

"Will you stay with me tonight?" He let his need for her show.

"Where?"

Nodding toward the cliff, he said, "In cabin ten. It's still dusty, but I swept up in there this morning." He tilted his head to the side. "I also stored a blow-up mattress in there. Just in case."

At her sexy smile, he added, "As well as candles...champagne, strawberries..."

She put a hand over his mouth. "Did you set up a seduction scene for me?"

He didn't think she was complaining, but he wanted to make his intentions clear. He held her chin between his thumb and fore-finger, making sure she didn't look away. "It doesn't have to be anything more than you're ready for. But I'm not ready for the day to end. That said"—he pulled in a deep breath and plunged ahead—"I'm also not making promises I don't know if I can keep. That I don't know if I'm *capable* of." He touched his thumb to her bottom lip, and he got lost in her eyes. "I don't ever want to mislead you, Meg. So, right now, I'm only making the promise to *try*."

She gazed back at him, the lowering sun reflecting off her hair and making the dark strands look burnished. And he saw the same need he felt reflected back at him. "Do you *want* to be capable of more?"

He nodded. "I very much do."

"Then that's enough for me right now."

He couldn't have been more grateful.

Putting his hands to her hips, he pulled her in to him, and then he kissed her again. This time when he did, he let a little more of the fire he'd been holding in all day show, and when her arms hooked around his neck and one leg inched up the outside of his thigh as it had at her place, he gripped her under the butt and pulled her up to his groin.

"You make me crazy, Megan Manning. You make me instantly hard and completely unable to have any ability to think."

She nipped at his bottom lip and locked her ankles behind

his waist. "The best way to have a man is hard and without the ability to think."

He laughed, the free and light feeling inside him one he couldn't ever remember having, then he started up the path with her in his arms. They'd gotten halfway up when he could make out the point to the roof that covered the second-floor deck off the master bedroom, and he suddenly stopped. That's the bedroom that had always been his dad's.

When Megan looked at him questioningly, he let her slide to the ground, but he kept an arm around her shoulders. His dad would never be in that room again. He was relegated to the first floor now. And it was Nate's fault.

"I couldn't bring myself to visit him while he was in rehab," he said, "because it was my fault he was there to begin with."

She immediately understood where the conversation had gone. "How could it have been your fault? You didn't know he was sick. None of us did."

"But I knew something was wrong."

He stared down at her. "Deep down, I'd known it for weeks. We'd had a bad ice storm once when I was a kid. One that took out quite a few trees. And Dad was worried then, too. But he didn't go out to check on them every morning. And never once before daylight. Nothing required that kind of scrutiny because there's nothing you can do for the trees once the damage is done."

"That still doesn't—"

She stopped talking when he held up a hand, and he looked back at the house and continued. "I knew he was getting up every morning this time. And I'd tried to talk him out of it. Tried telling him it was ridiculous to do so, but he wouldn't listen. So that last week, I met him downstairs every morning. I didn't offer to do the check in his place. Instead, I was waiting for him to *ask* me. And if he'd just asked, I would have. I'd have been out there in an instant," he gritted out, still mad that no one had ever considered that he might want to be a part of running things. "If he'd just needed me.

"I knew something was wrong," he went on. "I hadn't been able to put my finger on it, but he had moments where he just seemed to be somewhere else. And the morning of the accident, he had one of those moments." He dragged his gaze back to Megan's again, not wanting her to see his guilt, but at the same time, needing to show it to someone. "He was talking to the door when I came downstairs, Megan. Dear God. And I swear he thought it was talking back to him. So, I offered." He pulled in a breath and kept going. "I didn't think 'gee, something is obviously wrong with Dad, and I need to make *sure* he doesn't go out on the tractor this morning.' No, I just offered to go for him. And when he said no . . . when it felt like he'd pushed me aside because I couldn't possibly do the job as good as he could . . . I stormed out and left him to it."

He didn't say anything else for a moment, the back of his nose burning with tears that wanted to come out. But he didn't let Megan see his tears. Just his guilt.

However, when she pressed a kiss right over his heart and wrapped her arms tight around his waist, he couldn't keep in two lone drops that slid down his cheeks.

"I sat at the diner mad at the man that morning, Megan. Mad and ready to leave Birch Bay because no one here needed me. And I should have forced him to go get help. I should have taken the damned tractor key away from him and never let him get on it again. Because I *knew*, dammit. I *knew* something was wrong. But I was too damned worried about my own feelings to care."

MEGAN STOOD with her arms around Nate until his heart rate slowed back to a normal range, and when she lifted her head to peer at him, he seemed to be all out of words. Instead, he stared back at her with need in his eyes. It seemed to be a combination of needing her to *not* think too badly of him, while also needing her to hold on tight. So, she did both.

Reaching up, she gripped his face and brought it down to hers, and after she'd put all the feeling and the comfort she could into a single kiss, she turned and led him the rest of the way up the hill.

Cabin 10 sat waiting the farthest from them, and she could see a dim light coming from inside. There weren't any light fixtures installed yet, but he'd clearly brought out something to keep them from being in the dark tonight. And when they reached the cabin and she led him inside, her heart melted at what she found. Six fake candles sat glowing around the living room floor, with the blow-up mattress positioned inside them. A cooler had been brought into the room, as well, and when she peeked inside, she found the promised champagne—on ice—and strawberries. She then turned to the man who was the last person she'd ever thought she'd want to be with.

"Make love to me, Nate." She pulled her sweatshirt over her head. "Make love to me like you've never done to another woman before."

Her request seemed to be all he'd been waiting for, as he put his hands to her sides. He didn't move fast, though. Instead, everything about him said that he intended to linger. His fingers trailed slowly over her ribs as his hands slid upward. And as they reached her breasts, the pad of a lone finger slid, first, along the edge of the lace covering her left breast, then repeated with her right. A shiver tingled through her as that same finger dipped between her breasts, its rougher texture a distinct contrast to the plump flesh on either side of it, and then that finger curled into the front material of her bra, right between the underwires, and he tugged. Her chest bumped against him, and her breath got stuck in the back of her throat.

"Meg," he whispered her name, his eyes hot liquid pools of blue, and she caught her bottom lip between her teeth.

"Yes?" she breathed out.

"Thank you." His palm cupped her cheek, the heat of it reaching inside her until it touched her all the way to her toes. "For sharing the hard things with me earlier. For letting *me* share with you."

She nodded, unable to find words.

"And thank you for trusting me like this. For giving me a chance."

"Giving *us* a chance," she corrected, and he nodded.

"Us," he agreed. Then he went back to worshipping her body.

His hand, fingers splayed wide, slid down over her throat, causing her to arch away from him so he had better access, and her heart thudded behind her breastbone as both hands passed along the outsides of her breasts. Every place that he touched turn to fire.

"I want to take my time," he admitted. Both hands dragged down and slid around to her back. "But the longer I touch you" —he lifted her so she was flush with his body—"the harder it becomes to go slow."

She wound her arms around his neck. "It feels like going slow isn't the only thing that's hard," she teased, and one corner of his mouth tilted up. His length jutted into her abdomen, leaving her with the kind of ache that instantly pooled in her jeans. "Let's forget about slow." She nipped at his neck, her breasts aching to be touched. "Slow can be so overrated."

He shook his head back and forth. "Slow . . . savoring . . . showing you what this means to me . . ." He brought his mouth to hers and captured it, exposing his desire in the greedy way he took control. "We need slow this first time, Meg. We need no mistakes that this isn't only sex. For either of us."

She had to agree. So, they continued with slow.

He picked up her, her legs draping over one of his arms, then stepping around the candles, he gently placed her in the middle of the mattress. Then he settled in beside her. Unfastening her jeans, he reached for the pull of her zipper, and though she felt vulnerable lying there before him, she didn't dare move. Instead, she watched him as he undressed her. And she knew that this was exactly where she was supposed to be.

The slide of her zipper sounded loud in the room, with the only other noise that of their breathing. She lifted her hips as he tugged at the material.

She had the urge to rush him, then. Screw slow. She wanted the man stripped and naked, and both of them stretched out together. She wanted him plunging deep inside her.

Instead, he remained determined. He bared her cream-colored bikini panties, his thumbs skimming over the lace just as the denim slid away. The tops of her thighs were next. Then her calves. And finally—after yanking off her boots with little more than quick jerks of the laces and a grip of the heels—he dragged the denim over her feet. Then he rose and stood above her, tall and proud, and simply gazed down.

"You're beautiful, Meg. As beautiful as I knew you would be. Both inside and out."

"I'm also feeling at a slight disadvantage," she murmured. Her hands shook when she lifted them, intending to reach out and beg him to come to her, so she dropped them back to her sides. He'd been right. Slow *could* be good. As well as both of them knowing that this was definitely more than sex.

But Lord, she was going to explode if he didn't pick up a little speed soon.

"Make love to me, Nate," she pleaded. "Come back down here. Touch me. Let *me* touch you."

"We're about to." His voice had gone tight, and she could see that his restraint was truly being tested. "I just need to decide where I want to touch you *first.*" So, she helped him with his decision.

She reached behind her and unclasped her bra. Then she tossed it to the floor.

"Awww, Meg." His gaze latched on to her chest. "That's not playing fair at all."

"And I told you before. I play to win."

He nodded and dragged his gaze back to hers. "I guess I should have known better."

He went into motion then, pulling his own sweatshirt over his head, leaving his hair mussed and standing on end. Then he quickly shed his jeans. Two seconds later, he was back beside her. The heat from his bared limbs touched her. His mouth crashed into hers. And when one large hand finally slid up her belly and circled her breast, she sobbed out a sigh of relief.

"I want to worship every inch of you," he mumbled against her mouth before trailing his lips along her jawline. "I want to take my time and touch and explore." He flicked her nipple with his thumb and kissed her behind the ear. "I want to leave you boneless before I even *begin* to make you come."

But then his mouth suddenly took its worship to where his thumb played at her breast, and the unexpected move had her back straining off the mattress.

"Nate!" His name burst out of her as little more than a whisper, and then his teeth gently tugged at her nipple.

"Yes, dear?" He was enjoying his torture way too much.

"It's already too late," she told him. She ached everywhere, but mostly between her legs. "You may not have meant to, but you're *already* about to make me come."

His head lifted from her then, and a smug gleam shone down from sexy blue eyes. And she knew . . . he'd *definitely* meant to. He slid a leg over her thighs and rose up above her. "Will you come if I touch you?" His hands grasped either side of her panties and pulled them down. "Or do I need to put my mouth on you first?"

Her gaze dropped to his mouth.

Then it lowered to where his erection remained hidden behind his boxers.

"I guess that depends on how long you can hold out." She exposed him, his long length standing at full attention, and taking him into her hand, she stroked up and down. She was already lost in the feel of the silky hardness against her palm as she rose up, seeking out his mouth. They met in the middle, lips fused, tongues dueling, and though she both wanted to get her mouth on him and his on her, that wasn't what she wanted at the moment.

What she wanted was him inside her.

And she wanted it *now*.

"There's a backpack behind your head," he said as he pulled away. "I have condoms in there."

He stretched out over her, fumbling with the zipper of the bag, and she nipped at his own nipple that now hovered above her.

"Meg," he groaned. "I just need a—"

"You *need* to be inside me," she demanded. "And if you're clean . . ."

He went still. Then lifted up far enough so he could look down at her.

"Well . . ." She offered a tiny smile. "I'm just saying that *I'm* clean. And I'm also on the pill." She'd never quit taking them since she'd broken up with Jaden. And she hadn't been with anyone else in over four years.

She suspected similar thoughts were going through Nate's head at that very moment, and she held her breath, slightly worried that the reminder of who she'd been with before might slam on the brakes. It didn't, though. Instead, he dropped the backpack and slid back down next to her.

"You're sure?" he asked. He stroked a finger along the curve of her cheek, and she could see the honor that she'd allow that written in his eyes. "You'd let me do that? You'd trust me?"

"I do trust you."

He looked down the length of her body, his fingers whispering over her from chest to thigh. "I'm clean, too," he promised. "And I've never been with a woman without that kind of protection."

Now *she* felt honored.

"Then make love to me, Nate." She brought his hand to her

mouth and kissed his palm. "*Now*. Make love to me and show me that this isn't just sex."

He nodded, but before he did anything else, he kissed her again. And the kiss was long and drawn-out, and it showed her all the things this night was about. It held trust and respect. Passion and need. And it held hope. It was bursting wide open with hope.

Then Nate's body covered hers again, and while still kissing her, he slid deep inside her. He waited for a moment, neither of them in a hurry to move. And when those first waves of pleasure began to subside and they were both ready for more, they started moving as one.

Their earlier pace returned, neither of them in a hurry for this first time to end, and they took their time worshipping each other. They each touched, kissed, and pleasured the other until both coiled tight with the need for release, and when it finally happened, Megan noted that Nate's arms held her as tightly as hers held him.

They clung to each other until their breathing calmed, then Nate dropped his forehead to her shoulder.

"Did I already say thanks for that?" he murmured.

She let out a soft laugh. "I think I'm the one who needs to be saying thank you."

"No." He shook his head, but he didn't lift it so she could see him. "It's me. Trust me."

He didn't say anything else, and neither did she, and a couple of hours later she woke, realizing they'd remained wrapped in each other's arms. She looked up at him. He'd rolled to his back, and she'd curled into his side. And she found him watching her.

"Did you not sleep?" she asked.

"I did. Someone drained me, and I passed out like a baby."

That made her smile. "Want to be drained again?"

He barked out a laugh before hugging her tight. "I absolutely do. But first, let's have some food. We skipped the strawberries and champagne earlier, you know? And there's also cheese and summer sausage in there."

"Ah, yes, the seduction scene." She pushed up off him, and it suddenly occurred to her they were in a cabin with no installed bathroom fixtures. "I don't think the seduction was required," she teased.

"Still"—he reached for the backpack that rested at the head of the bed—"I hope you appreciate the effort." Pulling out a button-down shirt and a flashlight, he handed them over. "Your 'robe,' my dear." He announced the intended purpose of the shirt that would hang to her thighs. "And your flashlight to find the porta-pot."

Understanding dawned. The man had thought of practically everything.

He rummaged in the bag again and pulled out a pack of disposable wet washcloths, and her prior thought changed. He'd thought of *everything*.

"I also came out earlier with a disinfectant spray and cleaned the damned porta-pot. Guys are disgusting, in case you weren't aware. I couldn't have you using that."

She laughed as he shuddered with the memory, the sound loud and clear, and slipped into her "robe." "You're sweet, Nate Wilde. Has anyone ever told you that?"

He winked at her. "I think I'm just infatuated."

"Either one, I'll take it." She gave him a kiss before rising and pulling on her boots, and as she made her way in the moonlight to the blue porta-pot, she stopped and looked back.

That definitely hadn't just been sex in there. Not for either of them. And though, on the one hand, the mere idea of that scared her senseless—because the last thing she needed was to fall head over heels for a guy already on his way out of town—on the other hand, whatever it was had a life of its own, and she didn't know if she could stop it if she wanted to.

What a surprise Nate was turning out to be. And *whatever* this was, she'd take it one day at a time.

Chapter Eighteen

❦

The gauzy haze of pre-dawn light filtered through the uncovered windows in the small room early the next morning, and Nate lay on the low mattress, Megan tucked in at his side, and stared at the unfinished ceilings. The night had been more perfect than their day. And he couldn't imagine letting this woman go.

At the same time, how was he supposed to go to his brother and tell him that he was falling for her?

He couldn't. It was that simple. At least not yet. It was possible this was just post-sex glow, and that things weren't really as good as he thought. So, no need to rock any boats within his family just yet. He'd see what Megan thought about the whole situation, and then they'd go from there.

But when he turned his head to catch a glimpse of her sleeping, he saw that she'd already awakened and was watching him. And she looked as gobsmacked as he felt.

"Morning," he rumbled. God, he wanted to make love to her again. The three times the night before hadn't been nearly enough.

"Morning," she repeated. Then she turned into his body, and

all of her nakedness pressed against all of his, and he couldn't think about anything but putting his hands back on her.

She rolled on top of him before he could so much as offer a good-morning kiss and positioned herself over him, and in a matter of seconds, he was once again sliding inside her.

"Ahhhh." He couldn't hold in the groan. She was so wet this morning.

"Did you sleep well?" she asked as she set them on a slow pace.

"I slept like a man who'd had a night of exceptional sex." His fingers dug into her hips, and he held on.

"Funny," she breathed out. She leaned forward, her neck arching back, and her breasts swung in front of him. "I slept like a woman who'd had the same."

Her slow, steady rhythm was rapidly destroying him.

He strained upward, reaching for a beaded nipple, but managed nothing more than a hard swipe of his tongue across one tip. That brought her gaze to his.

"I love your mouth on my breasts," she told him, and then she angled a shoulder down so he could catch one in his mouth. His teeth closed around a nipple, and her inner muscles clenched around him. "I also love the feel of you inside me." She moaned as her rhythm picked up, and her movements became more intense. "Don't stop what you're doing, Nate." She rode him hard then, her breast still in his mouth, her whole body tense. "Don't . . . oh . . ."

Her hands pressed into the wall behind them, her breast coming free and both of them swinging unencumbered, and her body ground into his. Bringing a hand up, he caught her other breast and pulled it to his mouth, and when he sucked hard, her lower back arched.

"Nate!"

She came apart in his arms then, her body shaking with need and with release, and he quickly followed her over the edge. And when both of them were spent, when there wasn't an ounce either of them had left to give, she collapsed onto his chest. And as he had when he'd first opened his eyes ten minutes before, he stared at the unfinished ceiling.

"*Oh. My. God.*" He moaned the words out as much as saying them, but good Lord, that was a way to wake up.

"Ditto," she said from where her face lay buried in his chest.

They remained there for several more minutes, both of them trying to catch their breaths, and when she finally propped her elbows onto his chest and offered him a heart-melting smile, he knew that the day was going to come that he'd have to tell his brother he was dating his ex.

"You're beautiful in the morning," he told her.

"And you remain a charmer even in the wee hours." She blew him a kiss and then rolled off his body, but she didn't go anywhere. Instead, she remained tucked in the crook of his shoulder. "I've been thinking," she said, and his initial thought was *uh-oh.* But then he heard the excitement in her voice.

"Do you normally do a lot of thinking before the sun comes up?"

"It's often when I do my best thinking." She picked up his hand and pressed her palm flat to it, showcasing the vast difference in their sizes. "The barn," she said and looked at him. "It would be the perfect venue for weddings."

She was lying there thinking about business after riding him like a bull?

"Weddings?" He hadn't quite caught up with her yet.

"It would need to be renovated, of course, but brides love the rustic touch. You could do destinations weddings where the bridal party or guests rent out the cabins, and then weddings could be performed in the barn. Or possibly outdoor weddings, with receptions held in the barn. Or both." She rolled to her stomach and pushed up to her elbows, and all romance disappeared. "Can't you see it? Lights strung from the rafters, tulle everywhere. There are a couple of great caterers in town you could contract with. And you could even close up some of the space in the barn and create meeting rooms, too. Then you could host events that need meeting space."

The woman had good ideas. He reoriented himself so that he was propped up, as well. "What kind of events are you thinking?"

"Well, for one, Arsula could use it."

He didn't follow. "How?"

"We got her intuitive coaching website kicked off in April, and business is starting to pick up. In fact, so much so that she'll probably quit working for Dani within a couple of months. She's got clients now from all over the country, and even a few in other parts of the world, and what she hopes to eventually do is host a retreat or two every year. But she needs the right location for something like that. A space with lodging *and* meeting space. And if it happened to be in a peaceful locale with lake and mountain views . . ."

He'd never thought about anything like that. He'd only ever imagined lodging and excursions. But the idea was solid. *Very.* The potential revenue would be great.

He sat up and crossed his legs. "Something like that couldn't happen this year. At least not initially. We won't get the cabins open until July, so we couldn't start on that phase until then. But at the same time, we also wouldn't want to be doing noisy renovations while our guests are getting their very first looks. It might garner bad reviews for people to come into a brand-new place with the sound of hammering and sawing still going on."

"True," she agreed. "Maybe phase two happens in the fall before tourism picks back up for winter activities, but we could have sketches done for this season so visitors could see what'll be coming next year."

He smiled at the fact she'd said "we." She seemed to be taking as much ownership as he was. And he was okay with that.

"Any chance you might be able to bring some of the same guys back in for phase two?" she asked. "Not that there aren't people around here willing to work, but your guys are good. They get the job done."

He nodded. "Chances are excellent."

She looked at him then, her mind obviously coming back from visions of taking over the hospitality world, and a tiny line formed between her eyes. "How is it that so many guys were willing to drop everything and come help you out like they did, anyway?"

He gave a small shrug. "You know . . . good money buys beer."

"Oh, come on." She sat up like he had. "I might have only really spent time with a couple of them, but they admire you. I can tell. They're happy to be here. Pleased to be working for you."

"It's nothing."

"It's obviously something, Nate." She took his hands. "Tell me," she pleaded, and he let out an exaggerated sigh.

"*Fine.*" He might have known she'd get this out of him. "Most of them have worked for me before, okay?"

"What do you mean *worked* for you?"

"In the off-season. I have contracting businesses set up in a few different parts of the country, each run by a local manager, and these are some of the guys who've—"

"Wait." She held up a hand to stop him. "You *own* several businesses? How did you . . . what . . ." Her words dried up, and she just sat there staring at him.

He knew she'd make a bigger deal of it than it was. "It's actually all under one umbrella," he told her. "And they're small businesses in each location. They're in places where I've lived or spent time in, and most have done really well."

"And how long have you been doing this?"

"For a few years."

She still seemed as poleaxed as when the conversation began. "You just decided to start a business one day?"

"I did." He didn't see what the big deal was. "I actually

earned a business degree several years ago, and since the idea of a nine-to-five and four walls has never appealed to me, I started bidding on some construction jobs here and there. I'd always done that kind of work when not out on a crab boat, anyway, so it was the natural thing to do. One thing led to another, I filed for a tax ID, and now I have a business."

She sat there, totally naked, gaping at him. *"Nate."*

"What?"

"This is amazing. I had no idea. Does your family know about this?"

"No. Well, Nick knows that I got the degree. The rest just think I took a class or two."

Her mouth continued to hang open. "A class or two?"

"Right."

"Why didn't you tell them that you finished the degree? That you started a successful business?"

"Because it's not important, Meg. It's not what I want to do with my life."

"Well, what do you want to do with your life?"

He wasn't really sure.

He *wanted* to come home.

"I guess I'll know it when I see it."

"I CAN'T WAIT to get a good look at this man I've supposedly been having a fling with for the last two weeks." Brooke grinned like she had a secret no one else did, and Megan rolled her eyes as she drove down the road.

"Please don't say anything like that while we're out here."

"But what if someone asks?"

Megan shot her friend a look. "Then *change* the subject."

It was Monday morning. Brooke had no summer classes to teach and The Cherry Basket wasn't open, so the two of them were heading to Wilde Cherry Orchard—soon to also be Wilde

Cabins and Adventures—so Brooke could meet Nate in person. She'd "met" his truck several times over the last couple of weeks. In order to keep Megan's and Nate's relationship quiet, they'd often parked his truck at Brooke's place, and then she'd snuck him into her apartment for the night.

The whole thing was silly to some extent. They were grown adults, and there was no reason for them to be sneaking around. But at the same time, she was also fine with it. She knew that he needed time to come to grips with having a relationship with his brother's ex, and to be truthful, she wasn't exactly ready to share with everyone that they were spending time together, anyway. It was kind of special as it was. No one could judge them or get in their way. And that had given them plenty of time just to continue getting to know each other.

He hadn't wanted to be away from the house every night, of course. He liked being there to help out with his dad when needed. But for the most part, Gloria and Max were fine on their own. And when Nate *had* stayed over at Megan's, he'd been sure to keep his phone on him at all times. Gloria knew he was just a phone call away, and he'd taken that responsibility seriously.

Megan did suspect that Gloria and Max might have figured out where he was spending his time, though. After all, her car had stayed at their house all night that first night. She'd also stopped by the house several times over the last two weeks, and though neither Max nor Gloria had said anything, she'd seen the looks pass between them.

Arsula hadn't said anything else to her, either. She neither asked about it nor guessed out loud again that Megan was dating Nate. But every time she'd seen Megan, she did watch her with a gleam in her eyes similar to the one Gloria wore.

"We're really going to run the wood chipper today?" Brooke asked as Megan turned off the main road and headed up the driveway.

"He promised he'd saved us some trees." There'd been a couple of areas where the dead trees hadn't been taken down yet, but since they'd hired a guy to mow and weed around the remaining good trees, they'd also gotten him to finish taking down the dead ones. "And he'd *better* have saved some trees," she added. "He knows how badly I've been wanting to get ahold of that machine."

As they proceeded up the driveway, she could make out fat, plump green cherries now hanging off all the trees still in sight. At least the place hadn't been a total loss. She couldn't imagine this land with no cherry trees at all.

Sprinklers kicked on to their right, causing Brooke to jump in surprise, then she laughed out loud. "You know, I can't believe I've never been out here," she said. "Everyone in town has always known the Wildes. Or, at least known of them. I was young when their mom died, of course, but I remember her, too. She'd come into Mom and Dad's meat market every week."

Megan glanced over. "Was Nate ever with her?"

"Who knows? Often at least one of the kids was, but since he was a twin, when one of them *was* there, I never knew who I was looking at. They were hot even back then, though."

"I can only imagine. Poor little pre-teenage girls."

"You got that right." Brooke fanned herself with her hand, smiling as if one of the Wilde brothers were right there in the car with her. "We're going out to get a look at the cabins before we start working, right?"

Megan followed her train of thought perfectly, even though Brooke hadn't expressly stated it. "You mean are we going to get a look at the eleven good-looking guys working for Nate before you get all dirty and sweaty?"

"Well, yeah. That too."

Megan chuckled. "He said the pile of trees has been moved out there."

They pulled up to the house, and Brooke whistled under her breath. "Man . . . the way that man looks at you."

Nate was standing in front of the barn and had turned their way when she'd pulled up. "You can tell that from this distance?"

"I can. As well as every time I peek out when you two are leaving his truck at my place."

Megan smirked, imagining her friend hiding behind a curtain and peeking out at the two of them. "I suppose you could have just stepped out and said hello."

"What? And ruin the fun of spying?" She made a face. "Never."

They both stayed in the car as Nate made his way to them, and as he approached, Megan rolled down her window. She inhaled a deep breath, wanting to pull his scent into her lungs, and as she did, she heard Brooke snort in disgust. Her friend knew *exactly* what she was doing.

"You're pathetic," Brooke mumbled. She then leaned over and reached a hand out to Nate. "Hi. You must be the man whose truck I'm having an affair with."

Nate tossed a quick look Megan's way, humor filling his eyes as he captured Brooke's hand. "And you must be the friend who needs to check up on her friend's boyfriend."

Megan swooned inside at the term boyfriend.

"Good start." Brooke acknowledged. "He calls them like he sees them."

"I wouldn't want it any other way."

Nate squatted to bring his face eye level with them, and Megan thought for a minute that he was going to lean in and kiss her. They were sitting just outside the house, though, and anyone could see.

"Don't mind me." Brooke waved them on. "I'll just look out this window over here."

Both corners of Nate's mouth hitched up, but he didn't kiss her. Instead, he just looked her over, as if reminding himself exactly what every part of her tasted like—and silently promising that he would be tasting all those parts again—and dang, if that wasn't as hot as a kiss.

"You're evil," she whispered.

"I'm horny," he replied. "I haven't seen you in four hours."

"Well, geez, people." Brooke fanned herself again. "Let me out of the car first."

Nate laughed along with Brooke, while Megan rolled her eyes yet again, and then he headed for his truck with her promise to follow. She put her car back into gear and took off down the path behind him, and Brooke let out a long sigh.

"He really does have it bad for you, doesn't he?"

Megan looked over. "You think?"

"Sweetie." Brooke stared at her. "You're not stupid. You see what I see."

Yeah, she saw it. She just didn't know if him having it bad meant he'd seriously given thought to staying or not. They hadn't talked about it since they'd started going out, but there had been the occasional mention of "future" things that might happen here at the farm. And the whole family had loved the idea of the barn as a wedding venue, so plans for that were already in the works. But would that be enough to keep him here for good?

He'd said he didn't know what he wanted to do with his life. Could she convince him that whatever it was, he could do it here?

They made it out to the construction site, and as she turned off her car, she looked over at her friend again. "Fair warning," she said. "These cabins are scheduled to be finished in three weeks, and at that time, I'm going to drag you back out here to help me load in the décor. I've got a storage room full of stuff waiting at this point."

"Just tell me when and where, and I'll be there. But for the record, I still find it kind of hilarious that you volunteered to do that."

"Why?" Megan asked. They climbed from her car. "I'm loving it."

"Well . . . the way I see it, you quit a high-paying, one-hundred-percent work-from-home position with a Fortune 500 company to hire on as a manager of a local retail store. Then you get into interior design, and you've offered to handle registrations until they hire a full-time person. While *also* still doing the occasional website, of course."

"Don't forget that I also wrote a new app just last week." The app writing was a hobby, though, and it was a good way to pass the time instead of just sitting around thinking about Nate.

"I'm just saying that you're all over the place," Brooke went on. "And it seems a little odd to me. That's all."

"I guess I just don't want to get tied down to one thing." She'd never really thought about it the way Brooke laid it out. It did seem sort of like she was all over the place.

"Or maybe you haven't yet found 'the thing' that you need to truly tie you down."

She stopped walking and looked at her friend. Because that was an interesting idea. She was very happy as things were. She loved Birch Bay, and she loved managing the store. But as her assistant had taken on more responsibility, *she'd* found herself doing mostly backend tasks and not handling the day-to-day as much. And she certainly didn't want to go back to a tech job— no matter what her dad might think. But was it possible she hadn't found who *she* wanted to be yet? To this point, she'd just been focusing mostly on staying in Birch Bay. But maybe her focus needed to be more on *her*.

That was certainly something to give consideration to.

"Well, hello, ladies," Cade called out from an open window in one of the cabins, and suddenly all construction noise ceased. The men were now aware there were women on the premises.

Brooke grinned beside her. "Well, hello, construction boys."

"God, you're such a flirt," Megan muttered.

"Hey. I'm not the one in a relationship. I can flirt with all eleven of them if I want to."

Megan waved her on. "Then have at it, lady. Enjoy yourself."

Megan and Brooke were led through the almost-finished cabins, as well as getting a good look at the areas where the fire pits and any outdoor games would be set up. And all in all, it was impressive. Even without seeing the finished product. And

Brooke agreed. This had been an excellent idea on Nate's part, and once the wedding venue was in place, the whole setup would only get better.

After they saw the cabins, Megan finally got her turn at running the wood chipper. And as she and Brooke squealed and laughed each time one of them fed a tree into the hopper, Megan also caught sight of way more than Nate watching them. They seemed to be disrupting work a fair amount today. Therefore, she decided the two of them needed to leave. She didn't want Nate and his guys getting behind.

Dusting tree bits from her jeans, she headed for her car and watched as Brooke breezed between Chris and Conner, a teasing smile on her face. Then *she* offered Dre a smile as he came over to her.

"How are you?" Megan asked.

"Staying busy." He cocked his head, taking her in, then tossed a quick look over his shoulder. "That's what I thought," he said as he turned back. "You and Nate."

"No." She shook her head, but she knew she'd failed to pull it off. Her denial had been too quick, and the deer-in-the-head-lights look clearly indicated she'd been lying. She didn't give in, though. "You're mistaken, Dre. We're just friends."

"I don't think so, cutie." He took her hand in his, and over his shoulder, she caught Nate stand up from where he'd had a hip hitched against a wooden sawhorse. Dre tugged her in closer and whispered in her ear. "Good luck with him," he said. "He's a good man, and he's totally worth the trouble."

Happiness swelled in her chest. She loved that Nate's friend had his back. Everyone needed that kind of support in their life.

"He just needs the right woman to make *him* see all the good inside him," Dre continued. He pulled back slightly and peered down at her. "Is that you, Megan?"

She nodded, this time having no need to lie. "I'd like for it to be. And for the record, *I* see the good in him. And I'm trying my best to make sure he sees it, too."

"I thought you might be."

He pulled her in for a hug and headed back to work, but as soon as he walked away, Nate stood in his place. And he didn't look happy.

"Goodness." She picked a piece of wood out of her hair. "You're cute when you're jealous, Wilde. Anyone ever told you that before?"

He scowled. "Who says I'm jealous?"

"I did, and I can prove it. What were you just thinking about?"

When he didn't immediately answer, she propped her hands on her hips and pierced him with a look.

Finally, he shrugged. "I wasn't thinking about much. Just killing my best friend."

"*Hmmm.* Yep. Like I said. Cute."

He stepped in closer, and the backs of his fingers swept over the backs of hers. "I suppose some people might call it that. I wouldn't know. I've never been jealous before."

"Never?" She found that hard to believe. "Have you not had a serious relationship before?"

"Not really."

She stared up at him. "What does not really mean?"

"It means . . . not really." His expression went blank then, and he glanced back in the direction of the house. When he looked back at her, he offered another shrug. "I might have thought I was heading in that direction once. But I was too young to know what was going on. Too stupid and selfish to care."

"Selfish for wanting a lasting relationship?"

His eyes remained unreadable. "Among other things."

She watched him for a moment, considered pushing for more details. But this wasn't a man who liked to be pushed. And she wasn't in any hurry, anyway. She was enjoying their time together, and though anxious to see where it might go, she also knew that pushing would likely only derail things.

"Can you put something on your calendar for me?" he asked then, and she immediately nodded.

"Anything you want."

His eyes heated at the suggestive tone she'd used, and his hand brushed across hers once again. He wanted to touch her as much as she wanted to be touched.

"Father's Day," he said. "It's two weeks from yesterday."

"I know when it is."

"We're having a get-together for Dad, and I want you to come."

She held her breath at the implication. Was he ready to tell his family?

"It'll be mostly family," he explained. "Maybe Doc Hamm and a few other close family friends, and you'll get an invite anyway. Dad and Gloria think the world of you. But I'd like to bring you as my date."

"Nate." Her voice barely whispered between them. "Do you think you'll be ready?" And if he was, did that mean a potential future for them was more likely?

"I know that I want to be." He slipped two fingers between hers and inched a little closer. "You'll be there to help me through it, right?"

"Always," she promised.

"Then it's a date."

Chapter Nineteen

❦

"Well, Lila . . ." Nate looked down at his notes, ensuring he hadn't forgotten to cover anything. This was the second interview for Lila, who was currently a manager for a nearby hotel. "I'll tell you outright, you're our current front-runner."

"Really?" Lila Ferguson's smile was wide and bright, and she had a competent and friendly demeanor. She touched a hand to her chest. "I'd love that so much, Mr. Wilde."

"Nate. Please."

They were sitting on the back deck, both with a half-consumed glass of lemonade on the table in front of them, and it was nearing six o'clock. Lila had gotten stuck on a call earlier, making it difficult to head their way on time, and when Nate had replied to her text, letting her know to take her time, that he'd be here whenever she made it, he could tell it had relieved her. The whole situation had given him even more reason to want to hire her to manage the new business. She'd been anxious to get out there today, yes. And she sincerely seemed to want the job. But she hadn't walked out on an existing responsibility to ensure she got it.

He liked that kind of loyalty.

He rose from his chair. "I'll talk to Jaden and my other brothers and sister, and we'll be in touch."

"Thank you." She rose and held out her hand. "I look forward to hearing from you."

After Lila pulled away from the house, Nate caught Gloria peeking out the back door, and he motioned for her to come on out.

"Did you still like her?" Gloria had met Lila during her first interview.

"A lot." Nate picked up the two glasses. Jaden had also been in the first interview, but he'd taken their father into town for a physical therapy appointment that afternoon, and they hadn't made it back yet. "And she says she could start the week before we'd be opening for guests."

"That would work out great." She wiped off the table where the glasses had sat. "And I liked her, too. She'd be a pleasure to have around."

"Good to know." The last thing he'd want would be someone on the property who didn't fit in with his family. Granted, they'd be bringing in a trailer as a temporary office for whoever was hired, at least until the barn could be renovated and a permanent one constructed inside, but still, the new manager would likely come into contact with any member of his family on any given day.

"You're sure you don't want to stay home and run it, though?" Gloria cast him a side-eye as she headed back for the door. "I still think that would be the best option. And it would get you back home with us for good." She offered a smile as he reached for the door.

"Come on, Gloria. I'm a crab fisherman. I work in construction. I'm not an in-the-office kind of guy."

"You're not a crab fisherman anymore."

True. And he also couldn't say the thought of sticking around to help with the new venture hadn't crossed his mind since she'd first brought it up. Because like he'd told Megan a couple of weeks ago, running construction wasn't exactly his life's calling.

But he didn't know that running vacation rentals would be, either.

However, sticking around . . . He mentally sighed. He hadn't allowed himself to think about sticking around one way or the other lately. Because what if he stuck and he screwed something up again? What if he hurt Megan in the process?

What if Megan didn't even *want* him to stick around?

What if he stuck, and by some chance his past came back to bite him? To bite all of them?

No. Not a topic he was ready to think about. Not yet. They still had almost three weeks before the cabins would be done. He'd see where things went from there. And then there was the barn project scheduled for the fall . . . If he wanted to take that one on himself.

"Well, I still say you should think about it." Gloria took the glasses from his hands when they reached the kitchen. "You've got a good head on your shoulders, I can tell. Because those cabins out there aren't coming together by magic."

"Thanks, Gloria." He took the glasses back, then emptied and put them in the dishwasher himself. "And thank you for bringing out drinks while Lila was here. I'll give everyone a call later, and we'll probably make her an offer in the next couple of days." He hitched a thumb toward the door. "I have to run. Got to catch one of the guys and I need to do it now in case he plans to head into town later."

She patted him on the cheek. "You tell those boys I said hi. They're good boys. And will you be going into town tonight, yourself?"

She wore an unreadable expression as she asked the question, but he had no doubt what she meant. Because that's exactly how both she and his father always asked. If he was "going into town." But he knew they were aware of where he'd been spending so many nights. How could they not? He couldn't contain a damned smile any time Megan showed up out there. And he'd caught his dad noticing that fact, too.

He'd also caught his dad giving him an approving nod one day after she'd driven away.

He appreciated their privacy on the subject, and he pushed the guilt of sneaking around with her and not telling anyone to the side. He'd tell them eventually. In a week and a half, in fact. And then, he supposed he'd see how it all fell out.

"Not tonight," he told her. "I'll be back after I discuss a few things with Dre."

He'd *wanted* to go back over to Megan's tonight. Hell, he wanted to be over there *every* night. But he'd gotten a call earlier from one of his businesses. The construction manager in Round Rock, Texas, might be having some legal issues that would pull him away from the job for a while. They weren't his issues, per se, but his oldest daughter's. And it sounded like if things didn't get settled out of court, a lengthy trial would be ahead. And soon.

And, of course, they'd just signed one of their biggest contracts to date in Round Rock. So, things couldn't very well run without a construction manager. And Dre had held that position for Nate, himself, more than once.

He headed back outside and hurried through the line of trees separating the two properties, texting his friend as he went. He wasn't in the mood to deal with all the guys tonight, so he opted not to go to the house. Instead, he bypassed the sprawling one-story and asked Dre to meet him out by the cliff on the back of the property. The spot that he'd told Megan would be a perfect place for a house.

He'd no more gotten there, than Dre showed up behind him. "What's up?" Dre asked.

"Need to discuss something with you."

"It's about damned time."

Nate looked up from his phone, where he'd been checking to make sure he hadn't missed any texts from Megan—she did that sometimes, texted just to say hi—and caught the half-perturbed, half-laughing look on Dre's face.

"About time?" Nate repeated. "For what?"

Dre gave him a stop-shitting-me look. "Really? So, you *didn't* bring me out here, away from all the guys, just to confess your sins and to tell me that I was right?"

Nate tried to think what he might be right about.

And then Dre's half-laughing look was back, and he suddenly got it. *Megan.*

Clearly, Dre had figured it out. Likely, that's why the man had been hugging on her when she and Brooke had been out there two days ago.

He'd been meaning to have this conversation, if only to clear the air since Dre had gone out with her—and since *he* had professed that nothing would ever happen between the two of them—but he'd barely had a minute alone lately to so much as catch a breath. Much less to admit to his best friend that he'd been totally wrong.

"Oh yeah," he finally said. *"That."*

Dre snorted and slugged Nate in the arm. "Yeah. *That.*" He shook his head, his half-laughing look now turning to one of pure happiness. "Congrats, man. She's a great lady. And she might just be exactly what you need." He looked down his nose at Nate then, and he repeated the words Nate had previously said to him. "But hurt her, and you'll answer to *me.*"

～

"YOU ARE INSANE, NATE WILDE! CERTIFIABLE."

"Just hold still and everything will be fine."

"You're going to get me hurt."

Nate let go of her hips to make sure she wasn't correct, letting the skirt of her dress fall back into place, and he took a step back. He angled his head from one side to the other, checking things out from his position, but from the way he saw it, there was nothing wrong with what he was attempting. Everyone should have sex against a pole—assuming there happened to be a pole in their apartment—and his way of attempting that should work just fine.

Megan peeked back over her shoulders, her long hair draping over her cheeks. "You ready to let me up now?"

He shook his head. "Not even close."

She laughed, then hung her head between her outstretched arms. They were upstairs in her bedroom, and though he'd been threatening to take her up against the pole for weeks now, he'd never done it. But he'd awoken that morning, and as she'd been getting ready to go to his dad's house for Father's Day, he'd suddenly been unable to leave her place without trying it.

"I could fall through the hole in the floor," she pointed out.

"Not if you don't move your feet and you keep your hands where I put them."

Her legs were spread wide at the edge of the fireman's hole, and her hands gripped the pole at waist height in front of her. Her rear was poked toward him, currently covered by the dress she wore, and she was bent at a ninety-degree angle at the waist.

"It looks perfect to me," he told her.

"It looks like one hard thrust and I'm going down the hole."

He slid his hands back up her thighs, and he palmed her bare cheeks under the dress. He'd helped her out of her panties before he'd gotten her positioned, as well as shedding his own clothes. "Then I'm just going to have to thrust nice and slow."

More laughter floated out of her, and his dick pulsed at the sound. He loved making her laugh. Hell, he loved most everything about her. It had been a great last four weeks, and the idea of telling his brother—his whole family—that they were dating later today still terrified him. So, he supposed that might be playing into the physical gymnastics he had going on now. But he didn't stop. He wanted her like this.

"One last change," he announced. Then he helped her to stand, but he kept her feet spread apart. "I thought I wanted to do this with your dress on, so you'd be sure to think of me all day."

She shot him a look. "You think I *won't* be thinking of you all day?"

"I hope you will." He planted a kiss on the tip of her nose. "I know I'll be thinking of you."

"So then, why isn't the way you had me good enough?"

He gripped the hem of her dress and pulled it over her head. "Because I need your gorgeous breasts swinging freely as I'm slowly thrusting behind you."

Her eyes went molten at his words, and he unsnapped her bra. Then he tossed it down the hole in front of her, so she'd be staring at it the whole time he made love to her.

"Now bend over, woman." He nudged his penis against her backside, and he fit his chest to her back. "Because I want to make love to you like this," he whispered in her ear as one hand slid around her, and he rubbed a finger against her clit. "And I want to hear you screaming my name as you come."

Pulling his hand back from her core, he gripped her hip to make sure she didn't fall, and then with his other hand, pushed her head down until she reached out and held tight to the pole. She might have been acting like she didn't want this, but she quivered in his hands. And not from fear.

"Do it, Nate," she whispered as she pushed her ass back toward him. "*Now.* I want you inside me."

He wanted to be there too.

Gripping both her hips, he spread his own legs slightly to be better positioned to meet her height, and when the wet tip of him nudged at her again, she whimpered in front of him.

"Hang on, baby," he coaxed. A bead of sweat tracked down the middle of his back.

He had to release her long enough to get himself positioned at her entrance, and when he did that, he felt her clench at the head of his dick. His heart thundered.

"Hang on," he gritted out. "Fuck, you're hot like this."

And then he took her hips back in his hands, and he slowly slid home.

"Oh shit," she whispered. She didn't attempt to move, leaving him to do all the work, and as he got a good rhythm going, he decided that the next time they did this, he'd need to put a mirror on the other side of them so they both could watch.

"Meg?" He thrust again, long and slow, and groaned every time he pulled out and her juices glistened on his dick. "You okay, baby?"

She nodded, the movement quick, and he felt her push her hips back again.

"Harder?" he asked.

"Yes."

So he increased his rhythm.

He wanted to reach around and touch her again, but he was afraid to turn loose of her. So, he had another idea. "You're strong, right?"

She peeked back at him. "What?"

"Strong." He nodded as if that would make her understand. "You could do this with only one hand on the pole, right?"

He kept pumping, never letting up.

"What are you talking about?"

He nudged his chin toward her outstretched arms. "Take one of your hands," he panted. "And touch yourself with it."

The shock in her eyes said that the idea was both terrifying and hot. He nodded again and clenched his fingers harder into her hips.

"I've got you," he promised her. "And there's no way I'll let you go. But, sweetheart, I'm going to have an orgasm soon, and I want you there with me."

She looked back at her outstretched arms, where both hands were clenched tightly around the pole, and he saw the minute she decided to do it. The line of her back stiffened slightly, and she nodded her head. "I'm strong enough for that," she declared.

Then one hand let go of the pole, and he almost lost control of himself at that very second.

He managed to hang on, though, and as her fingers began to work herself and soft moans slipped from her lips, his erection surged.

"Hurry, baby." He kept going, unable to stop if he'd had to.

"I'm close."

He could see the side of her breast jiggling with each thrust, and her head had dropped as if she no longer had the strength to hold it up.

Her inner muscles clenched, and she angled herself farther back, then a low sound started coming from somewhere inside her.

"Nate," she begged, and he kept pumping.

"Ready?"

Her head jerked again, and he took that for a nod. "Now," she said, the word coming out soft. But the next words were spoken louder. "Now, Nate. *Now!*"

He thrust hard, his hands pulling her back at the same time he pounded her forward, and within seconds, both of them were roaring so loudly the room seemed too small to hold their shouts. But soon, they each quieted, each breathing harder than a simple round of sex should leave two people, and he gently brought her to her feet.

He wrapped both arms around her from behind, baby-stepping her away from the hole, and held her tight. "That was amazing." He kissed her neck before leaving a trail of kisses up her cheek. "That was fucking unreal."

A giggle slipped out of her, and she rested her head back against his chest. "It was. And I think I might want to do it again sometime."

"Yeah?" He nipped at her ear. "Picture doing it with a mirror on the other side of you."

"*Mmmm.*"

The slam of a door sounded from outside before he could

convince her that he could hunt up a giant mirror right now, and both of them went still. "Was that here?" he asked.

"It sounded like it. But I don't know who it could be." She grabbed her dress and tiptoed over to the window to peek out . . . and then she whirled back to him, her eyes wide. "It's my *dad*."

She quickly dragged the dress over her head.

"My dad is here, Nate." She searched around for her panties. "*Why?*"

Why now? he wanted to ask. But he held his question. He'd never met the man, but he already didn't care for him. What dad didn't have time for his youngest daughter? What dad cancelled on her, then didn't even get in touch with her again for another seven weeks?

"What are you going to do?" he asked, and she looked at him in shock.

"I'm going to go answer the door."

"Okay." He nodded as she stepped into her panties, and at the same time her dad pounded on the door below. "But what about me?" he asked. "*Us? This?*" He motioned between them and then to his nakedness, and she seemed to get the point.

"Put your clothes on, and I'll introduce you." She gave him a quick kiss. "I guess it's a day for telling our parents, huh? I love you."

She was gone then, sliding down the pole, and he was left standing there—naked . . . *confused*—watching her pick her bra up off the living room floor.

She loved him?

Chapter Twenty

❧❀❧

M egan straightened, bra in hand, and looked around for some place to hide it. So much excitement raced through her that her hands were shaking.

And then she realized what she'd just said.

She looked up.

There was no sign of Nate above her, though. All she could make out was the ceiling of her bedroom. But she could hear him up there. Water ran in the bathroom. Footsteps sounded on the floor.

She loved him?

When had that happened?

Or was she just so excited about her dad being there that that's what had come out?

Pounding came from the door again. "Megan? Are you in there? It's your father."

She loved Nate.

She blinked as the words settled into her heart . . . then she smiled as the feeling spread throughout her limbs. She did. She loved him.

Of course she loved him! He was all the things she'd been looking for in a man. He was sweet and gentle. Kind. Hot. Fun.

Smart and talented. *Sensual.* And he had a good heart. But most of all, he was her person. He was the passion and the joy she'd been searching for. And he made her happy.

She smiled wider. She was in love with Nate Wilde. And she'd just told him!

The doorknob rattled ten feet in front of her, and she jumped.

"Crap." She'd forgotten her father was there. "Coming," she shouted.

Grabbing the bag that she often used as a purse off the floor in front of the couch, she shoved the bra inside and rezipped the pack, then for the first time realized that she was about to open the door to her father while not wearing a bra. And likely smelling of sex.

She sniffed.

Then she shook her head and moved to the door. No time to worry about that now.

But *then* she remembered where her hand had been just a few minutes before, and she stared at the guilty appendage. *"Oh . . . crap."*

"Meg?" her dad said from the other side of the door? "Is everything okay?"

"Everything is . . ." She let the words trail off as she looked longingly toward the kitchen, but when the doorknob rattled yet again—with pounding at the same time—she closed her hand around the knob and opened the door.

"Dad." This time she had to force a smile. "It's so great to see you."

Her father stood on the other side of the threshold, sky-blue golf shirt perfectly tucked into khaki pants and hair precisely combed, looking more than a little concerned. "Are you okay?" He looked past her as if knowing someone was there.

She peeked as well, wondering if Nate had already made it downstairs, but the room remained empty. "Of course I'm okay. Please." She took a step back and motioned him inside. "Come in. Just give me one minute. I was doing something in the kitchen."

Hurrying to the kitchen, she turned on the water and noisily rummaged through her utensil drawer before her dad could make it in far enough to see that she hadn't actually been doing anything.

By the time he'd stepped several feet into the room, she had both hands under the water, with her right one doused with a liberal amount of liquid soap. "Just make yourself at home," she said a little too loudly. "And tell me what you're doing here."

Finally, her worry over what she must look—*and smell*—like subsided enough that her earlier enthusiasm for seeing her dad returned.

She dried her hands on a dish towel. "What a great surprise."

"Yeah?" Her dad finally smiled. "I was hoping you'd say that."

He was a good-looking man, and she'd always been proud to know that she held many of his features. "What are you doing here, Dad?" She crossed back over to him, and this time she pulled him in for a hug. "And why didn't you call and tell me you were coming?"

"I did call." He motioned back toward the door. "Several times, in fact. Then I finally ran across the store you said you've been helping with, and some lady passing by with her dog caught me peeking in the windows."

"You were peeking in the windows?" She laughed lightly. "We're closed today, but I can take you back up there if you want to see it."

"No. I was just looking for you. I didn't have your address."

"Oh." A little of her enthusiasm waned. He *hadn't* been checking out the store. Of course he hadn't. He had no idea how important it was to her. "Well, how did you find me, then?"

"A lady with the dog came by, and she knew you. And she knows Jaden. So, she called him and asked where you live."

"Some lady on the street just handed out Megan's address to a stranger?" The question came from Nate, who'd just descended the stairs. He was dressed in the jeans and pullover he'd had on before they'd started their sexual gymnastics, and his hair was pushed back from his face, slightly damp, as if he'd run wet hands through it while trying to get the strands to lie down.

Her dad looked back at her. "Who is this?" he asked.

"Who handed out her address?" Nate replied.

"*Meg?*"

This was not how she'd ever foreseen introducing Nate to her dad. Or to anyone else!

She slipped her arm through her dad's and turned him toward Nate. "Dad. I want you to meet someone."

"No." Nate stopped her. "I want to know who handed out your address to a stranger."

Her dad sighed. "She made me show her my driver's license to prove who I am. I explained that I couldn't get Megan on her phone, and she said her name was Janette. That she worked with Jaden."

Megan nodded. "That's Janette Wangler." She looked over to Nate. "That's who he works with."

"I know who Dr. Wangler is." The scowl had yet to leave his face. "I'm just trying to decide if this is okay or not. He could have been anybody with the same last name."

She laughed at that. "Look at us, Nate." She waved her hand between herself and her father. They both had the same dark hair and same facial features. Their eye color didn't match, but that barely made a difference. She looked just like her dad. "Janette stops in the store all the time. She knows me, and she'd have recognized the similarity without any trouble."

His jaw finally loosened. "I suppose so."

"I *know* so." She held her other hand out toward him. "Now come over here. I want to introduce you to my dad."

At her words, Nate's demeanor changed from protectant to man about to meet his girlfriend's father for the first time, and he pasted a polite smile on his face. He walked over to them and held out a hand. "It's nice to meet you, sir. I'm Nate Wilde."

"Wilde?" Her dad simply stared at him. "As in, Jaden Wilde?"

"Shake his hand, Dad," she gritted out. "You're being rude."

"I'm being your *dad*."

Nate dropped his hand and shoved them both in his front pockets. His brows went up. "I'm one of Jaden's brothers, sir. Yes. Two years older than him."

"He's one of the twins," she offered, not that she expected her dad to remember the details of Nate's family. She'd spoken of them only once, the first time he and Jaden had met.

Her dad didn't say anything else. He just checked Nate out, and Megan could see the judgment without him uttering a single word.

"Nate and I are dating. We have been for a while." She released her dad's arm and moved to Nate's side, then she forced another smile to her face. "I'm glad he was here when you arrived so you two could get a chance to meet."

"I'm glad, too," Nate added, and as they stood there before her dad, he dropped a hand to his side and took hers. She glanced at him and saw support shining back, and the look made her remember what she'd said upstairs. What did he think about it?

Did he love her, too?

If he didn't, did he think he ever could?

Then she remembered her dad again. She turned back to him. "So, to what do I owe this pleasure, Dad? You didn't say before. And I thought you were out of the country."

"I was out of the country," her dad finally spoke. He shifted his eyes from Nate to her. "I was needed back in Seattle for a week, so I decided to catch a flight through here and talk to you about another company I can get you an interview at. They've filled the position in Chicago."

Her heart sank. He was just here to try to get her to leave Birch Bay?

"I also thought I might take you out for a late lunch." He looked at his watch, and Megan flicked a glance to the clock in the kitchen. It was two o'clock, and Max's party would be starting at three. "I have a flight back out at seven, so I don't have a lot of time."

"You leave in only five hours, and the airport is an hour from here? That barely leaves time for lunch."

"I told you. I have to be in Seattle."

She almost told him that he shouldn't have bothered coming at all if that's all the time he could afford. She didn't, though, because saying that might make it the *last* time he ever came to visit. And that might be worse than only having a couple of hours.

"So, can I take you to lunch?"

The problem with that finally hit her. She could either go with her dad to lunch, or she could go with Nate to tell his family they were seeing each other. That wasn't a decision she wanted to make.

"It's okay," Nate said softly, as if he understood. He squeezed her hand again. "You go to lunch. I'll go to my dad's."

"But we're going to—"

"And we still will." He nodded, but his eyes had gone unreadable again. Like they'd been before she'd really started getting to know him. "You can come out later, if you want to. We'll be there all afternoon."

"Yeah?" The last thing she wanted him to do was tell his family about them alone. But she also couldn't exactly tell her dad to come back tomorrow.

"Yeah." His tone went soft, and he pressed a kiss to the side of her head. "You have a good day with your dad, and I'll see you later." His voice lowered to a whisper then. "But I do need to borrow your car key so I can go pick up my truck."

Oh, geez. She hadn't even thought of that. His truck was parked at Brooke's. "Sure." She didn't look at either of them as she rummaged through her bag and came up with her keys. "Just don't mess up my mess in there," she teased him, aware that he found it hilarious that for a woman who kept lists and could be so methodical about some things, her organizational system for the stuff inside her car was nil.

"I'll be sure and do that," he said drolly. He kissed the side of her head again, nodded to her dad, and said, "It was nice meeting you, Mr. Manning," then he was gone. And she was left facing her dad alone.

"Wilde?" he repeated, and the judgmental tone suddenly made her snap.

"Yes," she bit out. "Wilde. *Nate* Wilde. And I love him, Dad. And you were rude and a jerk to him."

"I wasn't anything to him."

"And that was rude," she tossed back. She slung an arm out toward the picture window in the living room as her little red car drove off on the other side of it, and her voice took on even more heat. "You could have shown some decency and been polite to the man that I'm dating."

"And you could quit acting like your mother and chasing men all over the country."

MEGAN WAS STILL FUMING. After her father had accused her of chasing men all over the country, she'd calmly explained that she hadn't *chased* Jaden anywhere. They'd made a decision as a couple to move somewhere together, and they'd done that only after she'd first visited the town and had fallen in love with it. They'd never even discussed it before that. And then she'd *stayed* because she'd fallen in love with the town even more. With the people. But the man still wasn't getting it. He was still trying to sell her on the new position he was certain he could get for her.

They'd left her place shortly after her explanation and had headed for the café in town, and as she'd sat while her father had eaten—while he was *still* eating—she'd tried to work up the courage to tell him that she'd decided to move out of that field completely.

He wouldn't let her get in two words, though. He just kept talking about how much she could accomplish if only she'd situate herself within the right company.

"Dad."

He finally looked up from his soup. "What?"

"I quit my programming job."

"You what?" He put down his spoon. "That's fine, I suppose. You'd have to eventually anyway."

"No. I quit it three months ago. I don't want to be in that field anymore." She'd thought that maybe the direct approach would be best, but if she were to guess from the look on his face, he still didn't get it.

"I don't understand," he said. "If you don't have a job, then why didn't you send me your resume for that AI position in Chicago?"

When he started to scoop up more soup, she reached over and placed her hand over his, and his gaze met hers.

"I do not want to be in the computer field. No science field. Not technology of any sort."

"But you're good at it. I've talked to your professors."

At that, she sat back. "You talked to what professors?"

"From college. And grad school. You're good. You had several job offers from your first round of resumes. Your rate of success was unheard of."

She'd had no idea he'd ever talked to anyone she'd taken a class from. Nor that he'd paid attention to the email where she'd listed the offers she'd once gotten. He'd barely replied with a simple "congrats."

"I am good," she agreed. "But it's not what I want to do with my life."

"And what do you want to do?" He seemed to think about his own question for a moment, then his brow wrinkled. "You want to do retail? Is that why you moved here?"

"I moved here because I loved the town," she explained again. "Because it was the first place in a long time that felt like home." And that felt like a place she wanted to *make* a home.

"But you had a home."

"Really?" she asked. "Where?"

He went quiet for a moment, his brow remaining ridged. Then he said, *"Seattle."*

She shook her head. "Not Seattle. I lived in Seattle because that's where I was going to school. And do you want to know *why* I went to school in Seattle?"

"I would assume because you liked what the school had to offer."

She shook her head again. "The school was fine. Their offerings were fine. But I could have liked many schools. I chose Seattle because that's where you were. Because I'd hoped to get to see you more often. I'd hoped you'd want to see *me."*

"Of course I wanted to see you."

"When?"

Again, he went quiet, and she just sat there, refusing to fill the void. She wanted an answer to her question. When, exactly, had he wanted to see her?

"When, Dad?"

"I . . ." He seemed to be thinking back. Realizing that he'd rarely put her first. And not at all in a very long time.

"You didn't. And I still don't understand why. I've tried my best to make you happy, but nothing ever changed."

"But I've always been happy with you."

She didn't have a response for that. She could say that actions speak louder than words, but she suspected he knew it. He just hadn't fully accepted it yet.

"I've tried my best," she said again. "And I've never felt like I succeeded. So, I'm finished trying." She thought about what Brooke had said to her a couple of weeks before. About what her friend's words had implied. She was hanging in limbo, reaching out, trying anything and everything that interested her. But she still wasn't fully happy. She still hadn't found her thing. "I'm not helping at The Cherry Basket, Dad. I'm running it. And I *enjoy* doing that. But no, retail isn't what I want to do with my life, either. The thing is, I don't know what I want to do. Because I was always so busy trying to win your approval."

When he remained silent, she went on. "So, I'm going to work on winning my own approval now. I'm going to find my own path. Figure out what makes me happy. And when I do, I'd love to have your support no matter what it is."

When he opened his mouth to speak, she held up her hand.

"And by having your support, that means that I don't have to explain why I chose what I did. That if I want to do something drastic like start over in school, then you'll merely say 'go get 'em' and not 'why don't you use the education you already have.' And having your support also means that I never again have to beg to see you. Because I won't, Dad. I'll let you know where I am, and if you'll do the same, then I'll make sure to visit you on occasion, too. But I won't be made to feel like I'm not enough anymore. Because I am."

It took a couple seconds of silence, but she could finally see that she was getting through to him. She didn't know if her siblings saw him on any regular basis, nor if they wanted to. And she didn't care what any of their relationships might be. But she *needed* a relationship with her father. She either needed one or she needed him to quit pretending and get out of her life for good. And at this point, she'd take either.

"I was lonely," he said, and sadness filled his eyes. "After your mother and I divorced. I was lonely, and I was hurt. So, I traveled more. I pushed myself more. But my doing that only hurt you. It only made you as lonely as me. And I think I've avoided you for that reason. Because I didn't want to see how I hurt my girl."

Tears sat in Megan's eyes.

"And for that, I'll regret my actions for as long as I live," he added. "I'll regret not only causing you pain, but also not being there for you when you needed me. For not letting you know that *I* needed *you*, too."

His last sentence had her blinking, and that had the wetness spilling over onto her cheeks.

"Don't cry," he whispered. "Not for me." He shook his head. "Never for me. But I promise you that I have missed you. That I've needed you, too. I just didn't know how to fix it."

They left the café shortly after that and climbed back into his rental, and they didn't talk much as she directed him to Brooke's house. But when she opened the passenger door to go to her car, her dad stopped her.

"Can I give you a hug, Meg?"

She looked across the seat. "You can always give me a hug, Dad."

He nodded. "Then that's what I want to do."

He got out of the car before she could lean toward him and waited for her in front of the hood, and when she reached him, his arms held her tighter than she could ever remember them holding her. Only . . . that wasn't true.

They'd also held her that tight the day he'd left their home for good. When she'd been ten and had begged him to take her with him. He'd hurt along with her, and she'd never known.

"I love you, Dad," she whispered into his chest.

"And I love you, Megan. So much more than I deserve to."

When the hug ended, he took her hands in his. "Tell me about Nate," he said. "You really love him?"

She laughed at his question. That's the last thing she'd expected to hear.

Then she nodded. "I do really love him, Dad. More than I even knew was possible. His family doesn't know we're dating yet, though. We'd planned to tell them together today."

His brow lifted at that. "Then I think you'd better get out there." He squeezed her fingers in his. "And good luck, Meggie. I hope it goes well. Will you call me later and let me know how it went?"

She couldn't remember him asking before for her to call and catch him up on something. "I'd love to."

"Thank you." He cupped her cheek in his hand. "I'll do better, Meggie. I'll come see you more often, and I'll stay longer when I do."

She smiled against the touch of his palm. "That would be nice. And I'll do better, too."

"No. You're perfect as you are. You always have been. But *I'll* do better." He nodded. "And someday, maybe I'll even make up for some of my past absence a little. I don't expect my sins to be forgiven easily or quickly, but I'll work hard to get there all the same."

He pulled her back in for another hug then, and that time she held on as tightly as him.

"Happy Father's Day, Dad. I love you."

Chapter Twenty-One

Nate sat by the fireplace on a straight-backed chair that had been pulled from the kitchen, his family the only people remaining from the party, and couldn't help but worry about Megan. Her dad would have needed to leave a short while ago in order to get back to the airport to catch his flight, yet Nate still hadn't heard anything from her. And that made him wonder if things with her father had gone even worse than he'd feared.

He'd hated to leave her on her own earlier, but at the same time, he'd also felt the two of them needed *their* time alone— what little time the man had been willing to give, anyway. But now, with several hours of silence ticking between them, he was regretting his decision. He should have stayed. Stood by her.

He should have made sure the man made her feel as special as she was.

He should go to her now in case she was so upset she hadn't felt like coming on over to the house.

Decision made, he stood at the precise moment a knock sounded from the front door, and Gloria jerked around at the sound.

"Well, who could that be?" She headed up the hallway, and Nate lowered back to the chair. Surely it would be Megan.

The party had been low-key, with only a handful of guests outside of the immediate family, but their dad had worn himself out. He'd excused himself thirty minutes earlier, needing a few minutes to recharge, while the rest of them were waiting. Gabe had mentioned that he and Erica had a special Father's Day present they'd like everyone to stick around for, then Nick and Harper had said something similar. It made Nate wonder if he'd missed out on a family memo. He had no idea what kind of special gift two of his brothers might have picked up.

"Megan," Gloria said from down the hall. "I'm so glad you could make it."

"I'm sorry I'm late. I wanted to be here earlier, but I—"

"No worries," Gloria cut her off, then the two of them appeared in the hallway. "Let me get you a chair," Gloria offered and disappeared back down the way she'd come, while Nate couldn't take his eyes off Megan.

She'd said she loved him earlier.

He'd never heard those words from anyone before.

"Here you go, dear." Gloria reappeared, pushing a rolling desk chair, and Gabe hopped to his feet.

"Here. Let me do that for you."

Gloria waved him off. "I've got it. You sit back down. You boys did all the grilling for everyone today, so you take a rest. I'm perfectly capable of getting a chair." She then shouldered Gabe out of the way when he continued to try to take the chair from her and kept on her mission. Her mission being to park the seat to Nate's immediate left. "The perfect spot," she hummed out. Then she patted Meg's shoulder.

He caught the older woman's gaze as she took a step back and gave her a thankful smile. She *did* know what was going on. He'd known it. And he appreciated the help.

"Did I hear Meg come in?" His dad's voice carried from the renovated bedroom, and once again Gabe jumped to his feet. Cord followed.

"Sit down, boys," their dad said as he made his way up the hall. "I'm broken, but I'm not out."

They all made a path for him to get back to his recliner. He'd come out on crutches instead of using his chair. Then the voices in the room picked back up.

As everyone else talked, Nate cast a glance toward Megan.

Everything okay? he tried to ask with a look.

She replied with a small smile and a quick nod.

Good. I missed you.

He didn't know if she understood his last message, but he had missed her today. Terribly. It didn't feel right to be in the middle of everyone else like this any longer without her.

He wanted to reach over and take her hand, but he held off. Now that she was here, they'd tell his family about their relationship. Then soon, they could head back to her place, and they could talk about what she'd said earlier today.

She loved him.

Had she really meant that?

He was almost too afraid to hope.

"So, Erica and I have an announcement to make," Gabe said, and the noise in the room ceased. He looked over and took his wife's hand, and Nate suddenly understood what the announcement would be. "We were saving this to share today for Father's Day, Dad, so I hope it makes you happy. We're pregnant," Gabe added. "Due sometime around the third week of December."

"I'm going to be a big sister!" Jenna announced. Her grin showed one missing tooth and one that was halfway in and slightly crooked. "I held the secret all day." She was so proud of herself, as was everyone else in the room.

Haley jabbed the little girl in the side, and both of them snickered as if they were aware that Jenna *hadn't* held that secret from everyone all day, and congratulations for the baby to come went around the room. It was also stated—to his father's disappointment—that the sex of the baby wasn't yet known. Then Nick cleared his throat to get everyone's attention once again.

He held up a hand. "Us, too," he confirmed, and Gloria gasped.

"Seriously?" Erica asked at the same time that Gloria said, "Two babies?"

Harper smiled, her face practically beaming. "Seriously. And actually, it'll be three babies. I seem to be pregnant with twins."

More gasping echoed around the room, and Nate watched as Jenna's and Haley's mouths dropped open, and their eyes went wide. He was getting a kick out of those two, and for the first time in his life, he wondered what a kid of his own would be like. And what they'd look like.

He glanced over at Megan at the same time she looked at him, and he wanted to know what she was thinking.

"And when are *you* due?" Nate's father asked.

Nick and Harper both smiled and spoke at the same time. "The third week of December."

This time it was his father and Gloria whose eyes went round. Then everyone howled with laughter.

"And before you ask," Nick tacked on once the room was again under control, "no. We don't know the sex yet either. And we were actually thinking about *not* finding out. Kind of wanting it to be a big surprise for everyone at Christmastime."

"Meaning, that if you *are* giving me a grandson, you want to make me wait to find out?"

Harper grinned, and Nick nodded. "Exactly, Dad. We figured that since we're giving you two chances for a grandson, then it only seems fitting to make you wait to find out."

"I really like that idea," Erica announced. She looked over at Gabe. "I think we should do the same thing. It'll be a race to not only see who delivers first, but also when—or *if*—a boy comes out."

"Sounds like a plan to me," Gabe added. Their dad groaned.

"Then, I guess we can do the same as well," Dani said, and everyone's gazes swiveled to her. They all looked questioningly at her, though, as if not completely clueing in to what she'd just said. Seven-month-old Mia sat, babbling happily, on her lap. "Yeah." Dani nodded. "Ben and I are pregnant again. It wasn't exactly planned, but it looks like Haley and Mia are going to have a baby brother or sister of their own soon. And it looks like *soon* will be . . . *sometime around the third week of December.*"

Instead of more laughter, everyone simply looked dumbfounded. Then they all looked expectantly at Arsula.

She held up both hands. "*Not me!* We're not even married yet. *Nor* are we planning a wedding yet. We've got plenty of time."

"Yeah," Jaden agreed. "We'll just play with their kids for now."

"Four babies," Nate's dad murmured, and Nate could see the utter shock on his face.

"And all at the same time," Gloria added.

"Well, I just want to know what happened here about three months ago," Cord said. "Because I want to make damned certain that if it ever happens again, I'm not anywhere near this place."

The mood in the room suddenly sobered. "The arctic blast," their dad said. "It came through in late March."

All the expectant parents nodded, and Nate felt Megan's knee bump against his then stay there. Out of something that had brought his family so much grief and worry, beauty was growing.

"Then God bless the arctic blast," Gloria declared.

"God bless the arctic blast," Jenna and Haley echoed.

"Maybe all the babies will wait and come a week late," his dad suggested, and when the three expectant mothers all gawked at him, he nodded toward Cord. "That way Cord could be home for Christmas, and he could deliver them for you."

Cord's brows went skyward. "I don't make a habit of delivering babies in my practice, Dad. Nor do I especially *want* to deliver them for my sisters-in-law"—he shot Dani a droll look—"*nor* my sister." He shuddered, and the rest of them laughed, and once again the room turned lighthearted and fun. It was proving to be a really good day.

So, now it was Nate's turn, he supposed. And his mouth went dry.

Holding up a finger in order to gain attention, he silently prayed that this would be seen as a good thing. And when no one noticed his attempt, he finally blurted out, "I have an announcement of my own to make, too."

Immediate silence followed, along with surprised looks, and his hand tingled to reach out and take Megan's.

"Actually," he restarted. "*Megan* and I have—"

"You're dating her," Jaden guessed before Nate could get it out. The words came out flat. "And what? Is *she* pregnant, too?"

"What?" Nate said. "*No.* She's not pregnant." At least, he didn't think so. He looked at Megan.

"But you are dating her?" Nick asked. "You and Megan?"

Nate turned back to the room, then he reached for Meg's hand. "I *am* dating her. *We're* dating each other."

"Why?" Jaden asked.

Nate jolted. "What do you mean why? Why are you dating Arsula? Why does anyone date anybody?" What kind of question was that?

"I know why *I* date someone," Jaden replied. "And I know that I'm in love with Arsula. That we intend to continue growing our relationship and are engaged to be married. So, I'm simply asking, *why* you two are dating?"

Nate stared in disbelief. "Are you asking if I intend to marry her?" They'd just started dating a month ago.

"I'm asking what your intentions are."

"Why? Do you think you're her father or something?"

Gabe held up a hand. "Guys—"

"I think I'm her *friend*," Jaden answered with vehemence. He looked at Megan then, studied her for a moment before coming back to Nate. And Nate could now see that he'd put on his counselor face. "But I'm also *your* brother."

"Well, *my* brother can say congrats and move the hell on."

Megan scooted to the edge of her chair. "What are you getting at, Jay?"

Nate could hear her anger building.

Jaden paused for a moment before answering her and seemed to be considering his words. When he restarted, he rephrased his question. "All I'm asking is if this is a real, want-it-to-go-somewhere relationship? Is it *legit?*"

"Of course it's legit," she snapped. "What? Do you think you can find someone else super quick, but I can't?"

Nate looked over at her, surprised. Clearly it had bothered her, at least a little, that Jaden and Arsula had gotten engaged so quickly. Then Jaden said, "This isn't actually about *you*, Meg." He looked apologetic. "Other than I want to make sure you don't get hurt. And I'm sorry it currently feels that way."

"I don't need you to be—"

"What *is* it about, then?" Nate's question came out cold. Because he was finished with this conversation. And he didn't like that it was upsetting Megan.

Jaden stared at him, the look on his face reminding Nate of the handful of times Jaden had brought up a certain subject, and Nate suddenly understood what Jaden's answer would be before he said it. "It's about your past. Have you dealt with it yet?"

"I don't have anything to deal with, Jay." His lips barely moved as he spoke.

"And I'm saying that I think you do."

"What past?" Gabe seemed to understand that Jaden felt he had something real to say. At the same time as Gabe spoke, Nick quietly motioned toward Harper.

"*Oh.*" She jumped to her feet. "Here." She reached both hands toward Jenna and Haley. "Come with me, girls. Let's go outside for a while, okay?"

"Why?" Jenna asked, but she rose and followed Haley and Harper anyway.

"The grown-ups need to talk," Harper said in a rush as she

herded the girls toward the back door. Clearly, Nick had filled his wife in on Nate's past.

Once the door closed behind the trio, Gabe turned back, and his expression had grown cautious. In fact, everyone in the room now wore expressions of caution. They all remained seated, unmoving, and all gazes bounced from Jaden to Nate.

"All right." Gabe addressed Jaden first. "What's going on? What past are you talking about?"

"Don't go there, Jay."

Jaden looked at him. "I *have* to go there. You need to deal with this. It won't ever be fair to Meg if you don't."

"I don't need to deal with *anything*. I'm perfectly fine. *We're* perfectly fine."

"What's he talking about, Nate?" Megan's voice had lost its heat, and her hand now felt small inside of his. "What do you need to deal with?"

Nate didn't answer. He couldn't believe his brother was going to say it out loud. That he would bring it up here. Now.

Jaden shifted his gaze to Meg. Then to Gabe. "Michelle."

Gabe's whole body tensed. "What *about* Michelle?"

Michelle was Gabe's ex-wife and Jenna's mother and had been fully out of the picture only since last year. She was also an exact replica of their mother. Narcissistic to her core.

Jaden looked almost regretful. Not enough to keep his mouth shut, apparently. But slightly mollified. He then opened his mouth and announced Nate's worst act. "He slept with her."

Gasps sounded in the room.

"He . . . *what?*" Gabe looked at Nate with shock.

"*And* he fell in love with her," Jaden added, and Nate could have gladly killed his baby brother.

He didn't say a word in defense of the accusation, though. Because what was there to say, anyway?

He also noticed that Megan let go of his hand. He didn't look over at her. He didn't want to see what she now thought about him. She'd loved him that morning.

"Is that true?" Gabe still hadn't moved. "Did you sleep with her?" He didn't look angry so much as disbelieving. And good Lord, Nate wanted to say no. He wanted to do that more than he'd ever wanted anything. He wanted to ignore the question and rewind the clock. And he wanted a complete do-over.

Do-overs didn't come with life, though. Only a person's own fuck-ups and Karma breathing down their neck.

So, Nate answered the question. It was time to pay the price. "Yes."

Gabe jerked as if he'd been hit. "When?"

"On my eighteenth birthday."

The answer made the entire room somehow go even quieter. They all now knew. They got it.

"That's why you left," his dad said.

Nate nodded, but he didn't take his eyes off Gabe. "I couldn't stick around after that, could I? After I'd slept with my brother's wife? While under the same roof?"

The words had Gabe's jaw tensing. "It happened in this house?"

"In my bedroom, yes. But only that one time."

Gabe tilted his head back then, as if visually measuring the distance down the upper hallway from the master suite—where he and Michelle had slept at the time—to the bedroom Nate had shared with Nick.

"It's not as bad as it sounds," Nick interrupted. "At least not from Nate's perspective."

"Don't," Nate told him. "Don't take up for me. I did it. I participated. And it can't be undone."

Gabe was now staring at Nick. Then he looked at Jaden again. "And you *both* knew about this?" Anger finally made an appearance, fighting with the shock already marring their oldest brother's face. He took in the rest of them. "Did the rest of you know, too? Have we all just been lying to each other about everything for years?"

"*No.*" Dani jumped up, baby in her arms. "We didn't all know. And we don't all lie to each other."

Which wasn't exactly the truth. Or it hadn't always been. Because back before Dani had quit blocking memories out of how terribly their mother had treated them, the rest of the family had intentionally kept that knowledge from her. For *years.*

"Plus," Dani added, "it's not exactly a lie to withhold something that could hurt someone so terribly. I'm sure Nick and Jaden were just trying to protect you."

"Yet you didn't like it when we were all trying to protect you from the memory of our mother's abuse," Gabe shot back, and Dani went still. He had her there.

Instead of saying anything else, she sat back down. And she snuggled her baby close.

"What happened?" Gabe turned back to Nate. His hands rested on his thighs, his palms intentionally flat, and his fingers spread wide. "You slept with my wife." Revulsion painted his features. "Why would you do that, Nate? And why would you tell *anybody* about it after the fact? The only person you should have ever told was *me.* And funny, this is the first time that I'm hearing about it."

"He didn't actually tell us," Nick spoke up before Nate could.

"Shut up," Nate replied.

"You *need* to talk about it," Jaden urged from the other side of the room. "Holding this in for so long isn't healthy. It'll never allow you to have a viable relationship with anyone."

Nate finally snapped, and he surged to his feet. "I don't fucking want to talk about it, okay? It was nine years ago. It's not part of my life now. And Gabe isn't married to her anymore, so *thankfully,* it's not part of his life, either. And, yes . . ." He faced Gabe again, his breathing now coming hard. "I slept with your wife. I'm an ass. I slept with her *while* you were married. *While* you were in bed down the hall from us. And I will *forever* hate myself for that. But talking about it won't help because it can't be undone. And though Lord knows I'm sorry, I also know that I can never apologize for it enough. I can't take it away, and I can't make up for it. Nor can I make up for the fact that I didn't just screw you over *that* night. I've let down all of you over and over again. My whole damned life. Because that's what I do. That's why Dad lost a fucking leg, for Christ's sake! That's why I should never—*ever*—stay in this town again!"

He stormed out of the room, the back door slamming behind him so hard that it shook the house, and five seconds later, his truck roared to life and sped down the driveway.

Megan looked from face to face, trying to digest everything she'd just heard. Everything those words had implied. All the while, telling herself that Nate just needed time to calm down. That he *would* be back.

But something about the finality of his words stripped her bare. And she found herself fearing the worst.

"What did he mean?" Max's voice broke into the silence. His words shook. "Why does Nate think my injury was his fault?"

Chapter Twenty-Two

꧁❀꧂

Megan had had to explain Nate's feelings of guilt to his entire family. They'd agreed with her, of course, that Max's accident had not been Nate's fault. She'd tried to express that very sentiment to Nate more than once since they'd started dating, but he'd always refused to budge. And seeing as how he'd stormed out of his family home a week before with those words hovering in his wake, his opinion clearly hadn't changed.

She stepped back from the wall where she'd just hung a piece of artwork in Cabin 7 and studied the room as a whole. The work on the cabins had been finished the prior Thursday, and after a crew had come in to do a deep clean the next day, Megan, Brooke, all of Nate's family, Dre, and the remaining guys who'd wanted to stay through the weekend had spent the last two days loading everything in.

It had been a long, hard couple of days. But it had been completely worth it.

"You're good at this, Meg."

Megan turned to Brooke, who'd just stepped into the cabin. "Thanks. Doing this was even more fun than I thought it would be."

"Yeah?" Brooke walked around the space, admiring the more

masculine plaids Megan had used in this cabin. It had been harder than Megan would have guessed to add all the finishing touches without Nate being there. To do anything without Nate, really. But as far as she was concerned, he was a grown man, and if what he wanted to do was storm out of his house and leave town without so much as a thought for her, then he could lie in the bed he'd made.

To be fair, Dre *did* know where he was. Nate had apparently texted the other man sometime Sunday night, asking him to see that the cabins got finished. Dre had offered to tell her where Nate could be found, but she'd declined the information. She didn't plan on chasing any man around the country. Not even Nate.

"I think you should do more interior design work," Brooke announced as she came back from exploring the single bedroom. "Get yourself yet another side gig going."

Megan laughed halfheartedly. "I could probably use another gig or two." It wasn't like she wouldn't have the time when she was going home alone every night.

"I'm not kidding." Brooke stopped at her side, and together they gazed upon the wrapped canvas of an expansive open Montana range that Megan had found. "You're very good. And you've never even had official training."

"I guess I've always just had an eye for things."

"I can see that. So, take a class or two, why don't you? See if you like it."

Megan looked over at her, realizing that her friend really was being serious. "What are you doing? Trying to help me find ways to spend all my empty hours?"

"No. I'm just trying to help you find *you*, babe."

Along with sharing the details of what had happened at the Wilde house the week before, Megan had also told Brooke about her dad's visit. *And* she'd provided far more details about her family than her friend had likely ever really wanted to know. They'd been good talks, though, and it had helped their friendship to grow even closer. But with all the sharing, she'd admitted that she had no real idea what she wanted to do with her life now. It was as if the whole world had suddenly been opened to her. Yet, so far, nothing looked all that appealing.

"Smile, girls."

They looked over as Dre stepped into the room, cell phone out in front of him, and smiled for the picture. He'd been taking several over the weekend as the cabins had come together. They'd be used as part of a portfolio for bidding on future jobs, she supposed. But she had no idea why he'd include one of her and Brooke.

Or one with just her, for that matter. Which Brooke had caught him taking earlier in the weekend.

"He's not going to turn around and ask you out again, is he?" Brooke spoke under her breath as Dre disappeared back outside. "Because I'd think that would feel really awkward at this point."

Megan made a face. "He's leaving town in a couple of days. He wouldn't have time to take me out even if he asked me."

"Not that you'd go, anyway."

Megan shook her head. "Not that I'd go, anyway."

The reality was, she was destroyed over Nate's leaving. Watching him walk away like that, and then sitting there listening to his family discuss what had just happened had only solidified her gut instinct. That Nate wouldn't be coming back. At least not anytime soon.

The situation Jaden had been referring to had been Michelle repeatedly playing mind games with a vulnerable seventeen-year-old, then slipping into his room on his eighteenth birthday with one thing on her mind. She'd taken advantage of him, and he'd been unable to deal with the guilt of staying after that.

Megan had been disgusted. And not just by that one story, but by everything that had been shared of Gabe's ex. And hearing those stories had made her feel even worse for Nate.

However, Nate had known what he was doing when he'd

walked out of the house that night. Then it had been three long days before she'd heard a word from him. And when she had?

It had been a single text.

I'm sorry. You deserve better.

She hadn't known if he'd been talking about his actions of that evening or about him in general. And she hadn't replied to find out. She didn't want to have a relationship by text. She didn't want to have a relationship where a man walked away without so much as a thought about her. And she wouldn't allow their next words to be via text or phone. He could either come home and deal with life like a grown-ass adult. Apologize for the way he'd walked out.

Or he could sulk his days away wherever the heck he was and be alone forever.

"Should I pick up wine and ice cream for tonight?" Brooke asked, and Megan smiled. They'd spent more than one night like that over the past week.

"How about we go out for a real meal tonight? To celebrate a job well done? My treat."

"Well, if it's your treat . . ."

They turned together and walked out of the cabin. But before she stepped off the small porch, she stood there and took in the beauty spread out before her. The water and the mountains. The peace of that very spot and of so many dotted throughout the town. This place was special. Just as she'd known it to be the first time she'd visited. And though her heart was currently crushed, she had a feeling that views like this and the community she'd befriended since moving there would pull her through.

Her phone buzzed, and she pulled it out to see that it was another text from Nate.

He'd not only texted that first time, but he'd sent two additional messages, as well. Both of which she'd also ignored. The first had been another declaration.

You probably think I'm an ass.

Again, was he an ass because he'd left town without saying a word to her or because he'd slept with Gabe's ex-wife? And either way, yes.

Well, the sleeping with Michelle thing . . . he'd been an already emotionally damaged teenager, and Michelle had actively set out to screw with him. So, the verdict was still out on exactly how big of an ass he'd been in that situation. Possibly none.

But, still.

The next text had been him finally sounding a bit more concerned for her well-being.

Would you please at least reply to me?
Let me know you're okay?

No, she would not, and she did not. He didn't get to know anything at all about her. And if he really wanted to know how she was, then he knew where she lived.

And now she had this one. And it broke her heart a little more.

Could I call you?

She stared at the message. It broke her heart because she'd *wanted* to call him. She wanted to talk to him. She missed him. She loved him. And she wanted to ask if *he* was okay. His family certainly didn't blame him for Michelle's behavior, and Max had thought the entire idea that his accident might have anything to do with Nate to be ludicrous. So, yeah. She'd love to talk to Nate. She'd love to make sure he understood that, even if nothing else came from the conversation.

But she also wasn't *ready* to talk to him. He'd hurt her. She knew that he'd been hurting that day, himself, and she could have totally understood him needing to get out of the house in that moment. She could even understand him flying out of there the way he had without thinking about her. Sort of. But she couldn't understand him not seeking her out.

She couldn't understand it taking him three days to reach out to her.

So, no. She wasn't ready to talk. And she wasn't going to be forced into it.

She slid the phone back into her pocket, then she took in the newly landscaped yard surrounding the cabin and breathed in a deep lungful of fresh air. And she turned to her friend.

"You good?" Brooke asked.

"I'm good. I *will* be good," she corrected.

"Then it sounds like you're exactly where you should be at this point."

NATE STARED AT HIS PHONE. He looked for any missed calls. Missed text messages. But he found nothing. Not from Meg. And he supposed that told him everything he needed to know. He'd tried to text her the week before. He'd asked if he could call her two days before. And he'd gotten nothing in reply. Not that her silence surprised him. And not that he'd even known what he would've said if she *had* agreed to talk to him. He'd just wanted to hear her voice. Badly enough that he'd asked.

But her silence said no. So, he'd have to be okay with that.

And it would be best, anyway. He'd stay away, and he'd let her move on.

He slid the phone into his pocket and swiped a line of sweat from his brow, then he grabbed his clipboard from the front seat of his truck and headed back to the forty-year-old home his team was currently renovating. He was in Round Rock, Texas, there to relieve his construction manager as the man supported his daughter in court, and where he'd head to next, he wasn't yet sure. Nor did he know if it would even matter. He was tired of going. Tired of not knowing *where* to go. But he didn't know how to do anything else.

As he entered through the open garage, he pulled his phone back out, unable to keep from looking at it one more time. He'd been gone from Birch Bay for over a week, and though he'd basically had no conversations with anyone, this small piece of electronics had been his lifeline. It wasn't unusual for him to go several weeks without speaking to any of his siblings when he wasn't at home. And that's what he'd expected this time. But he'd been surprised to see that they'd all reached out to him at some point over the last week.

He scrolled through the messages, pulling up the ones from Nick first.

Are you okay?

Nate had replied to that one. Yes. The question had been simple, as well as the reply. Nick had simply needed to know that he was alive. That he'd made it to wherever he'd been headed. It had come in Monday morning, then Nate hadn't gotten another text from Nick until late Friday.

Come home, man. For good. It's time to stop doing this bullshit.

He *hadn't* replied to that one, because what was he supposed to say? Would anyone actually want him there if he did go home? Especially after the way he'd left. All he did when he was around was cause problems. And it wasn't as if he contributed in any real way when he was there. Not that they couldn't replace him by either hiring out or doing something themselves. They didn't need him.

He'd also gotten a message from Cord on Wednesday.

```
That was a nice scene, bro. You about
done yet?
```

On Sunday night, Dani had said, `We're always`
`going to be here for you. You know that,`
`don't you? No one loves you any less,`
`and we never will.`

He didn't know if he believed that one. Gabe had to love him less. Gabe *should* hate him.

Jaden had even reached out.

```
I apologize for the way it went down,
but I don't apologize for it happening.
You needed to process what happened back
then. I'm sure you still need to process
it. Please call me.
```

Jaden had been trying to get him to talk about Michelle ever since Nate had threatened to tell Gabe what happened. Nate had left the house that next morning, riddled with guilt that he'd let himself fall for her, that he'd let himself have sex with her, and he'd wandered around for months. He'd started drinking during that time. In certain areas, it was easy for an eighteen-year-old to get beer. Then, about three months after he'd left home, he'd called Michelle.

I'm going to tell Gabe. What we did was wrong. He needs to know.

Of course, she'd instantly gone into a rage. She would destroy him with *all* of his siblings way before he could even get Gabe on the phone. She'd make it clear that it had been *he* who instigated things. Not her. She'd yell rape. She supposedly even had pictures of the bruises he'd put on her.

It hadn't mattered that she'd come into his room where his

brother had been sleeping. Nor that Nick had apparently been awake to hear the whole thing. She'd take Nick down with him. Say they were in on it together. That they both raped her.

The next day, Jaden had called. Michelle was saying that Nate raped her, and he'd left because she'd threatened to go to the police. Was it true?

She'd apparently only shared that lie with Jaden at that point. So, he'd kept his mouth shut from that day forward. He'd explained the truth to his then sixteen-year-old brother, making him promise to keep it to himself. He'd also made him promise to lock his bedroom door at night and to never be in a room alone with Michelle. Then he'd gone back to drinking and had given up the idea of confessing. He'd done the deed, so he would live with the guilt. And he *wouldn't* bring his family down because of it.

He scrolled through his texts some more. He hadn't replied to Jaden, Dani, nor Cord. They'd know that he was alive because Nick would have told them. He hadn't responded to his dad's message, either. His dad had left a voice mail.

What is this nonsense that you think my accident was your fault?

It wasn't nonsense, and he hadn't been about to get on a call with the man to explain it. The message had contained enough details, though, that it had been clear Megan had filled them in on his beliefs. If he hadn't been such a bitch about nobody ever needing his help around there, then he would have seen that his dad was too ill to be out on a tractor instead of him storming off in a huff.

His dad hadn't detailed it quite in that fashion, of course. Nate was ad-libbing. But he could imagine his brothers thinking the exact same thing. And he could imagine Jaden, once again, wanting to help him deal with it. To fix it. But his screwups couldn't be fixed. That's what no one seemed to understand.

He caused the fuck-ups, so he had to pay. Exactly as his mother had always—

"Boss?" a voice yelled through the house and carried into the garage.

Nate looked up from his phone, his breath catching in his throat. "Yeah?"

"We need an opinion in here. The master closet. Can you come look?"

"Sure." He stared at his phone again, as if it held answers. "Heading that way," he mumbled.

But he didn't move. His *mother*?

He was living his life based upon how his mother had treated him? The things she'd said to him?

Why? He knew better.

He knew she'd manipulated all of them. He'd watched her do it. He'd known all her tricks.

So why in the hell would he have let her words, her hatred, linger with him all this time?

"Boss?"

He shoved his phone away. "Coming."

It was another two hours before he found another minute to be alone, and when he did, he went right back to where he'd left off. His mother.

He still believed the shit his mother had fed him.

The very idea of that ticked him off because that was a load of crap!

His phone dinged, and he yanked the thing out of his pocket. It was Dre.

```
Took these for you over the weekend. You
probably don't deserve them, but I
figure I'll share because it might help
you see what kind of stupid you're
being.
```

What the hell?

He looked at the two attached pictures. Then he tapped his finger on the first one.

Megan stood off to the side of the cabins, facing the lake at the top of the cliff, and the air had whipped her hair into her face. Dre caught her with her head tipped slightly back and her eyes closed, and she looked to be standing unnaturally still. The visual bothered Nate. He knew this was a single moment captured in time, and he knew she could have easily been in motion when the picture was taken. But she looked as if she'd been standing there frozen. Like she'd been trying to breathe in enough strength simply to keep going.

The other photo was one of her and Brooke, with both of them grinning in the middle of one of the cabins. And at first glance, the shot made him smile. Megan looked happy in this one. Like he wanted her to be. He liked Brooke, and it pleased him greatly to know that Meg had someone like that in her life. But then he looked more carefully at Megan.

Bringing the phone closer, he zoomed in on her face, and then he couldn't look away from what he saw there. It was in her eyes. In the way her mouth smiled, but nothing else seemed to. She looked as if the light burning from within her had been dimmed.

She'd been standing in the middle of a project she'd been excitedly working on for weeks, yet at the same time she looked utterly broken. Was that because of him?

He swiped back to the first picture again. Then to the second.

Then his heart began to ache even more.

He'd hurt her. Far worse than a text message could fix. And all along, he'd been telling himself that he'd done her a favor by leaving.

Yes, the way he'd left had been wrong. He should have spoken with her before simply driving out of town. He probably should have gone to her house and waited for her to come home. Told her goodbye properly. And *not* waited three days to reach out to her. But he'd honestly thought him stepping out of her life would be the best thing for her. And hell, maybe it would *still* be the best thing. But he hadn't wanted her to hurt. Not like this.

He went back to his list of texts again, intending to pull up Nick's last message and ask him to check in on Meg. She may not want to talk to *him*, but he needed to know that she was okay. As his fingers hovered over Nick's name, however, he realized yet one more fact that hadn't occurred to him before. Everyone in his family had texted him in the last week . . . except Gabe.

Except the other person he'd hurt terribly last week.

And damn. He had to fix that. This was his brother, and he should have come clean and apologized to him years ago.

He switched to his contact list and tapped on his oldest brother's name. He didn't want to go another day without cleaning up his past. At least, that part of it. And though doing it over the phone may not be ideal, at least it was a start. And maybe *starting* there would make it easier to fix other mistakes.

Chapter Twenty-Three

The sun dipped below the mountains on the far side of the water, casting a glow over the lake. Boats bobbed out in the middle of it, their passengers waiting for the fireworks that would start as soon as the sun fully set, and Megan snuggled deeper into the bench, tucking the wrap she'd brought out more securely around her. The night wasn't cold, but there was a definite briskness in the air, and the weight of the extra material gave Megan a more secure feel. Like a pair of loving arms wrapped tightly around her.

There weren't any loving arms there tonight, of course. She still hadn't heard from Nate, much less seen anything from him. No more texts, no requests to call her. He'd given up.

And the knowledge of that had hurt even more than watching him walk out of the Wilde house nearly two weeks before. He was gone. She was alone. And nothing had changed.

But then . . . that wasn't actually true. *She* had changed. And those changes were for the better.

Her relationship with her dad had changed, too. She'd just gotten off the phone with him. They'd already talked more since he'd been in town than they had in the last six months, so that was definitely a step in the right direction. And according to him, he planned to come see her and stay for a long weekend in September. That was still two months away, but spending Labor Day weekend with her dad would be fun. Maybe they'd cook out on her little back patio.

She sighed and sunk farther on the bench. The bench sat at the end of a little trail that started just off her patio and meandered through the trees and down to the lake. This had become one of her favorite places over the last couple of weeks, as she'd spent a fair amount of time there. It was better than sitting in the house alone.

A bottle rocket sounded off to her left, but she couldn't see it. She could hear people in the neighborhood on the other side of the trees, though. And to her right, several small groupings of people had gathered along the lake. There wasn't a large access to the water here, but enough to bring a handful of families down. She was all alone on her little bench, though, and she'd been trying to convince herself for the last hour that having it that way was exactly how she wanted it. After all, she'd had two invites to go somewhere else tonight.

Brooke had tried to get her to go out on the lake with her family, but Megan had declined. Although she was sure that watching the fireworks from the middle of the lake would be beautiful, she just hadn't been in the mood. Brooke had been such a good friend since Nate left, and Megan hadn't wanted to risk bringing down the mood tonight.

She'd also been invited over to the Wilde house. It was the first weekend of reservations for the cabins, and unless things had changed since she'd handed the information over to the new manager earlier in the week, all ten cabins were booked for the weekend. The new business venture looked to be starting off to a great success.

Another bottle rocket sounded, and this time a couple of roman candles went up with it. She smiled as kids she couldn't see cheered. It wasn't dark enough for the official show to begin yet, but it was certainly dark enough for the kids who were anxious to see the bursts of colors and noises.

She turned her hand over to look at the face of her phone and saw that there had been no messages while she'd been sitting there. Which she'd known. She'd pretty much been holding her phone nonstop for the last few days, as if hoping for a text. Or maybe a call. And she knew that was silly. But she hadn't been ready to let Nate go yet. She'd been hurt when he'd left, then she'd gotten mad when he hadn't put out a true effort to get in touch with her. But in the back of her mind, she'd thought he'd keep trying. She'd *wanted* him to keep trying. And now, there had been nothing for six days.

Her nose burned, and in the next instant, tears slipped over her cheeks. And she didn't even try to wipe them away. She'd started crying over the last few days. At the drop of a hat. Which was yet another reason she hadn't wanted to be around anyone tonight. She didn't want anyone to see how broken she was. Especially not Nate's family.

More tears fell, and she lowered her head as if in shame. She hated the idea of sitting there crying over a man.

She hated even more that twice that week she'd typed out a text message to Dre, asking where Nate could be found. Because she was ready to go to him. She was ready to beg.

She'd deleted the texts both times before she could send them. But she was considering typing up another one tonight.

Another family showed up about twenty feet to her right, and the mother must have caught sight of Megan's tears when Megan glanced over. The woman wore a concerned expression and took a moment to send Meg a questioning look, asking if everything was okay.

Meg nodded. Then she dug out a fresh tissue from her jeans' pocket and blew her nose.

And then more tears fell.

More light filtered from the sky, leaving longer, darker shadows stretching out onto the lake, and she closed her eyes and dropped her head back to rest against the bench. Until the show started, she'd just sit there and daydream. And what she daydreamed about was that instead of sitting on her little bench, she was stretched out on a blanket on Wild Horse Island. And that fireworks were exploding in the night sky above her, raining down wide arcs of magical bright colors. And on that blanket with her was a man she loved. And he loved her, too.

And he told her that he'd never leave her again.

A boom sounded in the distance, and she opened her eyes to see the start of the show. But what she saw instead was Nate standing in front of her. And he looked as uncertain as she was miserable.

"Hi, Meg."

Her nose burned again. "Hi."

She couldn't get anything else out. Just one tiny syllable.

A burst of red, white, and blue exploded in the distance over Nate's head.

"Would it be okay if I talked to you for a minute?" he said, and she gave a little nod. The movement had been small, and everything inside of her felt deflated, but she managed to inch herself over to one side of the bench. Then she nodded toward the newly created space.

"Have a seat," she somehow managed. She then turned her gaze back out to the lake.

"Thanks." He joined her on the bench, his hard thigh pressing against hers in the cramped space, and leaned forward. As he shifted into place, Meg pulled her gaze back from the water and watched him. He rested his elbows on his knees, cupped his hands together in front of him, then he stared out at the water, same as she had. "How are you?" he said, and as if turning off one faucet and opening another full blast, her weepiness was quickly replaced with her prior anger.

"How am I?" she parroted. "That question's about as useful as 'how's the weather,' isn't it?"

Nate turned his head to look at her. She stared a hole through him.

"Should I start with an apology instead?" He asked the question hesitantly.

"Only if you want this conversation to go beyond your next words." Explosions continued in the sky behind him, but she didn't pay any attention. "It's your move, Wilde. Do you want to stay and play the game or forfeit straight out of the gate?"

She much preferred her anger to the weepy, crying mess she'd been the last few days.

Nate swallowed, then he opened his mouth again. "I'm the biggest idiot on this planet, and I never should have driven out of town the way I did. And then after I did drive out of town, I should have turned my truck around and driven right back. Right to your place. And I should have told you that day, same as you did to me, that I love you, too. That I don't know how it happened so quickly, and that three months ago, I couldn't have fathomed how someone's feelings for another could change so drastically in such a short span of time, but that I'm living proof they can. And then I should have begged your forgiveness for every mistake I've made to date plus the ones I know are to come. Because I do screw up. We both know that. But what you may not also know is that I definitely want to learn to do better."

Megan blinked. That had been a lot. And she wasn't quite sure what to do with it all yet.

So, she turned her gaze back to the sky, and she focused on the fireworks. "That's a better first attempt," she said without looking at him. "It's enough to let you stay for round two."

A soft burst of air sounded from him, sort of like a laugh-sigh, and something inside Megan softened. She closed her eyes, attempting to keep any threatening weepiness at bay, and let herself feel the sounds of the fireworks instead of see them. It wasn't Wild Horse Island, but she was now with a man who'd just professed to love her. That had to be a good sign.

"Why'd you come back?" she asked. She wasn't about to take anything for granted.

"Two reasons."

She glanced at him. "And the first one?"

"To apologize to my family."

He hadn't shaved in a few days, and she found herself focusing on the whiskers running along his jawline. "For?"

"Basically for ghosting them. For leaving without sticking around to face the fire about everything that had gone down, and then for not doing anything more than letting them know I was alive for over a week."

"So, they basically got the same treatment I did."

"They got less at first. I, at least, texted you. Tried to talk to you."

"It wasn't a hard enough try."

"I know that. And I'm not making excuses for it."

The fireworks show was still going, so she redirected her attention back to the sky once again. She'd also noticed that the woman who'd caught her crying earlier was now watching them, probably hoping to eavesdrop.

"So, your family got *more* than I did in the end?" she asked. He'd said they got less than her at first.

"I called Gabe Tuesday afternoon. Needed to apologize, and I decided it couldn't wait. I'd waited too long as it was. Then I called Dad to apologize for not taking his tractor keys away from him."

"And how did those calls go?"

Her gaze had drifted back to his again, and he seemingly hadn't taken his off her since he'd started talking. "Gabe told me it was water under the bridge. We had a long talk. I'm still not sure I deserve his forgiveness, but he's accepted my apology, and I've accepted his forgiveness."

That was good to hear. She'd known there wouldn't be any

lingering issues there. Not after all she'd learned about Michelle after Nate had left.

"And your dad?" she said. "Did he set you straight, too?"

The corners of Nate's mouth curled slightly. "He tried."

"You don't believe him?"

His gaze lowered to her hands then, where she had them gripping the edges of her wrap, her arms now crossed in a protective X over her chest. "The thing is," he said, then he stopped and seemed to need a moment to get himself under control. He turned his head, and this time it was he who stared at the sky. But then he turned back. "I apparently have more lingering issues from my mother than I'd realized. She always blamed me, right?" His shoulders scrunched in a little before he continued. "Well, I think I do the same thing. I blame myself for more than I should."

"You do," she told him. "You probably should talk to someone about that."

"That's exactly what Jaden said."

"He's not wrong."

"I know. And I took several numbers from him of people I plan to reach out to next week."

That one shocked her. He must have had some sort of serious come-to-Jesus talk with himself while he'd been gone or something.

She forced the tension in her shoulders to ease somewhat and let herself quit sitting so stiffly. She still wasn't going to get her hopes up too far too soon, but he didn't appear to be the exact same man he'd been when he'd left two weeks ago.

"There's something else, too," he told her, and he licked his lips as if his mouth had gone dry.

"What's that?"

He didn't move as he spoke. "I think all that time that I spent hating my mother and knowing that she hated me, too, I might have actually been wishing for her to love me instead."

Megan's eyes went wide. That one was deep.

And that one sounded like something Jaden would come up with. It made sense, though.

"Or," Nate went on. "I could be wrong. I haven't discussed that theory with anyone else. But I have done a lot of thinking the last few days. And that's kind of what it feels like. And I think that might have transferred in some way when it came to Michelle."

~

NATE WAITED to see if she'd say anything to that. Because that one brought him right back to what had made him leave town to begin with. *Michelle.*

The lines of her face softened. "You've done all this thinking while you were gone?"

"I had a lot of time on my hands." He wanted desperately to reach out and take one of her hands, but they remained clenched around her blanket. "I was at a worksite in Texas," he told her. "I knew we needed someone to fill in down there for a couple of weeks, so when I left, that's where I went. But I couldn't avoid thinking about the past. And for the first time, I didn't want to avoid it any longer. I also didn't want to run from it. I just wanted it to get out of the way, you know? Kind of bulldoze over it and be done with it."

She nodded, and he could see that she was getting it.

"Not that I thought I could, at first."

"Of course you wouldn't think that." The outermost edges of her lips twitched upward for the first time since he'd sat down.

"I seem to be set in my ways a little." When her lips twitched again, he went on. "Anyway, back to Michelle."

"Your family filled me in on what they knew, by the way."

He nodded. "And Nick and Jaden pretty much know all of it. Nick was there, and she dragged Jaden into it. I had to tell Jaden what truly happened just to make sure he could protect himself while he remained in the house." He studied her then, and he found himself surprised by something. "Jaden never told you any of this?"

"Never. I knew that no one liked Michelle, and during that first harvest when I was here, I remember watching you at one point and thinking that your hatred for her seemed to go a little deeper."

"I suspect it does. There's a fine line between love and hate, you know?"

"So, you really did love her?"

He could tell that she struggled with that concept. And he could understand why. Not only was she a bad person, but she'd been his brother's wife. "I thought I did at the time. But you've got to remember, I didn't exactly have a good role model for what love was. Our whole family was messed up."

"True."

He shifted on the seat, turning more toward her, and when his knee pressed into hers, he rested a hand on his thigh. "Let me start at the beginning. Michelle started coming on to me about the time I turned seventeen, doing little things when no one else was around. She'd act like she loved me. Hell, she eventually *told* me she loved me. That she wished she'd met me before she'd met Gabe."

"Wasn't she several years older than you?"

"A few, yes. And she was also just like our mother."

Megan's eyes narrowed. "But you didn't see her as a mother figure?"

"With the way she often dressed?" He let out a short laugh. "*No.* She dressed to provoke. Or her actions did the same. And then she would touch me. Sometimes just on the arm, sometimes my back, my thigh." He was encouraged by the way Megan didn't seem to be judging his actions.

"You were confused."

He nodded. "How's a teenage boy supposed to be anything else? Plus, I'd never had my mother's love. And unbeknownst to me, I apparently wanted love. Or so my theory goes."

"It sounds like a decent theory."

"I think I might be onto something. But still, what happened, it wasn't right. I might have been a stupid kid, but I did know wrong from right. And she was my brother's wife. And the thing is, it's not like I thought I would 'take' her from Gabe or anything. Hell, I didn't *want* her. Not like that. I wasn't thinking love and happily ever after."

"You just wanted love."

"I think I did. Or maybe I just wanted someone in which I could give *my* love." He paused as he said that, realizing that those words felt more right. He'd always had his love rejected by his mother. She'd hated him. It wouldn't have done any good to try to love her because she wasn't about to let him in. And then Michelle started acting like he meant something to her, so he . . .

He stared at Megan, not having said any of his thoughts out loud, but the way she watched him was almost as if she'd heard every one of them. Then finally, one of her hands released its clutch from her blanket, and it covered his. "I think that might be a better theory," she said. "And I think you probably do have a lot of love inside you to give."

Her words sounded promising. And he'd not felt overly promising at all since he'd shown up.

"I was wrong to have sex with her after she came into the room," he stated. "So wrong. I knew I shouldn't do it. I told myself to reject her and to think about my brother. But I just wanted to think about me in that moment."

"And then you couldn't think of anyone *but* your brother ever since."

He huffed out a sigh. "Pretty much. The shame I've carried . . ." He shook his head and briefly glanced away from her. The night was dark around them. "I don't have to see a psychologist to know that my shame was—*is*—unhealthy. To understand how much it's been weighing me down."

Her hand squeezed his, and his own heart clenched tight when she didn't release her grip.

"You may not want to hear it," she told him, "but I'm glad Jaden forced the issue that day. Not just for you and your mental health, but for your whole family. I think in the end it'll tighten your bonds."

"Well, I don't know about our bonds . . ." He shrugged after thinking about it. "*Maybe*. But I will say that the weight that's been lifted from my chest over the last few days"—he nodded, relishing the beginning feelings of freedom he'd been experiencing—"I'm glad he forced it, too. But you tell him that and I'll deny it 'til the day I die," he added quickly, and that got him the kind of smile he'd hoped he could pull from her tonight.

His heart swelled. He loved this woman. He'd known it before he'd driven away like a man with snarling beasts at his heels, but he hadn't let himself believe it. He hadn't let himself fully grasp that he *could* have that. With her.

And he still wasn't sure if he could have it. She might have loosened up a little since he'd first shown up there, but she hadn't exactly been inviting.

"So . . ." He glanced around them, unsure how to broach the next topic, and realized that everyone else in the vicinity was now packing up and leaving.

He turned his face to the sky and saw that the fireworks had ended.

"I'm sorry," he said, nodding toward the leaving families. "I made you miss the show."

"It's okay." Her smile softened even more. "This has been better than fireworks, anyway."

Once again, his heart clenched tight. He grinned at her. "You think so?"

She shot him a look as if to tell him not to be thinking that the way back to her was paved free and clear, before adding, "I'm happy that you're finding a new path, Nate. That you can hopefully put this in your past once and for all and move forward. I'm thrilled that you're beginning to see that you aren't just some bad guy. You're good. And your entire family loves you. They want you around."

He was beginning to believe that himself. It had felt that way when they'd all had a long talk earlier in the day. But he was also trying really hard to believe it *himself*. And he thought he just might get there some day.

First, though, he had another reason he'd come back. The most important reason.

He closed his other hand over the top of theirs, and he held her tight. "Please tell me what I can do, Meg. I know I messed up. I know I'm the world's worst boyfriend. But I need you back in my life. So badly. I need you by my side, and I want to be by yours. So please, tell me what I need to do to make things right, and I'll do it. I'll fall on my sword for you, baby."

She looked mildly impressed. "That was quite poetic—in a sense."

"You think?" He gave her a teasing smile. "Better than my opening monologue?"

"No." She immediately shook her head, but she wasn't returning his smile. "I don't know if you can top that one."

"Why not?"

"Because you said three words in that one that I kind of liked."

Hope instantly returned and bloomed inside him. He let out a long breath. "I'll say them again if you'll give me a second chance." He waited, not sure how serious she was, not knowing if she was teasing or still considering. Just . . . not knowing. But he did know that this would be totally her call. All he could do was wait.

"You're not going to run off and pull a disappearing act again?" she asked.

"Never. Not with you. Not with my family." He kept his hand over hers. "I've got all I need right here."

His last sentence seemed to surprise her. "You mean here, as in Birch Bay?"

Now he was confused. "Isn't that what we're talking about?"

"I'm just talking about being with you. *Wherever* that is. You said before that you didn't know what you really wanted to do with your life, so if you figure it out and it's not here, then let's talk about it. I'm not married to Birch Bay. Not like I thought I was."

"Then how about being married to me? *In* Birch Bay?"

The question caught her off guard, and he had the ring out of his pocket before she'd stopped gasping. "I want to live *here*, Meg. With my family. With you. And we can take things as fast or as slow as you need. Like I told you earlier, I get it now. I'm a firm believer that when a person finds what they want. Who they *need*. That they just know. So, I'm happy to wait. To take things slow. But I'm equally as happy to go fast. Because my mind isn't going to change."

He dropped down to one knee before giving her a chance to speak, and as he held up the ring, a large burst of fireworks suddenly exploded overhead.

"Will you marry me, Megan Manning?" He smiled at her, showing her all the love he felt inside of him, and all the love he wanted to share with her. "Will you be by my side from this day forward? Will you help me to not only build the type of tomorrow that I never thought I deserved, but the one that I never knew was possible to have? Would you do that for me, Megan?"

She shook her head, and as his brain registered the move, he mentally stumbled.

What?

"I won't do that for *you*, Nate. I'll do it for *us*." She nodded and reached her arms out to him. "Yes. *Yes*. Of course I'll marry you. I love you. I want to be a part of your life. For the *rest* of our lives."

"And I love you." He pulled her in his arms then, and they rose to their feet, and as he lowered his mouth to hers, finally closing the distance he'd wedged between them two weeks before, more fireworks exploded above them.

He pulled slightly back, looking down into her face as the bright colors lit up the night sky, and he knew that he'd found not only the person to *show* him love, to share her love with him, but also the one he wanted to share his with. For the rest of their lives.

Epilogue

Nate stared into the full-length mirror in his father's and Gloria's recently renovated guest room and slipped the second button of his navy suit jacket through the buttonhole. He smoothed his hands over the front of the jacket's material, appreciating the complementing colors of the navy with the soft-pink rose boutonniere, and envisioned what his bride might look like standing at the end of the aisle.

The summer had rolled through Birch Bay with Wilde Cabins and Adventures showing all signs of being the success he and his family had hoped for, and they were now not only planning to turn the barn into a wedding venue and add more cherry trees to the orchard, but they also had big plans for the main house.

A knock sounded on the bedroom door, and Nick stuck his head in. "You ready for this?"

"I've never been more ready for anything in my life."

Nick met his eyes, no doubt understanding how true the sentiment was, and as Nate stepped into the hallway of what had once been their next-door neighbor's property, he took in all four of his brothers in matching navy suits. His strong, fierce lone sister, wearing a flowing navy dress that covered her five-and-a-half-month baby bump, stood next to them, and all of them were ready to stand at his side.

His and Megan's wedding wouldn't be traditional in that there would only be men on Nate's side of the wedding party and women for Megan's, but it would hold all the traditions of bringing family together. On his side would stand his five siblings, while beside Megan would be Brooke, Erica, Arsula, Harper, and Dani's husband Ben. A true family affair. And even Megan's entire family had flown in for the event.

After the wedding, the reception would be held at Nick and Harper's house in lieu of their annual Labor Day cookout, then Nate and Megan would spend their first night as husband and wife in Cabin 10.

He and his siblings exited the house together without saying anything more and piled into the waiting golf carts. They then headed for the cliff at the back of the property that overlooked the lake.

After Nate had come back to town two months before, he'd already had in mind that he wanted to work a deal with the Wyndhams to buy the piece of their property where he wanted to build a house for him and Megan. But to his surprise, he'd discovered that his dad and Gloria had already signed a contract to buy both the house and land. They'd decided that the one-story home better suited their needs—with recent renovations led by Nate's company, of course—but they'd also been more than willing to invest the rest of the land back into the business. More cabins might be needed down the road. Or possibly more cherry trees.

But instead of rolling *all* the remaining land into the business, Nate had bought the spot at the cliff. He and Megan would be married today where their house would one day stand, then his crew in Birch Bay would break ground on the foundation next week.

He'd sold off his other construction businesses and had made an offer to Dre to run the newly created one in Birch Bay.

Because as Nate had told Megan before, construction wasn't what he'd always wanted to do with his life. He now knew, though, what he *did* want to do. He wanted to be a part of the family business.

And with that in mind, he was now managing partner of Wilde Cherry Orchard and Wilde Cabins and Adventures, while Megan had begun taking interior design and hospitality courses. She was also already accepting reservations and working on the details for the weddings and events they'd begin hosting starting the following year.

The light wind of the beautiful September day whispered over Nate's face as Gabe took his foot off the pedal and brought the cart to a stop. He'd positioned them at the crest of the path that allowed both properties to be seen at once, and after Cord and Dani rolled their carts to a stop behind them, as well, all six of them got out and turned to take in the construction already happening next door.

At their dad's suggestion, they were turning the house into a lodge so they could host more guests, as well as special events and retreats. Work would be completed by December, then his family would come together for the holiday one last time in the home where they'd grown up. After that, they would transition over to their father's and Gloria's new home, where they'd start new and improved traditions.

Cord pulled a decanter out of the back of his cart that Nate had asked him to put in there and poured and passed out five shots of whiskey and one of apple juice. Then he held his glass up in toast. "To Nate," he said.

The rest of them did the same, and Nate found himself utterly overcome with emotion. He looked at his family some days and couldn't believe how far they'd come.

"To *us*," he corrected before he held up his glass. "For so many years, all I ever wanted was for you all to be okay. For my *family* to be okay. And for most of that time, I didn't think I deserved to be a part of you. But at the *same* time, even through all the years that I stayed away or barely visited, I want you all to know that I would have done *anything* to make sure that 'we' didn't fall apart." He had to pull in a breath before continuing. "But now I see that 'we' honestly does include *me*, and that it never would have been right without me as an active part of it. So, from the bottom of my heart, I thank you all for never giving up on me." He looked at Dani. "For kicking my butt over the years when it was needed." To Jaden, he said, "For making me talk about things when you know that the last thing I ever want to do is talk." He turned to Nick. "For *always* being my other half and having my back no matter what." And to Gabe, he said, "And for forgiving me when I'd never known anyone who deserved to be forgiven less."

At the last part of his toast, he wrapped an arm around his soon-to-be only remaining single sibling, and he lifted his glass a little higher. "You're about to be the last man standing, Cord. The only single Wilde. So, I'd suggest you strap in and be prepared, because if I've learned anything over the course of the last few months, it's that while bumpy and sometimes treacherous, boarding this train was the best decision of my life."

They all drank to each other, and within minutes, Nate found himself standing at the end of an aisle with his siblings standing beside him and his father sitting in the row in front of him, and all of them never looking so proud in their lives.

The music started then, and he turned his gaze down the aisle. And there, on her father's arm, he saw the beginning of the best part of his life.

ABOUT THE AUTHOR

Photography by Amelia Moore

As a child, Kim Law cultivated a love for chocolate, anything purple, and creative writing. She penned her debut work, "The Gigantic Talking Raisin," in the sixth grade and got hooked on the delights of creating stories. Before settling into the writing life, however, she earned a college degree in mathematics, then worked as a computer programmer while raising her son. Now she's pursuing her lifelong dream of writing romance novels—none of which include talking raisins.

A native of Kentucky, Kim now resides in Middle Tennessee. You can visit Kim at www.KimLaw.com.

Made in the USA
Monee, IL
25 February 2022

91786733R10184